Sons a

No family celebrates birthd... ...s.
Every year, each person is ...ghts
(always homemade) from ...e family. But the twentieth birthday of a Daltry child is a special event. When a
Daltry turns twenty years old, Grandmother Minerva (a great
fan of classical mythology) assigns the young one a "labor," in
the tradition of the twelve labors of Hercules. Only three as-
pects of Minerva's challenges are predictable: the labor will
last one year, it will help to build her grandchild's character,
and it will not be easy . . .

The Matchmaker

Debra S. Cowan

JOVE BOOKS, NEW YORK

THE MATCHMAKER

A Jove Book / published by arrangement
with the author

PRINTING HISTORY
Jove edition / October 1995

ISBN: 0-515-11711-0

A JOVE BOOK®
Jove Books are published by The Berkley Publishing Group,
200 Madison Avenue, New York, New York 10016.
JOVE and the "J" design are trademarks
belonging to Jove Publications, Inc.

PRINTED IN THE UNITED STATES OF AMERICA

10 9 8 7 6 5 4 3 2 1

*To Marshall and Judy,
who accepted me into the family through their son,
but love me as if I were one of their own.*

Acknowledgments

In my experience, no book has ever been written without the generous help of others. Thanks to the following for their help with C. J.'s story:

Melinda Metz, for the opportunity to participate in this project, Kathleen Clarke for seeing it through and Jennifer Lata for the finishing touch.

Patsy Klingstedt, for going above and beyond the call more than once.

Maggie Price, for lending an ear and substantial brain-power during a crucial moment.

The other Daltry family authors who shared their vision and characters. Especially Lorraine Heath for her enormous help with the research and all her encouragement.

Prologue

A SHOTGUN BLAST RIPPED THE SUMMER AIR, SENDING THE SIX children catapulting away from the corral fence as though they'd been fired from a slingshot.

"Run! It's old man Peabody!" C. J. Daltry yelled.

Peabody raced out of his house, spindly arms waving like a scarecrow's. His bowlegs stretched across the flat red earth in an odd straddling gait.

The children scattered like the shot in Peabody's gun—except for Lizzie Colepepper.

She froze, huddled by the corral post closest to the barn, and her gaze darted back to find C. J.

He was gone! Everyone was gone!

They had all disappeared into the night without her. Pain stabbed, destroyed her newfound hope that she'd finally found some friends, that she finally belonged. Peabody rushed toward the corral, and she quickly dropped to the ground.

Her heart thumped in her chest like a scared rabbit's, but she plastered herself to the hot Texas dirt, sweat causing her new dress to stick to her. If she was caught, her stepfather would find out that she'd gone with the others to spook

Peabody's new bull. And if she embarrassed her stepfather . . .

She shuddered as Jude Menefee's strongest threat passed through her mind.

I'll put you on an orphan train.

She dragged her mind away from that thought and focused on huddling into the clump of grass that grew around the corral post. This day had been so perfect. She'd been allowed to enjoy all of the Independence Day festivities for the first time, including the barn dance and the fireworks.

And just before they had all sneaked away to bother old man Peabody's new bull, C. J. had kissed her. Her first kiss —only a quick buss on the cheek, but forward just the same.

She was finally being accepted. After two years in Paradise Plains, and despite her painful shyness, Lizzie had been included in all the day's games and was finally bestowed a coveted invitation to join the others.

It had been C. J.'s idea to tease Peabody's new bull, a breed called a Brahma. Of course C. J. had been first to dart into the corral and wave a red bandanna at the wicked-looking animal. Now the red kerchief lay on the ground, limp and hapless, just like Lizzie. She wished she could use it to cover her face, but she didn't dare move.

"Durn fool kids! Disturbin' my peace, rilin' up my bull." Mr. Peabody passed in front of her. His gun leveled out in the darkness like the long arm of God and exploded again.

She jerked, looking around. She had to get away and get back to town without him seeing her. If he caught her, he would drag her by the ear to Jude.

Peabody stopped at the edge of the barn, squinting into the darkness and muttering under his breath. Lizzie knew she must take her chance now.

Silently she rose to her feet and edged along the corral. Behind her, the bull stomped and snorted, his hot breath blowing against her backside.

Fear choked her, but she dared not look at the bull. Her

gaze stayed locked on Mr. Peabody. She was halfway down the corral length. She took another step. The bull snorted again.

She spun and sprinted to the far edge of the corral and darkness.

"Ho, there! You!"

Lizzie's legs pumped harder. She reached the far corner of the pen and wheeled around the protruding fence. Just a little farther and she could fade into the shadows.

A hand clamped onto the neck of her dress and lifted her into the air. She squealed, her hands clutching at his grimy wrist for balance. Legs dangling, gasping for air, Lizzie squeezed her eyes shut as old man Peabody turned her around for his inspection.

"The minister's daughter?" He squinted at her. Heavy smells of tobacco and wood smoke and beer floated around him. "Ach, he ain't gonna like this one little bit, missy."

She grimaced, fighting the fear that threatened to suck all the air from her lungs. As painful as the punishment she knew would surely follow was the knowledge that her new friends had deserted her.

An hour later, she stood in the front room of the small, spotless house she shared with her stepfather. The door closed behind Mr. Peabody, and Lizzie felt trapped, as cut off from light and air as if she had been sealed inside a tomb.

For a long minute, Jude Menefee said nothing. He simply stared. The anger built on his lean face until his hawkish features distorted into a sharp red mask.

She saw him reach for the quirt. Fear rushed through her. Reflexively she lunged to the right, but the thin whip caught her on the left side of the face.

She cried out once, then clamped her lips shut. Jude hadn't hit her in a couple of years, but she remembered that only silence would calm him. Her cheek and the line of her jaw throbbed and burned with icy heat.

Slowly she raised her hand to her face, careful to keep her gaze on her stepfather. Warm blood slicked her hand and oozed between her fingers. She bit back a sob.

She saw Jude's lips move, and as though from a distance, heard him screeching like a raven fighting for territory. She drowned out the words, knowing them by heart.

You've embarrassed me again, Lizzie. I won't have it. You'll conduct yourself as befits the daughter of a minister. The words were always the same and had lost some of their power to hurt, to belittle.

But circling through her mind, carving scars on her fragile, tender heart, was the thought that no one, not one of her new friends, had stayed to help her. Or even slowed down to see if she was with them.

Not even C. J. *Especially C. J.*

Jude's bony fingers bit into her arm, jerking her attention to his lean face. "You stay away from those heathens, you hear me?"

Stay away from them? "But Papa Jude—"

"Don't talk back to me!" The walls vibrated from the force of his words. His face, normally as pale as lime, turned florid. A vein bulged in his neck. "Flirting with the devil, the lot of ya. I ever catch you with those kids again, I'll put you on some orphan train. I swear I will."

His threat worked. It always did. Not because her stepfather was the only family Lizzie had left, but because Paradise Plains was the first real home she'd ever had.

The first ten years of her life had been spent traveling from town to town, settling nowhere. Even though her mother was now dead, Lizzie had a home, and she meant to keep it. Anger ebbed away, replaced by the cold gel of fear. "I'll be good, Papa Jude. I will."

"No more of those kids," he thundered.

She hesitated, then nodded. Her throat ached; misery pinched her insides.

"Swear it!" He raised his right hand, his gaze commanding, threatening.

She raised her right hand, her injured cheek throbbing beneath the fingers of her left. "I swear," she sobbed. "I swear."

One

LIZZIE HURRIED THROUGH TOWN TOWARD THE MERCANTILE, late as usual. Knowing the scar was covered by her hair, she refused to tuck her chin into her chest.

"Excuse me. Pardon me. Excuse me." She wove her way through the throng of people stationed outside the new Hercules Daltry Memorial Library, built just to the west of the church. Though the pristine Greek structure had been completed almost six months ago, a crowd still lingered to admire the exterior before going inside.

She passed Sally Orndorft's barbershop and Clay Masterson's newspaper office on her way to Hank and Maybelle's store. She sidestepped everyone, but managed to meet their gazes. A few people spoke to her.

After Jude's death nine months ago, Lizzie had determined to make some friends. She repeatedly told herself she had nothing to be ashamed of. One day she knew she would believe it. . . .

She was late. Hank and Maybelle wouldn't care, but Lizzie did. Halting in the street, her gaze locked on the storefront. HANK AND MAYBELLE'S MERCANTILE was painted in fading white letters.

The door was closed against the biting February air. Sunshine glittered off the polished windows. Inside, Lizzie could see the crush of boxes stacked against walls, the burnished gleam of the bells hanging in the doorway to announce customers.

The building was plain graying wood, the plate windows large, reaching up from the planked boardwalk to the top of the door. A wood awning slanted over the porch, providing a sloped extension that shaded the area. Rocking chairs sat in front of the windows, put there by Hank for the men who passed their time gossiping and whittling. Empty barrels crowded the space between the chairs.

All in all, the store looked cluttered and busy. Lizzie loved it. A sense of pride bloomed. She didn't own any part of it *yet*, but she felt a sense of satisfaction that she worked there and was saving her money to buy a portion from Hank and Maybelle.

Thank goodness for Hank, who appreciated Lizzie's ability with numbers and was more than willing to give her a chance to secure something for her future. Lizzie suspected that, due to Maybelle, he also knew how much it meant to her to be considered a valid part of something. Hank always made her feel needed.

At the door, she peered into the sparkling glass window and rearranged her hair again over her cheek. She didn't notice her bonnet or the new cameo she wore at her throat; she only took care that the scar was covered.

As usual, she felt unsettled when looking at herself, but preferred the murky image in window glass to the clearer one of a mirror. She had *no* mirrors at home, and hadn't since the night Jude had hit her with the quirt.

Her gaze skittered away from her reflection and she pushed open the door. She edged around Miss Lavender and her frilly concoction of a dress. Today the fragile-looking owner of The Hatbox wore a shirtwaist the yellow of chick down, frothing with white lace cuffs and collar and bows. She clucked over several bolts of rolled-out fabric.

Lizzie immediately knew Maybelle was gone, because she usually helped Miss Lavender with her fabric selection. Maybelle considered her Southern upbringing to be *the* authority on everything genteel, including fashion.

Hank, as round and stout as a Franklin stove, lumbered out from behind the counter. In the early daylight, his bald pate gleamed like a freshly laid egg. "Oh, Lizzie, good. I'm glad you're here."

"Where's Maybelle?" she asked breathlessly, her gaze meeting Hank's. Over the past few months, the three of them had become friends. She felt no threat from Hank. He looked into her eyes when he spoke to her, and didn't try to get a peek at her scar as so many others did.

The burly man who ran the mercantile untied his apron and thrust it under the counter. "She's taken Will to the doctor. The boy was coughing until all hours of the night and she's worried. I need to go over there myself and—"

"Perhaps I can go, while you stay here?" Lizzie cut him off, panic flaring. She knew what was coming.

He smiled and touched her shoulder. "I'll only be gone for a minute. I really do need to check on the little man."

"I—I know." Her gaze dropped, and she attempted a smile even though her heart had twisted into a painful knot. "You go on ahead. I'll mind things here."

"I promise I'll hurry," he said gently, his brown eyes meeting hers.

She felt ashamed, but she couldn't control the nervousness that caused a fine trickle of sweat between her breasts. She had never worked behind the counter before.

"It'll be good practice for when you become our new partner."

"Yes, it will." She squared her shoulders, determined to try. She would have to share equally in the responsibilities when she was able to buy a portion of the mercantile. With the money she had saved so far, it might be only another year before she had enough. "Go on. I'll be fine."

Hank winked and hurried out the door. Lizzie sneaked a look at Miss Lavender. The tiny woman muttered under her breath, holding a swatch of blue calico next to a red-and-white gingham.

Lizzie turned to put her reticule under the counter and take off her bonnet, careful to pull her thick black hair forward over her left shoulder so that it curtained her cheek. Her heart slowed to a less painful beat and she knelt down to open the change box.

"Good day, Miss Lavender." A voice rumbled through the store.

"Good day, C. J."

Lizzie froze. She would've known the voice without Miss Lavender's greeting. It was a voice she'd spent the last eight years avoiding.

His voice came again, deep and husky, with an innate warmth that hinted at ready laughter. He slapped a hand on the counter, causing a slight vibration. "Anybody back there? Hank? Maybelle?"

Lizzie took a deep breath. *Go away. Just go away.* Despite feeling like a coward, Lizzie huddled behind the counter, praying C. J. Daltry would give up and leave.

She should've known better.

She heard the creak of wood, felt another vibration above her, then a warm breath caressed her ear. "Hello, miss, are you all right down there? Is there something—Lizzie?"

She squeezed her eyes shut. *Drat. Blast. Damn.* She added the last curse simply because she could. Jude was gone now.

"Lizzie, is that you?"

Of all the bother! She surged to her feet, taking care to keep her hair in place. "There's no need for caterwauling. I'm not deaf. State your business."

C. J.'s blue eyes widened at the sight of her, but he quickly masked the surprise. He rested his elbows on the counter and leaned against it indolently. "Hello."

The soft whiskey timber of his voice caused a strange

tingle to feather up her spine and she snapped, "What do you need?"

His gaze rode over her, quick and assessing, but she could read nothing in the crystal blue depths. "I'm here to pick up a book from New York. On irrigation methods."

She gave a brusque nod and swept through the curtain to the back room. She found the book quickly, but hesitated, using the time to compose herself. She hadn't been this close to C. J. Daltry since that summer night eight years ago. If anything, he was more handsome. Drat him.

Oh, it wasn't as if she hadn't seen him about town in the past years, but she'd taken pains to avoid noticing him.

She couldn't avoid noticing now. The tall, gawky boy of twelve had grown into a devastatingly handsome man. His blond hair, colored to a wheat gold by the sun, hung two or three inches below the collar of his chambray work shirt. He wore a mustache now, and it was a darker gold, accenting the rugged tanned planes of his face. His aquiline nose kept him from being handsome in a fussy way.

He was lean-hipped, with long, muscular legs that stretched on forever. His eyes were still the brilliant blue of an unfettered Texas sky, but there was a hardness there now, a maturity created by pain. She knew his engagement to Diana Whitlaw had been broken two years ago and wondered if that had put the aloofness in his eyes.

"It is here, isn't it?" C. J.'s voice sounded nearer, as though he'd moved around the counter. "It's my birthday. Sort of a present to myself."

She jerked out of her reverie, grabbed the book from the shelf, and marched back to the counter. He stood at the end now, and she pushed the volume at him. "The ledger shows you've already paid for the book and the postage."

Her voice was stiff. Maybelle frequently warned her against that, but this time she couldn't seem to help it. She didn't *want* to help it with C. J. Daltry.

He smiled that dazzling smile that had earned him the

favor of the schoolteacher—and every other female in Paradise Plains. Except Lizzie. "Thank you."

"Good day." She turned, examining a row of canned goods, her ears straining for the sound of him walking out the door.

"Aren't you going to wish me a happy birthday?"

Grudgingly, she repeated the words. What would it be like to celebrate with a big family like his? Longing shot through her—longing to be part of a family—but she pushed it away.

"Lizzie?"

A hint of a plea tinged the word. Her spine tightened. She turned stiffly, as though someone else controlled her movements. "Yes?"

His gaze held hers. Pity, regret, uncertainty passed through his eyes. She read the emotions and fought not to scream at him. For a moment, she feared he would apologize. Again. Or bring up all the pain. Again.

When he spoke, his voice was low and gentle. "Thanks for the book. Have a nice day."

He touched his fingers to the brim of his sand-colored hat and walked out.

Lizzie stared after him, stunned. Emotions churned through her—regret, old pain, and a fierce stab of longing.

She'd done it again. Why couldn't she curb her sharp tongue? Ever since Maybelle had pointed it out, Lizzie had tried. But with C. J. . . .

She closed her eyes, refusing to let herself be swayed by the small amount of attention he'd paid her. Seeing him brought back memories of the summer of 1873, memories of that Independence Day, that fleeting kiss. She opened her eyes, shoving the thoughts to the back of her mind.

She and C. J. had been friends once. They weren't anymore. And that's the way she wanted it.

*   *   *

Apprehension lapped at him. C. J. sat in the immense dining room, surrounded by his family. All through his birthday dinner, he fought the urge to fidget, but he couldn't stop his gaze from traveling the length of the table to his grandmother at the other end.

The long oak table had been specially made by his father, as had most of the furniture in the house. Odie had made a new oak cabinet for C. J.'s birthday, to match the bed he'd made. It had been moved upstairs to the room C. J. shared with Atlas.

Minerva Daltry studied him often, her head tilted to one side, her gray eyes warm yet speculative. Sweat prickled his neck, but he ignored it. He didn't want Grandma to see how nervous he was. In an effort to remain calm, C. J. reminded himself he wasn't alone in this.

For generations, Daltrys had been given a special assignment on their twentieth birthday. Thanks to Grandma's life-long love of mythology, Pa and his siblings had been given tasks. Just as C. J. and all his siblings would be.

His father had accomplished his with ease, winning Jane in the process. C. J.'s older brother and sister had also found love. Lee and Persy had both managed to rise to the challenge, even beyond Grandma's expectations. Lee had married Meredith, a red-haired schoolteacher, while Persy had wed Jake Devlin, a former saloon owner from New York.

Not that C. J. wanted love. He had all the women he could handle. He'd just as soon have a new horse or a new bull. But it was common knowledge that Grandma never gave what one wished for.

Hoping to keep the anxiety at bay, he let his thoughts wander to Lizzie Colepepper. Even though he'd heard she worked for Hank and Maybelle, he'd been surprised to see her behind the counter at the mercantile today. Discomfort and regret soon choked out the surprise. Those were the emotions he most usually associated with Lizzie, ever since that July night eight years ago.

It had been almost that long since he'd really noticed her. Her eyes drew him. They were an unusually dark shade of blue and almost too big for her delicate features. But it was her hair that really captured his attention. Or rather the way she wore it.

She pulled the thick ebony mass over her left shoulder so that it draped her cheek and gleamed like satin. She wore it as though she were hiding her face. Which she was. And that was why C. J. felt so uncomfortable thinking about her.

The last strains of "Happy Birthday" faded away. An awed hush swathed the room and thoughts of Lizzie disappeared. All eyes moved to him.

Persy walked through the kitchen doors and toward him, placing a heart-shaped cinnamon cake in front of him. So they wouldn't miss C. J.'s birthday, she and Jake had cut short a trip to New York City, one of several large cities where they worked on behalf of needy children.

In honor of C. J.'s day, his sister had made heart-shaped biscuits for breakfast, heart-shaped tarts for a snack, and now this cake. Hearts, hearts everywhere. They only reminded C. J. of how his own had been broken.

He would never tell Persy, but hearts were one of the reasons he hated sharing his birthday with St. Valentine.

The other was that on the Christmas before his eighteenth birthday, he'd been kicked in the face by Ulysses, a black devil of a stallion. The resulting broken bones in his nose and jaw were the reason Diana Whitlaw had called off their engagement. She had believed C. J.'s features would be permanently distorted. On C. J.'s eighteenth birthday, she had run off with a railroad scout.

Across the table, Atlas and Allie whispered. Their gazes were bright, darting between him and Grandma.

Next to him, Persy cut the first piece of cake and placed it on his plate with a flourish. "Has she given a hint at all?"

C. J. shook his head, but kept his gaze glued on his grandmother. "I'm just hoping she won't try that schoolteacher thing on me that she pulled on Lee."

"At least you'd have Lee and Meredith to help you if she did. But you know Grandma never picks the same labor twice." Persy passed around slices of cake, and a natural silence fell as everyone ate their dessert.

From his position of honor at the head of the table, C. J. scanned the room. Everyone was here. Lee and his wife, Meredith, sat on C. J.'s left. Persy, as was her custom, served everyone. Her husband, Jake, sat next to Lee. C. J.'s father and mother sat on the other side of Meredith. Grandma sat at the opposite end of the table.

Allie sat on C. J.'s right, cramming cake into her mouth so she could say she ate faster than Atlas. Atlas was next to her, methodically eating each forkful. Jimmy, Lee and Meredith's adopted son, sat quietly beside Venus, who pulled on her gloves so as not to get the smell of cinnamon on her hands and began to nibble at the cake in front of her.

The whole family was gathered and waiting for the same thing C. J. was. Once dessert was finished, Persy and Jane rose to carry a stack of dirty dishes through the swinging doors and into the kitchen.

Allie leaned over and whispered something to Atlas. C. J.'s youngest sister then hopped up and disappeared into the kitchen with her plate. Venus pushed her plate aside and flipped through a stack of Valentine favors from her many beaux. Atlas, as usual, scratched away at a piece of paper. He shoved it across the table to C. J.

"Here's a list of what I think she might do," Atlas whispered, casting a surreptitious glance down the table toward his grandmother, who sat with Pa discussing the merits of fencing the ranch.

C. J. took the list from his fourteen-year-old brother and scanned it. He snorted. "Cooking? That's for girls."

"We thought teaching was, too, and she made Lee do it," Atlas pointed out in a fatalistic tone.

Lee raised his eyebrows and grinned.

C. J. grimaced and looked back at the list. "Tame a bull?"

"I bet that's never been done. If anybody could do it, you could."

"That seems too easy." He returned his attention to the list. "Carving, painting . . . *finding a unicorn?*" He shook his head, glancing at his brother. "How'd you come up with that?"

"I thought it might be something only Grandma would think of." Atlas glanced down the table, and C. J.'s gaze followed.

Minerva watched the three of them with a fond smile on her face that gave nothing away.

Lee rocked his chair back on two legs and crossed his bulky arms over his chest. "It won't be anything you're prepared for. I can guarantee you that."

C. J. knew he shouldn't waste his energy trying to guess, but he couldn't dismiss the thoughts. Neither Lee nor Persy had been prepared, true, but they had managed to complete their tasks and better themselves in the process.

C. J. knew his talents. He ran the ranch with a sure hand, a born instinct for decision-making and animals. Anything to do with the ranch would be too easy. And futile.

Lee was the eldest grandson, and he, not C. J., stood to inherit the Circle D when Grandma passed on. Even though Lee had worked like the devil to obtain his teaching certificate, he was still regarded as heir to the ranch.

The familiar burn of resentment streaked through C. J. He, not Lee, knew the bloodline of every animal on the place. He, not Lee, loved every blade of grass and grain of dirt. He, not Lee, slept, ate, and breathed the Circle D.

Lee excelled at teaching the slower-learning children in town. While he had done a fine job working the ranch, his heart really wasn't in it. C. J. gave the ranch his heart, his soul, his passion. In return, the land gave C. J. purpose and strength. After Diana had left, the ranch had been his solace, the one thing he could rely on.

Besides, he had few other skills he was as certain of. He could imitate birdcalls with such uncanny precision birds would answer him back. Sometimes the bobwhites would even come close enough to feed. But he couldn't see how birdcalls could be incorporated into any type of labor. Nor were his uncommon good looks, which thanks to Pa hadn't been ruined by the accident, particularly useful.

Odie had invented a wooden box that worked as a splint on the face, keeping the bone fragments pressed tightly together. Though he had looked mighty ridiculous for some months, C. J.'s injuries had healed without even a scar.

Jane, Persy, and Allie marched back into the dining room, their laughter quieting as they stopped at the table. He had asked that no gifts be given, so everyone had settled for dinner. All that remained of C. J.'s birthday was the assignment of his task from Grandma.

A hush filled the room and everyone looked at the matriarch of the family. She smiled, her gray eyes soft and warm as they lit on each family member in turn. "You've had a wonderful birthday, C. J."

"Yes, ma'am." The air suddenly grew thick and hot. His shirt, even though unbuttoned at the neck, seemed to choke him.

Using her cane for leverage, Minerva stood, and with her rose the air of expectancy. It pulsed in the room, thick and palpable. He realized he was holding his breath and released it in disgust. How bad could it be?

"I'm ready, Grandma."

"I hope so." Her gaze leveled on him. For an instant, he felt ten years old again, uncertain, tested. Fondness passed over her features and then a flicker of compassion. "Why don't you accompany me to the barn, Cupid?"

"The barn?" His nerves knotted. She had used his given name, which she did only when she was serious.

Atlas kicked him under the table. "That's a good sign. Maybe it's the bull."

Chairs scraped the floor as everyone rose to join Minerva and C. J.

Grandma halted them with an upraised hand. "Only Cupid, please."

"Only Cupid?" Lee's gaze swung from her to C. J. "But what about the rest of us? Everyone heard mine."

"And mine," Persy put in.

Minerva smiled, which made C. J.'s throat tighten. "Not this time, dearlings. I will tell C. J., and if he desires to tell you, then he may."

A solemn hush descended on the room. Lee's eyes narrowed in speculation. Odie looked stunned. Ma looked curious, Persy worried. Even Venus stopped fiddling with her favors and looked perplexed.

"Gosh," Allie breathed.

"Gol–ly," Atlas intoned in a grave voice. "What can it be?"

C. J. didn't want to admit to the pulling in his gut, but it was there all the same. By Thor, what was his task?

With a last dread-filled glance at his siblings, C. J. followed Minerva through the front room and held the door for her. The clapboard swung shut with a clatter. With a few long strides, he caught up to his grandmother.

She patted him on the arm. "Don't worry, my boy. It's nothing you can't accomplish."

"I don't understand why the others can't hear."

"You will." The words hummed like a dire prediction and killed any hope that his task might be an easy or familiar one.

He considered the possibilities, discarding Atlas's suggestions even as he wished fervently for one of them to be his assigned task. Why in blazes was Grandma taking him to the barn?

He knew she wouldn't talk until she was ready. Night

closed in around them with a frigid bite as they made their way around the house. Raw February air hurried their steps as they walked inside the barn.

C. J. shut the heavy door and was assaulted with the much-loved odors of leather, oats, and hay, and the rich warmth of horseflesh. The familiar sanctuary calmed him somewhat. He came here after every big moment in his life, to think, to triumph, to grieve. And Grandma knew that, he realized.

She walked toward a lantern hanging above a stall, her cane making hollow thumps on the earthen floor. She turned up the light, and the ripe odor of kerosene drifted over to C. J. Soft light gilded his grandmother's magnolia-smooth skin.

He waited, his throat dry and aching, his chest tight. Curiosity chewed at him.

She turned toward him, her eyes concerned and gentle. "Remember the night I found you here? The summer after you turned twelve. You were angry. So angry." She paused, fondness warming her voice. "I'd never seen you pitch so much hay, like a dervish you were."

Sudden alarm pricked him. C. J. lifted his head and his nostrils flared like those of a foal sensing danger. "Grandma—"

"Do you know the time I'm referring to?"

"Yes." The single word tore out of him, brought back all the memories. He'd seen Lizzie *that* day, too. Seen her face and known he was responsible.

Compassion flitted through Minerva's eyes. Dread tingled up his spine and made him shift from one foot to the other. "I had thought, with the years—" She broke off, sighing. "It's been eight years, Cupid. I had hoped either you or the girl would've patched things up, but it hasn't happened."

"She holds no grudge against me," he said carefully, warily. "She's assured me."

"I believe you. She isn't the one I'm concerned about. It's you."

"Me?" Surprise and shock billowed through him. Just as it had this morning, regret stabbed at him. Thoughts of Lizzie always made him feel as though he'd left something undone.

Minerva's voice floated to him, almost drowned out in the chaos of his thoughts. He tried to corral the memories she'd resurrected. "I know you feel guilty, Cupid. And I'm offering you the chance to do something about it."

"I tried to do something about it then." He ached to leap on Goliath and tear across the rolling hills beyond the ranch. "I apologized. I spoke to her stepfather. I did everything except beg on my knees."

It hadn't helped his attitude that she was the one girl who'd remained immune to his considerable masculine charms. Shy little rabbit Lizzie. She would have none of him, and after a while his pride got the better of him. As she'd asked, he quit going near her and eventually stopped talking to her.

Oh, he'd heard the taunts, the stories the other kids made up about the scar on her face. But he knew the truth, and he'd never told.

That was something they did share. Part of him understood that she had become aloof because she was embarrassed by what her stepfather had done to her. He had seen the shame in her eyes when she'd begged him to leave her alone. Finally he had. And now, after eight years, his grandmother wanted him to resurrect all that. "Grandma, I can apologize to Lizzie till the Judgment, but it won't do any good."

"I want you to find her a husband."

"She wants nothing to do with me. Or with anybody. You know how she keeps to herself all the time—you *what?*" C. J. stopped, his head pounding at what his grandmother had just revealed. A dull ache throbbed behind his eyes.

"You heard me."

"Grandma!" Panic thumped at him. He had to make Minerva understand. "Grandma, if it hadn't been for me, she never would have been out that night. Peabody never would have caught her. I ran off and left her at his mercy."

"You thought she had escaped with the others." Minerva looked down her nose at him, daring him to argue further. "You went straight back the minute you discovered she had not."

"And look what it cost her. Jude Menefee struck her. I didn't see her for a week. When I did—I as good as caused that scar, Grandma. Don't you see? She probably hates me."

"I'm not asking *you* to marry her," she returned calmly. "In fact, you're to keep your hands to yourself where she's concerned. No roaming."

"Grandma!" The heat of embarrassment stung his neck.

She shot him an exasperated look. "I love you dearly, C. J., but I'm not blind to your reputation. Your task is to find her a husband. The poor girl is the most solitary person in Paradise Plains."

"That's her choice."

"Perhaps, my dear, but there are always reasons. I would imagine hers are painful."

"This is ridiculous! Isn't there a rule that you can't fiddle with other people's lives?"

"I *make* the rules, Cupid."

He stared at her, shocked and stunned. "How am I supposed to do something like that?"

"That is strictly up to you."

"I don't have a lot of experience in finding husbands," he snapped.

Minerva gave a short, dry laugh. "The girl is smart. And quite stunning, despite the scar. I doubt you'll have much trouble finding interest among your friends."

Oh, but Grandma didn't know Lizzie as C. J. did. Or at

least the way he used to. One of the reasons Lizzie had no marriage prospects was her attitude, her "general deportment," as his mother would say. The girl made persimmons look sweet. Hell, he had a better chance of getting a colt out of a cow.

He thrust a hand through his hair. "Give me something else. Anything."

She shook her head.

"I can't do this."

"I think you can." She took a deep breath, her gaze boring into his. "You'll have a year to do it. You have to earn your prize the same way Lee and Persy earned theirs."

C. J.'s thoughts tangled. He wasn't using Lizzie to get his prize, was he? No, not if he didn't marry her himself.

As if she'd read his thoughts, Minerva said, "You may not marry her in order to win the prize."

"No danger of that," he said dryly. Marriage wasn't for him, and he supposed he could thank Diana for that revelation. Still, he hesitated, feeling unsettled and guilty.

Minerva tapped her cane on the ground and arched one eyebrow. "So? Do you accept or do you forfeit?"

"Forfeit?" His gaze shot to her. "No one's ever done that."

"That's right." Her gray eyes turned somber.

C. J. studied her. Perhaps he could convince her to assign him something else.

"If you forfeit, you forfeit it all. There will be no other chance." Her gray eyes speared him. "Well?"

C. J. met her gaze squarely, swallowing a sudden burst of apprehension. He couldn't be the first Daltry in two generations to refuse the task. It simply wasn't done.

And both he and Lizzie would profit from the task, wouldn't they? Somehow that reassurance didn't ease his anxiety.

He closed his eyes briefly, then rasped, "I accept."

"Excellent!" She rewarded him with a beaming smile. "In

full, the task is to find Lizzie Colepepper a husband. You have one year in which to accomplish this. Once done, you will receive your prize."

"A year?" he groaned. "How about twenty?"

Minerva laughed and patted his cheek. "You'll do fine. I doubt it will take you much time once you get warmed up. That Daltry charm isn't legendary for nothing, you know."

C. J. nodded and watched his grandmother walk out the door. Charm? His charm wouldn't amount to a hill of cow dung with Lizzie Colepepper. If his grandmother only knew how many times he'd tried.

Since that Fourth of July eight years ago, Lizzie had kept to herself. Any effort made to reach out to her was met just as it had been today, with brittleness or sharpness.

Just after the night at Peabody's, C. J. had tried to apologize, tried to make amends, tried to forget. His every attempt had been met with downcast eyes. Then she had finally begged him, *begged* him, to let her be. Almost as though she were afraid.

At the time, C. J. hadn't understood it, and he didn't understand it any better now. Nor did he want to. But he had honored her request.

As the years passed, they attended school together. He saw her at church or in town. But she rarely went to socials or local barn dances. The times she did, she was always in the company of her stepfather, and C. J. didn't dare approach her.

After a while, he managed to bury his guilt—first by telling himself she didn't matter, then by telling himself it had all been a childhood accident. No sense in reliving it. But Grandma was right about one thing.

Lizzie Colepepper had haunted him. And probably would until he tried one last time to set things right. He just wished he had a snowball's chance in Hades of succeeding.

C. J. could see it now—the first Daltry to fail. The gods would roar with laughter at that one.

Two

C. J. UNSADDLED GOLIATH AND BRUSHED DOWN THE PALOMINO stallion, then fed him some oats. For the past two hours, he had ridden like a possessed man all over the ranch. What was he going to do about Lizzie? How in hell was he supposed to find her a husband?

Frustration gnawed at him. Except for the soft glow of light in the upstairs windows, the house was dark. He was glad. He wasn't up to facing anyone tonight. Not after the shock Grandma had dealt him.

He stepped onto the porch of the two-story frame house. It was white with black trim, a big, practical house designed by his father. Black scrollwork over the porch entrance and slender white columns were the only fancy trimmings. In the twilight, the columns gleamed gray.

Chilly February air washed over him. Cold sweat glued his shirt to his chest and shoulders. From the corner of the porch, he looked over the Circle D, his gaze skimming the barn, corrals, and the stable.

The bunkhouse sat behind the house on the other side. All was dark and quiet for the night. The moon hung like a sliver of ice, translucent and white against the sable sky. Stars glittered on the pale frozen canvas. The land stretched and rolled in an endless blanket of grass, dotted here and there with the broad stripped skeletons of pecan and oak trees.

Close to the front porch were his mother's flower beds, dormant now for the winter. A few feet away sat the gazebo his father had made. It was fashioned like a Greek temple and circled by several stripling oaks.

Tonight, C. J.'s usual pride in his land and his home was pricked by frustration. He stared at the gazebo, its unique shape mocking him, and cursed having been born into a family with such a queer fascination for Greek mythology.

A chill filled him as he silently let himself into the house. He passed the dining room and kitchen on his right, the library on his left, then started up the stairs, unbuttoning his shirt.

A lantern hung at the top of the banister and he blew it out, thankful that his sisters' and parents' bedrooms were dark. Lee's old room sat dark, too, since he had his own home now. A sigh of relief escaped C. J.

He walked as softly as he could, his boots scraping faintly against the wood. Once past Grandma's and his parents' rooms, he opened the door to the one he shared with Atlas. Bright moonlight filtered in and illuminated the room—*and* Atlas and Allie.

"What are y'all doing?" C. J. demanded, annoyed to have discovered them there.

Allie lay on her stomach on C. J.'s bed, chin propped on her fists, feet crossed behind her. "We want to know what your task is."

Atlas sat on his bed, an exact copy of C. J.'s long, narrow one and stacked just beneath it. "Are you allowed to tell? It was the bull, wasn't it?"

"No, it was not the bull," C. J. mimicked roughly. He sighed, knowing it wasn't Atlas's fault he'd been given Lizzie as an assignment. "Sorry. I don't really want to talk about it."

"But maybe we can help." Atlas moved off the bed and stood in front of C. J.

Allie pushed herself to a sitting position. "Ah, horsefeathers, C. J. It can't be all that bad."

"It probably feels like it about now." Lee's voice came from the door, and C. J. pivoted.

"Well, why don't y'all make yourselves comfortable?" he drawled, fighting off feelings of apprehension and frustration. He yanked his shirt off and wadded it into a ball.

Lee grinned, his teeth flashing white in the moonlight. "That bad, huh?"

C. J.'s irritation dissolved and he shrugged. "Pretty confounded strange."

"Tell us," Allie and Atlas urged together.

He heard a door open and said, "Why don't we wait for Venus? I'm sure she'll be here directly."

Persy stuck her head around Lee's shoulder. "Did I miss it?"

"You, too!" C. J. exhaled, throwing the shirt into a corner.

"Not yet," Allie crowed. "He's just about to tell us."

"Should've charged admission," he muttered. "Is *everybody* up?"

"Just us." Lee leaned against the door frame. "Well?"

Persy filled the door on Lee's other side. "Yes?"

C. J. planted his hands on his hips and stared at his siblings. Reluctantly, he said, "My task is to find a husband for Lizzie Colepepper."

For several long seconds, silence filled the room.

Lee frowned. Persy arched her eyebrows. Allie and Atlas stared at each other. C. J. waited.

Then sound erupted.

"A husband?"

"Lizzie Colepepper?"

"That girl with the scar on her face?"

"I know. I know." He paced to the window, then turned

to face his brothers and sisters. "Since you're all in here, you might as well give me some idea as to how to do this."

"Oh, no, little brother," Lee laughed. "You're on your own this time."

"That's part of it, C. J." Persy smiled apologetically.

Lee shook his head. "I'm glad it's not me."

"Why don't you get Grandma to give you another task?" Allie suggested.

"She'll never do it," Lee and Persy chorused, exchanging knowing looks.

C. J. nodded, the task growing more daunting and grim in his mind. "I already tried that."

"Gosh," Allie breathed. "You've got to find someone for Lizzie—but how? Do you think it'll be hard?"

"Well, I can't exactly walk up to her and say, 'Lizzie, I need to find you a husband. Got anybody in mind?' "

"I guess you can't." Atlas sat cross-legged on the bed, resting his chin on one hand.

Venus poked her head over Persy's shoulder. "What did I miss?"

"C. J. has to find Lizzie Colepepper a husband," Allie announced. "Bub's trying to think of a way to help."

"Oh, pooh, C. J." Venus waved a hand dismissively. "How difficult can that be? You've already got every woman under fifty chasin' after you."

"*I'm* not supposed to marry her," C. J. snapped. "I'm supposed to find someone to marry her."

"Oh." Venus pursed her lips, then smoothed back her pale blond hair. "Well, I'm glad I don't have to do it. You'll think of somethin'. You always do." With that casual encouragement, she disappeared into the room she shared with Allie.

Lee, too, moved away from the door. "I'd better get back down to the cabin. Meredith will be wondering."

"Tell her if she has any ideas, I'd appreciate them."

"Will do. Good luck." Lee disappeared, his footsteps thundering down the stairs.

Persy's sweet smile eased some of his frustration. "You'll do fine. I remember how nervous I was."

Grateful for her kindness, he gave her a half smile and watched as she followed Lee.

Allie jumped off his bed and walked over to him. "Gosh, I was really hoping you'd get a new horse to break."

"Me, too." He rubbed the top of her head, even though she hated it.

She stuck out her tongue and skipped out the door.

Only Atlas remained. He stayed silent as C. J. shucked his boots and jeans and climbed into his bed. He lay on the top part of the odd-looking pair of beds his father had designed and built for them. The beds were narrow, but longer than usual to accommodate C. J.'s height. Though his bunk was stacked on top of Atlas's, he hardly noticed his brother below him anymore.

He watched the play of moonlight and shadow on the ceiling. Pictures of Lizzie flashed through his mind—the wariness in her eyes today at the store, and the eager pleasure he'd seen in those eyes all those years ago when he'd invited her to go along to old man Peabody's.

He grimaced. Grandma knew him well. He did feel responsible for Lizzie getting that scar on her face, but he didn't know that he owed her a husband. He also didn't know how he was supposed to find her one.

"I think I might be able to help," Atlas whispered in the still room.

He frowned. "No offense, Atlas, but you're only fourteen. As near as I can tell, you've never even courted a girl."

"Well, it seems to me that it would be just like anything else."

C. J. laughed. "Women aren't like *anything* else, little brother."

"What I mean is," Atlas continued irritably, "if you want

something, you need a plan to get it. And I'm real good at coming up with plans."

"That's a fact." The kid might come up with nothing. On the other hand, Atlas might be able to at least get C. J. started. "What do you think?"

"I think we need to make a list of the things she likes, then find someone who likes to do those same things."

"Makes sense."

"So what does she like?"

"Well, how should I know?" C. J. exploded.

Atlas kicked the bottom of C. J.'s bed. "Then that's what you have to find out." He snickered and added slyly, "Cupid, messenger of luuuv."

C. J. growled and whacked Atlas with a pillow.

C. J. rose at dawn, armed with a plan and a nagging headache. He gulped a cup of coffee on his way to the barn, saddled Goliath, and took off at a gallop for town.

Sometimes it paid to have a brother as methodical as Atlas. All C. J. had to do was find out what Lizzie liked, then he would be able to find her a husband from among his many friends.

He left Goliath at the livery with one of the twins who worked there—he could never tell them apart—and made his way next door to the mercantile. Hank stood on the front porch, sweeping the ever-present dust into the street. Glaring sunshine beat down on his bald head, making his pate shiny and red. He looked up as C. J. approached.

"Mornin', C. J." Hank stuck out a beefy hand and pumped C. J.'s hard, as was his custom. "Heard you picked up that book."

"Sure did. Thanks for ordering it. It'll come in mighty handy."

"You Daltrys thinking of buying up some more land? What with Lee settled down by the river, it seems the lot of you could own the whole of Taylor County if you was of a mind."

C. J. glanced inside the store and saw only Maybelle. She gave him a generous smile before she disappeared behind the curtain. Where was Lizzie? He didn't want to ask Hank, because the man asked too many questions. Even though the store owner was a good man, he told too many people what he learned.

"Guess you ain't decided about that yet," Hank concluded with a grunt. He jabbed a thumb in the direction of the store. "Got a new doohickey in there."

"What's a doohickey?" C. J. scanned the street. Was it possible that Lizzie was already in the store? Hank had just opened. Perhaps she had gone in the back way.

Hank laughed. "Well, I'm not as good at explaining it as Lizzie is, but she ain't here right now. Bless the girl, she's late every day of her life." He leaned the broom against the wall and motioned C. J. inside. He pulled a long tubular-looking instrument from one of the crowded shelves and handed it to C. J. "You look inside it and pretty pictures turn around."

Trying to bury his impatience, C. J. took the tube offered by Hank. He stuck it up to his eye and squinted. Vivid jewel-toned colors of emerald, sapphire, and ruby merged to become triangles, then spirals, then rings inside rings.

C. J. returned it to Hank. "What's it for?"

The other man frowned. "Just a pretty, I guess. Maybe you'd be more interested in—hey, where ya going?"

"I'll be right back." C. J. walked out and toward the north end of town. Lizzie lived beyond the new town library that had been built in Lee's name. C. J. waited on the rise behind the building until he saw her coming toward him.

"Good mornin', Lizzie," he called when she got within a few feet.

Wariness crept into her eyes. "Good morning."

He fell into step beside her and offered his most charming

smile, Minerva's edict ringing in his ears. "It's nice to see you."

"You just saw me yesterday." She stared straight ahead, tension coiling through her body.

He felt a tug of sadness at that, knowing why she wasn't glad to see him. But he was on a mission. "That's a pretty bonnet you're wearing today."

Surprise flared in her eyes, and they darkened to that odd shade of midnight blue. Her hand went up, but instead of touching her bonnet, she grazed her hair where it lay close to her cheek.

Guilt and remorse surged within him. "May I walk with you to the mercantile?"

She stopped and her head swerved toward him. Her gaze, confused and uncertain, held his. He offered what he hoped was a friendly and nonthreatening smile.

She looked quickly away and turned onto Main Street. "It's a public street. I guess you can walk anywhere you want to."

His hands were suddenly itchy with sweat. He and Lizzie passed the library, then the barbershop.

"Morning, Miss Orndorft." C. J. tipped his hat to the slender woman who was both barber and dentist in Paradise Plains. As usual, she wore pants and chaps and a dark cowboy hat over her braided graying brown hair.

"Morning, C. J., Lizzie."

Lizzie bobbed her head, but didn't speak.

C. J. watched her from the corner of his eye. She was nothing like any of the other girls he'd ever walked with. She didn't watch him covertly. Or try to walk closer to him or even make conversation with him. Maybe it was because it was morning and she wasn't completely awake. He remembered that she used to be shy. Maybe she still was.

He wished she would look at him, just once. He wanted to look at her scar without seeming to. He wanted to see what he was responsible for. But she kept her hair draped over the left side of her face.

They passed the boardinghouse. Mrs. Bennett's cheery voice floated through the front door as she greeted her boarders. The clickety-clack of the newspaper press echoed from the newspaper office, and C. J. knew Clay Masterson was already at work on the paper.

All his questions to Lizzie were met with one-syllable answers. She didn't look at him once. Irritation sprouted inside him, but he tamped it down. He couldn't expect her to accept him so easily after all these years. She would have to get to know him again. He wanted her to feel comfortable so she wouldn't bolt away from his friends.

They stepped up onto the porch of the mercantile, and out of habit, C. J. cupped her elbow to assist her. She jerked away, her neck flushing red. Her face drained to a pasty white.

He withdrew immediately, stunned at her panic. "I'm sorry, Lizzie. I didn't mean to startle you."

"It's—fine." She took a deep breath and stepped inside the store. The words were stilted. "Thank you, C. J. It wasn't necessary for you to walk me."

"You're welcome. Would you—"

Hank shuffled out from behind the counter, carrying a crate. "Oh, I see you found her."

Lizzie's gaze cut to C. J., then she turned to go.

"Would you like to have lunch?" He knew that was moving a mite fast, but he was no closer to finding out what she liked to do.

Her head snapped up and uncertainty clouded her blue eyes. "Lunch?" she squeaked. "With you?"

"Yes." He kept his voice even with an effort. No woman had ever responded to him as if his company were something undesirable.

He noticed that Hank stood inside the door, plainly listening, the broom forgotten in his hand. Maybelle watched from behind the counter. She halted in the midst of tying on her apron, her green eyes riveted on Lizzie.

Lizzie swallowed and her gaze skittered away. "No. No, I can't."

"All right." He smiled and his words were gentle, but his frustration mounted. He didn't need this—he stopped the thought. The only other choice was to forfeit, which wasn't a choice at all. "How about supper?"

He saw Hank shift closer. Maybelle's face brightened with hope.

A blush crawled up Lizzie's neck. "No," she choked out. She glanced around and saw Hank and Maybelle. "No, thank you. Please, just go."

"You have to eat sometime. There's no harm in eating with me, is there?" C. J. shifted from one foot to the other. Never having been turned down before, he wasn't sure what to do next.

She took a deep breath and turned a fierce look on him. Fierce and somehow pleading. Just as she had looked at him all those years ago and begged him to leave her alone. "Leave," she urged.

It was the reminder of her long-ago plea that had him backing toward the door. He had obviously upset her. There were no tears in her eyes, but he could see the pain and anger. He'd been right. Grandma didn't know *what* she was getting him into by asking him to find Lizzie a husband.

Lizzie turned and sailed behind the counter to push through the curtain that separated the store from the back room. C. J. looked at Hank, and for once the man didn't speak. His gaze followed Lizzie's retreat, then rested on Maybelle.

C. J. walked out. Not sure what to do next, he stood on the porch of the mercantile, haunted by the tortured look in her eyes. He'd hurt her enough. All those years ago, it had been his idea to go to old man Peabody's. He'd been the one to invite her. And he'd been the one to leave her.

Down the street, he saw Grandma's buggy pull to a stop in front of Wiley Vernon's office. The attorney's office was on the far side of The Hatbox, Miss Lavender's establishment. Wiley assisted Grandma from the buggy and ushered her inside. C. J. stepped off the porch and strode toward the office.

She would have to give him another task. She would understand when he told her about the pain in Lizzie's eyes.

He went through the door to Wiley's office, then closed it silently behind him. There was no sign of Grandma or the lawyer, but the low hum of voices beyond the room told C. J. they were already in Wiley's back office. C. J. would wait.

He removed his hat and fingered the brim. The front area of the office was fancy yet understated. Dark wood bookshelves with glass doors stood in a row along the far wall. Inside, leather-bound books were shelved in precise rows. Two black leather wing chairs sat in one corner, separated by a glossy mahogany table upon which rested an oil lamp.

On the wall was a portrait of Wiley's wife, Miranda, and on the far wall, above the fireplace, was a charcoal drawing of a river with sleek sailboats. Sunshine glinted through the windows, and C. J. examined the room, listening distractedly to the rise and fall of his grandmother's voice.

He moved closer to the desk in the far corner to study a map of Texas. Wiley's voice suddenly rose.

"You're sure about this, Minerva?"

"Absolutely." Her voice came clear and strong across the room.

Wiley spoke with a mixture of fondness and exasperation. "I know you have your reasons for doing this, and it's not my place to ask, but I'm surprised you want this deed changed."

C. J. grinned. Grandma surprised people all the time. Wiley should know that by now.

". . . always thought Lee would be the one."

Why were they talking about Lee? What were they talking about? C. J.'s spine stiffened. *What deed?*

"Lee has his teaching certificate now," his grandmother said. "And besides, he's never been tied to the ranch the way C. J. is."

"And you want me to do it now?" There was a thump, then the sound of shuffling papers.

"Yes," Minerva said. "I'm not sure when I'll give it to C. J., but I want it to be ready. It may not be for a year, but it might be sooner."

C. J. froze, shock slamming into him. His mind raced as he tried to piece together what he'd just heard. His grandmother was deeding the ranch over to him? Why? What had made her change—

The task.

That had to be it. Was the ranch to be his prize if he found Lizzie a husband?

He blinked, excitement unfurling with the shock. Could he really have heard her say that? He *had* heard her say it. Could he find Lizzie a husband? What if he hurt her further?

Determination squared his jaw. He *wouldn't* hurt her. And he wouldn't give up yet.

A chair scraped across the floor in the other room, and C. J. silently let himself out of Wiley's office. He was going to find Lizzie the best damn husband in Texas.

A little while later, he sat next to a window inside The Buccaneer. Was it cheating that he knew his prize? He didn't think so. The knowledge wouldn't help him find a husband for Lizzie, so it shouldn't matter, right?

The ranch? He still couldn't believe it. He wondered how Lee would feel about that.

He wasn't exactly sure how *he* felt about it. He was excited, yes, and definitely up for the challenge. But he couldn't dismiss the pain in Lizzie's eyes earlier. He had planned to try with her again tomorrow, but now he knew he couldn't go back to the ranch without seeing her today.

Until noon, he sat next to a window inside The Buc so he could see her when she left for lunch. *If* she left for lunch. He realized then that he didn't know even that much about her.

But at twelve-thirty, he saw her walk out the door. She glanced up and down the street, then headed up Main and past the library at a brisk walk.

He quickly shoved his money at Fritz, the restaurant owner, and went after her, determined to follow Atlas's suggestion.

She walked toward her house, a small white frame with black shutters. She disappeared between it and another white house with a fence.

C. J. stopped between the houses. A sharp gust of wind tunneled around him. He rubbed his hands together for warmth and scanned the area. Where had she gone? He walked farther back, past a small garden laid out in neat rows and a pecan tree with a wooden chair situated underneath for shade. Watery sunlight trickled through the spidery branches of the pecan tree, making a faint wobbly pattern on the ground. There was no sign of Lizzie. The only thing in view was a sturdy shed.

He halted, looking around. From the shed came a strange sound, like the flutter of wings. C. J. tried out a mockingbird whistle, but got no answer. He tried a bobwhite, but got only another feather ruffle.

He eased up to the shed and pulled the door open. It took a minute for his eyes to adjust, but when they did, he grinned. In one corner was a hoe and a shovel. But set around the small shed were sturdy cages, all open. Huddled inside were an owl, a possum, a hawk, and a black-and-white-spotted dog.

Did these animals belong to Lizzie? He stepped inside, ducking and shifting his shoulders to fit through the door. The roof was too low for him to stand upright. He hunched his shoulders and stepped toward the first cage. The hawk ruffled one wing in a threat.

The other animals eyed him warily, poised to flee if necessary. He clucked softly to them.

"What are you doing here?"

At her sharp voice, he spun and whacked his head on the roof. His hat fell to the ground.

He stooped to pick it up, rubbing the top of his head. "I'm sorry, Lizzie. I was looking for you."

"Most people would look in the house."

"Uh, well, y–yes, I meant to." Was he stuttering? No, couldn't be. "I thought I saw you come back here."

"You're trespassing." Her tone was flat, but edged with panic. Suspicion sharpened her eyes. "Were you following me?"

"Not exactly. I just want to talk."

She leveled a cold look at him. "You're scaring my animals. Come out."

"What are you doing with them?" C. J. glanced back at the cages, anxious to learn something, *anything,* about her. "Where did you find them?"

Some of the chill left her features. She walked inside and moved to the hawk, murmuring to quiet it. She stroked its head and the bird's eyes closed. "They're all injured. I'm just tending them until they can go on their way."

"That hawk looks pretty wild." C. J. eyed the bird's wicked talons, which curved into the wood of its cage. A white bandage was wrapped around one of its legs.

She shrugged. "She's fine with me." As if to prove it, Lizzie stroked the hawk's wings, then its head again.

C. J. moved nearer, drawn by her easy manner with the bird, wishing she could have that ease with people. The hawk was one bird he'd never managed to coax down from the sky. "Can I try?"

She hesitated, looking from him to the bird. "Be very still. Talk to her as you approach."

C. J. did as she directed, speaking in the soothing voice he used with his horses. The bird swiveled its head, sharp eyes boring into C. J. But it remained quiet under C. J.'s hand as he stroked it.

He smiled and looked down at Lizzie.

She looked away. "Why did you come?"

"I'd like to be friends." That was true, he realized. "I'm curious about you and what you're doing these days."

"You're curious." Her voice was flat, edged with impatience. "About the scar?"

"No!"

Mistrust blazed in her eyes. "Friends like how?"

He tried to smile reassuringly. "Well, like friends."

"Don't you have enough of those?" she asked sarcastically.

"You can never have too many friends." Sweat dampened his palms and he jammed them in the pocket of his overcoat.

She studied him warily, as if he were an uncontrollable animal and she was trying to decide the best way to handle him. "What do you expect out of this friendship?"

He couldn't help a grin. "Well, you'd have to speak to me on the street if you saw me."

Her gaze flicked over him. "What else?"

"You might have to like me a little." His grin widened. "Or act like you did."

She pursed her lips, her stare cold with no trace of teasing.

He laughed in disbelief. "It's not that hard to like me, is it?"

"I'm not sure."

Her head was tilted back and she stared up at him with confusion and questions in her eyes. Her hair had fallen away from her cheek and in the shaft of weak sunlight coming into the shed, he saw the scar.

Just on the upper side of her left jaw, it ran the length of her face and toward her chin, fading. It was thin, a barely noticeable imperfection in the creamy skin.

He had never seen it up close. After that night, she hadn't let him within ten feet of her. Seeing the scar after all these years pulled something tight in his gut. For that instant, he hated Jude Menefee and he hated himself.

Her features changed, closed against him. She jerked away and darted out the door. "It's time to go."

C. J. walked outside and settled his hat on his head as Lizzie closed the door to the shed.

She kept a wary distance from him. "I can't possibly see why you would want to be friends. We haven't talked in years."

As soon as she spoke, she looked away, as though mortified that she had said anything.

"I know." He softened his voice, feeling the sting of guilt again. He fought the urge to squirm. Caution flared, and he suddenly felt something great and important might be at stake—though he couldn't say what. "I thought it might be time to change that."

Horror widened her eyes as though he'd said he wanted her to strip naked and go swimming in the river.

"Hey, Lizzie—"

"I think you should go." The words were uttered in a shaky whisper. Her face was white as paper.

"I'd like to be friends again." At first he'd come because of Grandma, but now he was surprised to realize he really would like to have her friendship again. He hadn't realized how much until he'd seen her these last two days.

Her face mirrored the uncertainty in his voice. Dark blue eyes, clouded with pain and shyness, searched his face. She cleared her throat. "Good-bye."

"Lizzie—"

"Please." She turned and slipped back inside the shed.

C. J. thought about following her, but she had looked shaken, overwhelmed. She had known the exact moment he had noticed her scar. Even though he didn't think it looked bad, she was obviously self-conscious about it.

He had learned nothing about what she liked, except that she liked animals. He didn't know any men who took care of ailing wild creatures, especially hawks.

It didn't matter. C. J. felt sick, as if he'd intruded and glimpsed a private part of her he wasn't supposed to see. And he had the uneasy feeling he was going to hurt her, no matter how hard he tried not to.

Three

After lunch, Lizzie hurried back to the store, glancing over her shoulder every ten feet. So far, she was alone.

As she always was.

Disappointment stabbed her, but her newly raised suspicion washed it away. That suspicion had followed quickly on the heels of surprise after finding C. J. Daltry in her shed. What had he wanted? Why, after all this time, was he coming around?

Was it curiosity about *her,* as he'd said? Or the scar? Absently, she fingered the scar that ran the length of her left jaw. He had looked at her with pity in his eyes, just as he had all those years ago when he had first seen what Jude had done to her.

She stepped onto the porch of the mercantile and slipped inside, turning at the window to look for C. J. He was nowhere in sight, and relief eased the pressure around her chest. She turned.

Maybelle stood in front of her, green eyes sparkling, her petite figure swamped by the ceiling-high stacks of boxes and crates. She rolled up on tiptoe and peered over Lizzie's shoulder out the window. "Is he out there? I saw him follow you home at lunch."

"You did?" Irritation flared, but she couldn't expect Maybelle to tell C. J. to stay away.

The other woman grinned and stepped around Lizzie. "He's sweet on you, isn't he? I think you're the only girl in town he hasn't courted."

"Of course not." She jerked her head toward Maybelle, startled at her friend's conclusion.

"I think so, Lizzie. Well, except for Meredith Lewis, who married his brother. I think I'm right."

"I didn't mean that." She wove her way around a stack of Hank's new crates and headed for the back room, trying to keep her voice even. "He's not courting me." She gave a sharp laugh. "Absolutely not."

"Then what does he want?" Maybelle hurried to catch up.

Lizzie dropped the curtain and wished her friend would leave her alone.

Maybelle shoved the curtain out of the way, easing beside Lizzie. "Did he come to your house?"

She sighed, not wanting to be rude. Maybelle was one of her new friends, one of a very few. "Yes."

"And?"

"And?" She frowned, placing her reticule in the bottom drawer of Hank's immense oak desk. She sat down in the chair and pulled a ledger toward her.

Maybelle slapped a hand on the ledger, keeping it closed. "What did he want? What did you say? Honestly, Lizzie, tell me what happened."

She stared up at Maybelle's eager face. She didn't want to disappoint her friend, but had a feeling she would. "I told him to leave."

"You what?" Maybelle drew back, the expression on her face as mortified as if Lizzie had held him at gunpoint.

She opened the ledger, hoping to drop the subject.

"You're so shy. I'm sure that's the problem. Maybe he won't be discouraged. He knows that about you, doesn't he?"

"It doesn't matter." But the familiar sharp piercing in her chest told Lizzie it still did. "We were friends once. A long time ago."

"That's a good sign." Hank shouldered his wide bulk through the door. "It's a good place to start."

"Look, you two, I appreciate that you care." Lizzie glanced over her shoulder, wondering how much Hank had heard. "But there won't be anything between me and C. J. Daltry. It's nothing like that." She remembered the pity in his eyes and her jaw tightened.

There had been a time when she had developed a liking for him. But those were memories of a little girl, a little girl who was no longer. "It will never be anything like that," she added emphatically.

She ducked her head and pretended to study the numbers.

"Aw, now, come on, Lizzie." Hank patted her shoulder awkwardly. "I can't imagine why a fella like C. J. would come around if it wasn't for courting."

"Courting trouble, maybe?" Lizzie arched a brow.

Maybelle snapped her fingers. "Maybe he's heard how good you are with those little strays you take in."

She hid a smile. "I don't think so."

"Well, then, what the devil is it?" Hank boomed impatiently.

"Hello!" Miss Lavender's voice chirped from the front. "Hank! Maybelle!"

Hank gave a snort and pushed through the curtain.

"We'll figure it out." Maybelle patted Lizzie's hand, then followed her husband out of the room.

Lizzie hated disappointing them. Since she had begun working at the store after Jude's death, they had quickly become her friends.

She didn't know C. J.'s reasons for coming around, but she did know it *wasn't* for courting. Her fingers edged up to her jaw again. No, C. J. definitely wasn't coming around for courting.

For an instant, she heard again the echo of children's laughter from that long-ago night. The warmth of being included swept over her like a spring breeze. Just as quickly, it disappeared.

The cold, hard fact was that Lizzie had never been and would never be included. In anything.

She tried to keep her mind on the numbers, but memories squeezed in. She stilled, unable to stop the crush of the past. That night, her face had been swollen and bloody. It had been a week before she could go out of the house. By then, the scar was a thin red line and she had learned she could keep it covered with her hair.

She had gone to the livery to get a liniment for Jude's mare. Determined to keep her vow to Papa Jude and avoid people, she had walked home through the alleys.

But she hadn't been quick enough to escape C. J. He'd caught up to her behind the mercantile. When she faced him, his eyes grew wide with horror at her scar. He asked what had happened, but she ran for home.

The next day, he had waited outside her house until Papa Jude left to go to the church. She couldn't face him. He spoke through the door, somberly apologizing for having left her at Peabody's and inviting her to have lunch with him. Though she'd desperately wanted a friend, she'd refused. Just as she'd promised she would.

Terrified that Jude would hear of any association with C. J., she stayed clear of him. And the other children stayed clear of her.

Only Lily Brown and Ann Marie Hardin, the other two girls who'd been at old man Peabody's that night, tried to talk to her. They had come to her house and she had rebuked them. She would give Jude no reason to send her away.

When school started later that year, she had heard the

whispers, seen the stares. Some kids had taunted her, saying she'd been captured by Indians and tortured. George Bates had told everyone she was a witch and had the mark on her. It wasn't so hard to stay away from some of them after that.

Now, all these years later, she wondered if she shouldn't have left Paradise Plains, just as Jude had threatened to make her do. In another place, she might have had friends. But there was no use dwelling on what-ifs. Jude was dead now.

In the nine months since he had passed away—gunned down in Fort Worth by the very men he was trying to convert to a Christian life—Lizzie was trying new things and had even made friends of Hank and Maybelle. Perhaps she could make other friends as well. But not C. J. Daltry.

She didn't want his pity. Or his friendship. She wanted to steer clear of him.

No matter how hard Lizzie tried, she couldn't avoid C. J. He didn't follow her home again, but she saw him in the morning as she walked to the mercantile. She saw him at lunch, either at the corner of the mercantile or as she walked past the library. After work, he always managed to pass her on Main Street.

He always smiled, always said hello, but he didn't try to speak to her alone. That eased some of her nervousness, but she was too aware and too curious to be completely comfortable.

He was the most handsome man in the county, besides his brother, Lee, and Lizzie couldn't figure out why he was suddenly everywhere she went. She'd lived for years in the same town with him and managed to avoid seeing him, except for town gatherings and the occasional church service that he attended.

She was surprised to realize one morning that he wasn't around. She actually looked for him, going so far as to walk past the livery, until she realized what she was doing.

That had been last week, and now as Lizzie walked out onto the porch of the mercantile into the fresh March sunshine, she nearly tripped over him. He and George Bates were sprawled in a couple of rockers that Hank had set on the porch, just for "socializing."

C. J.'s sand-colored cowboy hat rode low on his head and his azure eyes, as vivid as the sky today, pierced her. Powerful, leanly muscled legs stretched out in front of him. His hands were folded across his belly. They were a dark bronze against the buff of his work shirt. "Lizzie."

"Hello." Her breath lodged in her throat. She felt suddenly self-conscious and . . . targeted. She turned quickly away and stepped off the porch.

She heard the creak of wood and the thud of boots. C. J. and George left their chairs to follow her.

Her heart stepped up its beat and small beads of sweat trickled between her breasts. She sneaked a glance first at George then at C. J. What did they want? C. J. smiled, and she jerked her gaze away.

"Hi, Lizzie." George held his hat in his hand, one finger absently stroking the brim.

"Hello," she replied huskily. She eyed him warily and looked away.

The familiar churn of nervousness assailed her. She didn't know what to say, how to act with these two boys. Men, she amended as she watched C. J.'s long shadow stretch out beside hers. They were children no longer.

"George and I were just talking about the spring dance." C. J.'s blue eyes settled on her, stirring a faint heat through her belly.

She swallowed and her gaze shifted to him. "Dance?"

"They have one every spring." There was a smile in his voice. "Remember? Since they built the school a few years back?"

"Oh. Of course." She had never thought about the dance because she had never gone.

"Were you planning on going with anyone?" George asked.

Lizzie halted so quickly her teeth snapped together. "Wh–what?"

George and C. J. stopped as well. George grinned, though it looked more like a painful grimace, and stepped closer. "Were you planning to go with anyone?"

Her chin came up. A sharp retort burned her tongue, but she bit back the words. She looked from George to C. J., expecting to see mockery. Instead she saw a sincere question.

She couldn't quite keep the edge from her voice. "My social calendar is simply too full."

C. J. grinned.

George looked confused. He turned his hat slowly in his hand. "I was wondering—maybe you'd go with me? That is, if you want to?"

Lizzie blinked, telling herself it was from the sharp blaze of the sun, not from the surprise that shot through her. Wasn't it George who'd said she was a witch? She arched a brow at him. "Aren't you afraid I'll turn you into a toad or something?"

"My, my, aren't we prickly?" C. J. murmured, laughter shining in his eyes.

George coughed. "All right—"

C. J. spoke up. "He was just a kid, Lizzie. You can't hold that against him."

She shot him a look, irritation spinning through her. "I suppose not." She looked at George. "Me? You?"

George smiled, though his eyes were cloudy with uncertainty.

Though she'd never noticed anything about George, she noted suddenly that he had very nice eyes, kind and velvety brown. And he was looking at her as if he really did want her company for the dance. But why would he want to take *her?* "Thank you, George, but I don't think so."

He looked surprised more than disappointed and turned as if to leave. "Well, if you're sure—"

"You already said you weren't going with anyone else," C. J. broke in.

"I'm not." She started walking again.

The two men fell into step beside her. C. J. demanded, "Then why won't you go?"

She frowned at his tone. "I've never—I don't see what all the fuss is about. It's just a dance."

"It could be a lot of fun," George wheedled.

Her stomach tied in knots, the way it always did when she was confronted with the unfamiliar. She could just imagine the look on Papa Jude's face if she announced she was going to the dance. The thought caused her to pause.

Papa Jude was dead. She could do whatever she wanted. And she had *never* been to the spring dance before.

Before she could lose her nerve, she swallowed hard. "George, thank you. I'd like to go."

He looked taken aback. Perhaps she had said the wrong thing. Perhaps a girl could only accept on the first request.

Then he smiled, though it didn't quite erase the dazed look in his eyes. "It will be a lot of fun. You'll see."

"Yeah. We can all go together." C. J.'s eyes gleamed, and Lizzie thought she detected relief there. "I'm taking Emma Samuels. You know her, don't you, Lizzie?"

"Not very well." Of course Lizzie could say that about nearly everyone in town. Why did she suddenly feel a wave of disappointment that C. J. wasn't the one who had asked her?

He slapped George on the shoulder. "We'll be going along now, Lizzie. You won't be sorry."

The two men touched their hats to her and strode off toward the livery.

She stood dazed in the street for several seconds, then shook herself. "Wait!" she called. "When is it?"

C. J. and George turned. C. J. stared intently at George,

who finally answered, "It's Saturday. Starts around seven. I'll call for you."

"All right." She watched them disappear into the livery. She licked her suddenly dry lips, feeling a mixture of excitement and apprehension.

She hadn't been able to avoid C. J. And now she was going to the spring dance. Nervousness fluttered in her stomach.

At least she wasn't going with C. J. She should be relieved, but she wasn't.

C. J. watched Lizzie walk away, her slim hips gently swaying. A familiar heat grew in his belly, the same feeling he'd experienced with several women. The realization pulled him up short and he frowned.

"Okay, I did it." George elbowed him.

"Yeah." He glanced over, remembering the distrust in Lizzie's blue eyes when George had asked her to the dance. But he'd also seen a flare of yearning.

"She looked scared to me."

"She wasn't. Maybe nervous." Soft color had suffused her cheeks, and C. J. found himself wondering what it would be like to have her look at him that way, full of wonder and anticipation. He shoved the thought away.

"I don't know if I want to do this."

His head whipped around. "You already said you would."

"Yeah, but—"

"How about I let you use Goliath twice?"

George's eyes widened. "Really?"

C. J. glanced back at Lizzie, wishing he didn't still smell her rosewater scent. "Really."

"Deal." George stuck out his hand.

C. J. turned, tearing his gaze from Lizzie to shake George's hand. Together they walked down the street to the livery.

"So when will you bring Goliath over?"

C. J. tried to escape thoughts of Lizzie's eyes, uncertain and guarded. They taunted him, and he wished George had asked her without any prodding from him. "Huh? Oh, whenever your mare's in heat."

"It'll probably be a couple of weeks." George rubbed his hands together. "That'll be some colt, huh?"

C. J. chewed the inside of his cheek. Ever since he'd offered Goliath to George in exchange for asking Lizzie to the dance, unease had skimmed along his nerves.

Bribery, plain and simple.

He'd had no other choice, he reminded himself. When he had first approached George, his friend had looked horrified, then burst out laughing, certain that C. J. was challenging him with a new dare. Only after the promise of Goliath standing stud would George agree to ask Lizzie to the dance.

C. J.'s gaze narrowed on his friend and he stopped in front of the livery. "You're not hooked up with Lily Brown, are you?"

George's features hardened. "You know I'm not. She hasn't paid a whit of attention to me in months."

"Good." He didn't want Lizzie becoming attached to someone already spoken for.

George shot him a sour look and muttered something under his breath.

C. J. leveled a gaze on him. "You better not forget to take her, either."

"I won't." He rolled his eyes. "As if you'd let me. What's going on, anyway? Why her?"

"All you need to worry about is earning the right to use Goliath," C. J. told him. He couldn't discuss the details with George, even though he was in no position to deny his friend anything right now. George would think his whole family was crazy. "This better stay between us, George. I don't want Lizzie's feelings to be hurt."

"Yeah. I wouldn't want her to find out about this."

C. J.'s jaw tightened. "You'd better show her a good time."

"I will." George shifted beside him and glanced back. "She's kinda pretty. In a subtle kind of way."

"Yes. She is." C. J. mentally measured the nip of her tiny waist, the noticeable spring in her step. She had looked pretty today, her hair sleek and shining with the sun twining through the midnight strands and her blue eyes warmed with pleasure. And her skin—had he ever noticed her porcelain skin before?

The scar, definitely, but not the rose-and-cream satin of it, the graceful sweep of her elegant neck. Unease nipped at him again.

George might be reluctant right now, but on the night of the dance he'd change his mind. Lizzie was smart. And good company, he hoped.

C. J. had done his part. All that remained was getting George to call for her on his own.

Four

THAT SATURDAY NIGHT, C. J. CALLED FOR EMMA IN THE GOOD carriage, then stopped for George.

The night was soft around them, but fringed with an early spring crispness. The sky was clear and inky, the moon a silver crescent. Stars scattered about like drops of mercury, as though sprinkled by Zeus. When C. J. pulled to a stop in front of Lizzie's house, George climbed down and straightened his brown string tie.

He walked to the door, but before he could knock, Lizzie opened it. C. J. turned his head at the creak of wood and sucked in his breath. Lantern light haloed her head and outlined her figure in soft amber. As though she stood behind a veil, he could see the blurred definition of slender shoulders, full breasts, and tiny, tiny waist. Caught just above her breast with a dark ribbon, her hair hung over her left shoulder. It shimmered, tempting a man to touch it, bury his face in it.

The thought hit him abruptly and he jerked his gaze away. Emma sat beside him in the carriage with her hand stuck slyly in his coat pocket. He stared at her classic profile—her high cheekbones, the pert nose with its slight upturn, her full, rosy lips.

He smiled at her and looked up as George and Lizzie approached the carriage.

"Emma, this is Lizzie Colepepper," George said.

"Good evening," Emma murmured.

George looked dazed, as though he wasn't quite sure this was the same Lizzie.

C. J. grinned. Everything was going exactly as he'd planned.

Up close, he thought Lizzie looked even more fetching. The dress she wore was deep purple and had elbow-length sleeves and a high white collar. The regal color made her skin look as translucent as moonlight, and she appeared almost fragile. Vulnerable. Guilt tightened in his gut again for the methods he'd used to get her here.

"We're taking a carriage to the school?" she exclaimed, clearly pleased. "It's only over the rise."

Some of C. J.'s guilt eased at her obvious pleasure. He looked over his shoulder and grinned at her. "We're going in style."

Emma's hand tightened in his pocket and he shifted his gaze to her. She smiled coaxingly, but the smile didn't reach her eyes.

She leaned close and whispered, "What do you think of my new dress?"

He looked down. Beneath her cloak, her blue satin dress was cut low and her breasts swelled over the line of the bodice. She stroked the creamy skin and smiled at C. J.

His groin burned. "Mmm, nice."

"And my hair?"

He didn't want to tear his gaze from her breasts, but he did. "Lovely."

She smiled and snuggled closer, pressing her breasts against his arm. C. J.'s aroused manhood surged against his britches. Anticipation washed over him, and for an instant he savored it.

Behind them, George spoke to Lizzie. "We're going in style."

C. J. grinned and clucked to the pair of bays. This might be easier than he'd imagined. George looked half-smitten already.

Two hours later, he stood with George and watched the dancers whirl by in a flash of color. A wooden deck had been erected beside the schoolhouse for dancing outside. Lanterns hung suspended from ropes and bathed the entire area in a rosy glow. The fiddler, banjo player, and mouth organist stood in the corner, diagonally across from C. J. and George. They launched into a lively reel.

The platform rattled from the weight of the dancers. Music and voices merged, creating a pleasant tangle.

C. J. gulped down his punch and spoke over the clapping hands and moving feet. "What do you think?"

Lee and Meredith whirled by and Lee gave C. J. a meaningful look. He followed Lee's gaze to see Lizzie. She was dancing with Hank, whom she'd danced with earlier. She smiled at something Hank said, and C. J. smiled, too.

George tore his eyes from the dance floor and blinked. "About Lizzie? She's . . . all right. She looks nice."

"Nice?" C. J. thought she looked more than nice. "So are you going to see her again?"

"Well, I don't know. Maybe." George's attention returned to the dance floor. He straightened, squaring his shoulders and lifting his chin, posturing just as C. J.'s stallion did when he scented a mare in heat.

C. J. glanced toward the dance floor, expecting to see Lizzie whirling by with Hank. Instead he saw Lily Brown, leading one of the twins from the livery around the floor and straight for George.

"Oh, no, you don't." He stepped in front of George to block his view.

Her gaze intent on George, Lily glided by. Something

white floated through the air over C. J.'s head and landed at George's feet.

C. J. spun in time to see his friend stumble as he bent to pick up Lily's lace handkerchief. The reel ended and George straightened. He shoved his punch glass into C. J.'s hand and followed Lily's come-hither gaze, answering the call of a siren with blind obedience.

"Damn it, George."

George ignored him, walking over to Lily and presenting her with the handkerchief. She smiled and tucked her hand through his arm, her lashes fluttering coyly.

C. J. searched the crowd and found Lizzie standing alone under a tree. She had a clear view of George and Lily. As the couple disappeared around the schoolhouse, C. J. saw hurt flit across Lizzie's face.

Regret stabbed him. This was his fault, and one of the reasons he didn't think Grandma should've assigned him this particular task. He didn't want Lizzie to get hurt. Not by him or George.

Emma was still dancing with Clay Masterson, so C. J. headed over to Lizzie.

"Hi." His voice sounded overly bright, but he wanted to wipe the loneliness from her face.

"Hello." She gave him a guarded smile.

It bolstered his courage. He stood next to her, not touching her but able to feel her heat and smell the faint tease of rose water. He crossed his arms in front of him and rocked on his heels. "Having a good time?"

"Yes, I am." She lifted her chin, daring him to dispute it.

Had she seen George leave with Lily? She must have. "I saw you dancing with my brother earlier."

"Yes." Her voice was cool, filled with warning. "And with Hank. Are you in charge of my dance card?"

"Certainly not." He laughed, inwardly cursing George for leaving her. Would she always be so defensive with him? Or was it because of George? "I did notice you danced with George, too."

"And George."

He could tell nothing from her soft tone. Her gaze shifted to him, speculative and judging. As though she knew his every secret, especially the one regarding the task. He noticed his hands were sweating and his gut knotted.

"Would you like to dance with me?" He found he wanted to lessen the hurt of George's leaving.

"You needn't feel obligated. I'm fine."

"I want to dance with you," he said firmly. And he did. Suddenly, surprisingly, he wanted to see how she would feel next to him.

She was going to refuse. He could tell. "It's the last waltz," he wheedled. "Don't break my heart."

She gave him a flat stare, then a hint of a smile. "I didn't know you had one."

"Ouch!" He offered his arm. "Shall we?"

Her gaze passed slowly over him, weighing and wary. Hesitation etched her features, then she shrugged. "All right."

He didn't cup her elbow to assist her up the steps to the dance floor, but did press close behind her. Her heat floated around him, soft and inviting.

They found a place in the middle of the crowded floor. The slight scent of roses filled his nostrils, mingled with the fresh new air of spring. Couples jostled and bumped against them and he pulled her closer, until her breasts nudged his chest and he could feel the warmth of her thighs against his. His muscles quivered suddenly and heat stroked up his spine.

He slid an arm around her waist and realized that she was built so small that he could splay one hand across her rib cage, just under the curve of her breast, if he desired.

A latent wanting sprang to raw life within him. Her breasts flattened against him, firm and caressing with each movement across the floor. A couple bumped into them, but C. J. barely noticed.

He tightened his hand around hers and pulled it to his chest, keeping their elbows drawn in. Her head came up and shock flitted through her eyes, as though he'd offended propriety. She glanced down, but he could see the flush in her cheeks. He wished she would look at him again.

The back of his hand nestled against her hair. Silky strands teased his knuckles, slipping slyly between his fingers to tickle his nerve endings, stroke his palm. She swayed against him in a teasing mimicry of the love act; they moved together then apart as the music dictated, a graceful thrust and parry of their bodies.

C. J. breathed deeply, intoxicated by the rose scent of her and a deeper warmth that hinted at passion and stolen kisses. He was drawn into a spell of touch and smell woven by Lizzie. He didn't know when, but they had stopped moving.

She raised her head and looked at him. Lantern light gilded her ebony hair and one half of her lovely face. In her eyes, he read the same uncertainty and flare of desire that he felt. His hand rested across her back, feeling the heat pool between them, wanting to prolong it. Her lips were moist and slightly parted as she stared up at him.

He wanted to kiss her. The thought flitted through his mind, then disappeared as sound trickled back. Feet shuffled across the planked floor. Punch glasses clinked. The music ebbed, then the banjo twanged as the player fingered a chord.

C. J. exhaled and forced a shaky smile, leading her off the dance floor. He couldn't meet her eyes. "George is probably wondering where you are. I'll go find him. You stay right here."

He escaped, frowning. What was wrong with him? He'd actually thought about kissing her. He wasn't supposed to want that—*George* was! By Thor, where was George? C. J.

searched through town, behind the school, even behind the library, but didn't find George and Lily.

As he headed back to the dance floor, he wondered what to tell Lizzie. Despite her silence on the subject, she had to know George had left with Lily. What could C. J. say to her? How could he apologize? The whole mess was his fault. And Grandma's, he thought hotly.

He stopped at the tree where he'd left Lizzie and was overcome with disappointment.

She was gone.

As Lizzie walked toward home, anger bubbled inside her. Part of it was directed at George for embarrassing her, but a larger part was aimed at C. J. She wondered why George had asked her to the dance, then left with Lily, but she wouldn't waste any tears over him. She had gone simply because she wanted to, not because of any feelings she had for him.

On the other hand, she didn't understand *what* she was feeling for C. J.

She had enjoyed her dance with him. So why was she angry? *He* hadn't asked her to the dance, then left with someone else.

She was humiliated by George's actions—the whole town had witnessed his departure with Lily Brown. But she couldn't stop reliving those moments in C. J.'s arms. She'd felt alive, graceful, almost . . . beautiful.

She walked faster, skirting a rut in the road. How could she feel those things? C. J. Daltry had his pick of women. He certainly would not want her.

And she wanted nothing to do with him. A little voice inside mocked her, but she pushed it away.

"Lizzie, wait!"

C. J.! *Of all the bother!* Lizzie tucked her chin into her chest and hurried toward her house, only several yards away now.

"Lizzie, please!"

She stopped, her face burning at the realization that C. J. probably felt she was his responsibility. She lifted her chin, determined to relieve him of that notion.

"I thought I told you to wait." He skidded to a stop in front of her, smiling, his breathing ragged and fast.

"I can see myself home," she said stiffly. "I've done it for a good many years. Good night."

His smile faded.

She went around him to walk toward the house.

He caught up to her. "I'd like to walk with you."

"Well, here we are," she said brightly as she stopped in front of her porch. "I had a nice time. Thank you." She turned to go in, wanting to escape his knowing blue eyes, the strange flutter in her stomach, the cloying sense of being trapped. "And tell George the same."

He halted in front of her, the moonlight sculpting his molded cheekbones and full lips and silvering his sandy mustache. "George got tied up."

"Yes, I saw the 'rope.' " Lizzie stepped onto her porch. "I know what happened to George. You don't have to coddle me, C. J." Although the idea did hold appeal.

He hesitated, then reached out and placed a hand on her arm. His touch burned through the fabric of her sleeve.

An unfamiliar warmth shot through her legs and tickled her belly. She slowly pulled away, her thoughts not on George but on the man beside her.

Moonlight fell on the porch and created a wedge of silver light. She could see uncertainty in his eyes, but didn't understand it.

Her gaze settled on his lips and she wondered what it would be like to be kissed by him. As Maybelle had said, almost every other girl in town already knew.

He shifted closer. "You look real pretty tonight. George is a fool."

She stared up at him, surprised and uncomfortable. Her

heart swelled. She clasped her hands tightly together in front of her. "You don't have to do that."

"Do what? Tell the truth?" He grinned, the smile spreading to his eyes and causing her to smile as well.

"You're the county's biggest flirt, C. J. Daltry," she accused, trying to keep a stern face. But even knowing it didn't lessen her pleasure. She'd never flirted in her life, and she couldn't keep the grin from her face.

"Couldn't deny that if I wanted to." His voice was husky, stroking her into a sudden stillness. His blue eyes settled on her lips and they tingled.

Confused and uncertain, she froze. A strange tension hummed in the air between them, new and unrelated to the past they shared.

He dragged his gaze away and looked down. When he looked at her again, there was no heat, only mild interest. "I'll say good night. I hope you enjoyed some part of tonight."

"I did. It's the first time I've ever been to the spring dance. Thank you for thinking of me."

He gave a half grin, bemused. "It wasn't me who asked you. It was George."

"So it was." Somehow C. J. had had something to do with that, but Lizzie wasn't sure exactly how.

He stood for a moment longer, watching her with an intense stillness. A quiver ran through her. "You'd better go. Emma will be waiting."

"I told her where I was going."

"Oh." She licked her suddenly dry lips.

"Well." He turned to go, then swung back to face her, his eyes serious. "Did you think I wouldn't come back?"

"I haven't been able to stop you so far," she said wryly.

He laughed. "No. I meant when I went to find George. Is that why you didn't wait like I asked you to? I know I left you once before—"

"That was a long time ago," she cut him off, assaulted by

memories of the past, not wanting to talk about them. She gripped the support post of the porch.

"I didn't leave you at Peabody's on purpose." The words rushed out, fervent and almost pleading. "When I realized what had happened, I came back for you, but it was too late. If I'd had any idea that he would catch us that night, I never would've invited you." His face was tight with guilt and remorse. "I'm not heartless."

"I never thought you were." In the face of his sincerity and obvious misery, her anger waned. She hesitated, then stepped off the porch toward him. "Is that why you've been coming around? Because you feel badly about that night? About my . . . scar?"

Reluctance shadowed his face. He tilted his head back and stared at the stars for a minute. His voice came hoarse and tight. "Partly."

Her heart sank. "I don't blame you for my scar," she said stiffly, drawing into herself again. "You can stop doing penance."

"It's not penance!" He shoved a hand through his blond hair and his gaze sought hers. "If I hadn't invited you, if I hadn't been showing off for you, it never would've happened."

Lizzie swallowed around the lump in her throat. She could see how responsible he felt. She didn't want him, *anyone,* feeling shunned and unloved as she had for so many years. "C. J., you had nothing to do with this scar."

"That's not really true, is it?" He held her gaze, his own full of anger meant for himself. "You got it that night because you were caught. You were caught because of me."

"That part is true, but—"

"If you didn't blame me, why wouldn't you see me anymore?"

"I couldn't." Alarms sounded in her head. *Go in, Lizzie. Go in now before you tell him everything.*

"I thought we were friends."

"So did I." Sadness shifted through her, for times lost as a young girl, possibilities lost now.

He frowned at her, an earnest desire to understand in his eyes. "If you didn't blame me, then it makes no sense."

"Stop!" Her voice rang out sharply. She gripped the post until splinters dug into her palm. The words tumbled out, spurred by the blame and guilt she now knew C. J. had carried. "My stepfather forbade me to see any of you."

"Why? Because we were caught? We were just kids, Lizzie. It was a stupid thing to do, I admit, but—"

"I embarrassed him," she said stiffly. Frustration raked through her. She didn't want to talk about Jude with C. J. or anyone else.

"Even at school?" C. J.'s confusion was evident as he struggled to understand. "He never would've known."

"He said he'd ship me out on an orphan train," she whispered, the hateful words slipping through her tight throat.

C. J. rocked back on his heels as though punched. "Hell . . . fire." Disbelief blazed in his eyes. Then pity crept in.

"I'd appreciate it if you'd keep this conversation to yourself," she said briskly, turning away from the sympathy on his face.

He stepped onto the porch, his voice close to her ear. "I really do want to renew our friendship. If you do. And I swear I won't tell anyone what you told me tonight."

Friendship? Yes, that's all she would ever have with C. J. Daltry. That's all she wanted, she told herself. He was involved with countless women. And Lizzie was, well—she was as alone as she'd always been.

A deep, secret part of her longed for more, longed for a friend, a . . . lover. But her dreams had slowly been killed by her rigid stepfather. *You're too clumsy, Lizzie. You're too loud. You have the devil's tongue.*

Her gaze held C. J.'s. Questions clouded his eyes as he waited. During their dance, she had thought she detected a flicker of desire. But there was nothing in his eyes now except earnestness. And an expectancy.

She had precious few friends and didn't want to resist any overtures. "Friends. I'd like that."

He grinned, a wide smile that flashed his perfect teeth and sent a tingle up her spine. She felt her own lips curve and wondered how he had managed to make her smile simply by smiling himself.

He took her hand and kissed it. His mustache tickled her skin, causing her nerves to jump and spawning a new hope in her breast.

As she watched him walk away, her smile faded. She had shared with him what she had with no one else. It left her feeling vulnerable and dissatisfied with her life. C. J.'s attention tonight had opened up possibilities in Lizzie's mind, possibilities she couldn't afford to ponder.

She had done just fine without him until now. One night wasn't going to change that. She hadn't been able to depend on C. J. back then. She told herself she wouldn't be able to now.

He'd almost told her the bloody truth. He could go to town now and tell her. The urge swept through C. J., strong enough to cause him to pull off his work gloves and turn toward the barn door.

How would she react if she found out his sudden interest in her was due to Grandma's edict? After what George had pulled last night on Lizzie, C. J. just hadn't been able to tell her the whole truth.

Anger churned inside him. He yanked the gloves back on and lifted a bridle from a peg on the wall. Since learning about Jude Menefee's cruel threat, C. J. had experienced an uncommon urge to go to her, to make certain she was all right, even though she had been fine when he'd left last night. He pulled a saddle from the sawhorse next to him.

"How tight are you gonna cinch that saddle?" Atlas stood

a few feet away, holding his new roan gelding, Zeus, on a lead rope.

C. J. blinked and looked down. His paint mare had puffed out her belly and the cinch cut into her like twine into sausage. He released the pressure and shook his head.

"What are you going to do about George leaving Lizzie at the dance?"

"How'd you know about that?" C. J. growled. Satisfied the saddle was fitted properly, he checked the stirrup length.

Atlas shrugged and offered a carrot to his horse. "I was down at Lee's a while ago. He and Meredith were talking about it."

"I don't know what to do. I've got to find somebody better than George. Somebody who won't run off like a low-down son of a snake."

"You're really mad, huh? How come?"

A flush heated his cheeks. C. J. wasn't exactly sure, but he hadn't been able to get Lizzie out of his mind all morning. Or last night. "I'd feel the same about anyone who treated a lady that way. It's just not right."

The sound of an approaching horse drew his attention. He turned and saw George. His anger exploded anew.

"Bates, get your scurvy butt off my land!" he bellowed, striding toward George and his bay mare.

George swung down off his horse, frowning. "What's wrong, Daltry? I came out to check on Goliath."

"You can just forget Goliath." C. J. leaned into George's face, staring him down. Blood roared in his ears.

Atlas's voice penetrated through C. J.'s anger. "Why is he checking on Goliath?"

George narrowed his eyes. "Daltry, you promised him to me. You can't back out on a promise. We shook on it."

"There is no deal. You didn't follow through."

"What deal?" Atlas sidled up beside C. J., looking from him to George.

George glared and pushed C. J. "You only said I had to ask her to the dance. I did that. So pay up."

"Nothin' doin'." C. J. shoved George back, knocking his friend back onto his heels. He wanted to ram his fist into George's face. "You left her alone there."

"You . . ." George faltered for a moment, then announced triumphantly, "You never said I had to see her home."

"Well, of course you were supposed to see her home!" C. J. landed a punch to George's stomach.

The other man doubled over, but brought his knee up. C. J. sidestepped, barely escaping a painful jab to the groin.

He roared and charged George, landing a stinging punch to the man's right jaw. George's fist slammed C. J. in the stomach and his breath whooshed out.

Atlas circled around them, dodging fists and knees. "C. J., you bribed George to ask Lizzie to the dance? You bribed him with Goliath?"

"Get outta here, Atlas." C. J.'s head pounded and the muscles in his stomach burned. He swung another blow at George, his arms and legs feeling weightless.

George blocked the punch, then stumbled back. Both men stared, panting. Blood oozed from a cut above George's eye and blood trickled from C. J.'s nose.

Atlas stared, his mouth hanging open. "C. J., I don't think that's fair. I don't think Grandma would—"

"Shut up!" C. J. spun and advanced on him. "Shut up, Atlas, right now, or I'll dunk you in the trough."

His brother backed up a step, then another, looking from C. J. to George. He pressed his lips together and nodded.

George bent at the waist, sucking in great gulps of air. "You can't go back on our deal, C. J. It'll be all over town that you don't honor your word."

"Damn it!" C. J. whirled, his fist itching to smash George's nose. He didn't need Atlas running to Grandma with this tale. Or George running back to town. Drawing in a deep breath, he swiped at the blood on his nose. "You can use him once. Only once."

"You said twice." George straightened, pressing a hand to his ribs.

C. J. advanced on him, each breath tearing out of him in a ragged pant. "Once because you asked her. You did not take her home. In fact you left her there—in front of the whole town—and took off with Lily." He paused for a breath, wincing at the sharpness in his lungs. "Once. And that only because I made the deal."

"Gol–ly." Atlas's voice whispered through the barn.

George hesitated, still glaring. "All right. I'll let you know when my mare's in heat."

"Fine." C. J. tilted his head back and pinched his nose to slow the bleeding.

George mounted, staring at C. J. as if he didn't recognize him. "Hell, the way you're defending her, you'd think you were in love with the girl or something."

The anger kicked up again, along with an unfamiliar surge of protectiveness. "You were wrong, George, and you know it."

George shot him a surly look, then wheeled his horse around and rode out.

C. J. picked up his gloves and tugged them on as he walked back to the paint.

"Gol–ly!" Atlas fell into step beside him. "You whacked him good."

"You don't need to be tellin' anybody. You hear?"

"I won't. I swear." Atlas crossed his heart. "You were really mad, huh?"

C. J. nodded and swung into the saddle.

"I can't believe George said you were in love with Lizzie." Atlas snorted, then sneaked a glance at C. J. "You're not, are you?"

"Of course not." C. J. thumped his little brother on the ear. "Just being a gentleman."

"Do gentlemen bribe other gentlemen to call for a lady?"

"You know they don't." C. J. shifted, uncomfortable with his brother's questions. "This was a special case. And it would really hurt Lizzie's feelings if she heard that, so keep it to yourself. All right?"

"All right." Atlas followed C. J. to the barn door. "What are you going to do now? Who will you get next?"

"I don't know," he muttered. "But whoever it is, I'll definitely be more specific."

He rode out, wishing he could get rid of a sudden urge to see Lizzie as easily as he'd gotten rid of his anger.

Five

Last night C. J. had actually sounded as if he truly cared. For just an instant Lizzie had let herself believe he did. Surprise had rippled through her and weakened her defenses. But he'd admitted he had sought her out because he felt badly about what had happened at Peabody's.

She touched her scar and tried to push C. J. out of her mind.

As she tended the animals in the shed, thoughts of him still hovered like a forbidden secret. She turned back to the dog and dipped a bandage into the buttermilk poultice she'd made. Midmorning sunshine streamed into the shed through the partially opened door. Lizzie liked to keep the animals themselves shaded, while letting them have fresh air. Today the air smelled of spring and new flowers and freshly turned earth, while inside the shed the ripe scent of animals was evident.

She tried to keep her thoughts from C. J., but she kept replaying the day she'd found him here in the shed. Despite the suspicion she'd felt at his sudden interest in her, she also felt a stirring of warmth, a desire that he might truly want to renew their friendship.

She wrapped the bandage around Domino's hind leg. He

whimpered once, but sat still under her ministrations. The infection was nearly gone, but she didn't want to take any chances.

Somehow the dog had gotten into a bois d'arc thorn bush. When Lizzie had found him almost two weeks ago, his leg had been swollen to twice its normal size. She had worked the thorn free and managed to slowly rid the dog of the infection. His black-and-white coat was shiny and smooth, free of the burrs and dirt he'd had when she found him. He watched her now with soft black eyes as she scratched him between the ears.

"You'll soon be running again, Domino." She had named him, as she did all the strays. "But maybe you'll decide to stay here."

She gave him a last pat and moved to the hawk. Speaking softly to the bird, she stroked its head. "How are you today, pretty girl?"

The hawk pressed its head into her hand, its feathers smooth and satiny against her palm.

"Yoo–hoo! Lizzie!"

The hawk's good wing jutted out in a panic and she struck out with her foot. One talon pricked Lizzie's hand.

She jerked her hand back and squinted to examine it. Her skin burned and blood welled from a small scratch. The hawk settled down with a ruffle of its feathers.

"Lizzie, are you out here?"

She pressed her apron against the wound and straightened. "In here."

The door swung open and Maybelle stepped inside. "Oooh! Ah–choo!" The other woman lifted a gloved hand to her nose and sneezed again. Will peered around the door, trapped on the other side of his mother's wide skirts.

"Good morning, Will." Lizzie smiled and motioned the little boy inside.

"It's so musty in here." Maybelle waved a hand delicately in front of her nose. "How do you stand it?"

"It's only dirt." Lizzie smiled at her friend's son. "What do you have today?"

"Kitty." The two year old squeezed a gray-and-white-striped kitten around its thin waist and thrust it at Lizzie. The kitten mewled in protest and Will's green eyes sparkled. "Kitty."

"He wanted you to see it." Maybelle stroked the boy's dark head. " 'Lizzie love,' he said."

"Yes, I do." She knelt and stroked the kitten's head. The fur tickled her nose. She held back a sneeze, but felt the familiar itching in her eyes and throat. Cats seemed to be the only animals to affect her this way, but she refused to ignore or avoid them because of it. "She's pretty, Will. What have you named her?"

"Kitty," he said, smiling up at Lizzie, then burying his nose in the kitten's soft fur.

"Did you hurt yourself?" Maybelle peered at Lizzie's hand.

She rose and pressed the apron tighter against the wound. Blood speckled the cloth. "The hawk scratched me."

"Should you have Sally Louise look at it?"

"I'll be fine." She touched Will's shoulder. "Come see Domino. He's getting much better."

The little boy walked over and solemnly stared at the dog. Domino sniffed at the kitten, then reached out with his tongue to swipe Will's face. The boy laughed and rubbed the dog's nose.

Lizzie picked up the bowl of buttermilk poultice and stepped outside.

Maybelle followed, glancing back at Will. "Well, tell me what happened," she whispered.

"What happened when?" Lizzie poured out the remainder of the poultice and frowned at her friend. Too late she realized what Maybelle was talking about.

"Last night. I saw George leave with Lily. Someone

should tan his hide." She eased closer to Lizzie. "Everyone saw C. J. come after you when you left."

"Oh, he wasn't coming after—"

"What happened?" Maybelle's eyes gleamed with excitement. "He walked you home, didn't he?"

"Well, yes, but—"

"And then?"

"And then?" She shook her head. Maybelle talked and thought too fast for her sometimes.

The other woman gripped Lizzie's arm and pulled her a few more feet from the shed, whispering, "Did he kiss you?"

"Absolutely not!" She pulled away, a flush heating her cheeks. "I told you there's nothing like that between us. There never will be."

"Then what is it?"

"What is *what?*"

"What is between you two?" The question was put to her in an annoyingly slow manner, as if Lizzie couldn't understand.

She stared, uncertain whether to laugh or to rebuke her friend. "If you have to call it something, I suppose we're friends. That's all."

"Then why did he walk you home?" Maybelle asked archly.

"Because he's a gentleman?"

"I hate it when you answer questions with questions."

Lizzie gentled her tone. "Don't look for things that aren't there, Maybelle."

"Maybe you're the only one who thinks there's nothing there. Everyone knows how much time he's been spending around the store lately."

"Maybe he needs supplies."

"You'd have to be dead not to notice C. J. Daltry. Why, every woman in the county—"

"I know, Maybelle." Lizzie cradled her injured hand and walked to the house.

The other woman checked on Will, then hurried after Lizzie. "Why won't you admit there could be something there?"

"Because there's not," she said sharply. Maybelle's eyes widened in hurt, and Lizzie softened her sharp tone. She wasn't angry at Maybelle; she was frustrated at C. J. "There will never be anything like that between us. I tried to tell you that once before."

"He's certainly acting like a man who's interested in a woman. I should know. I had more than my share of beaux before Hank."

Lizzie studied her friend, considering for the first time that she might tell someone about what had happened in the past between her and C. J. She looked down, fingering the edge of her apron. "I asked him last night why he was coming around."

"You did?" Maybelle breathed. She fluttered her hands. "And? And?"

"He said it was partly because he felt responsible for . . . my scar." Lizzie watched the other woman carefully. She had never talked about it with anyone. Never.

"The scar?" Maybelle frowned. "The scar on your face?"

"It's the only one I have," she retorted, feeling anxious.

Her friend's eyes widened. "Oh, my lands! C. J. did that? How could he?"

"Oh, no, C. J. didn't do it. My stepfather did."

"I don't understand. Is C. J. responsible or not for that scar?"

"Not that way." Lizzie suddenly found she wanted to tell Maybelle the whole story. She explained about the night C. J. had invited her out with the other children, and about the lot of them being surprised by Mr. Peabody and his gun. She added what she had just learned of C. J.'s return for her.

When she finished, Maybelle looked dazed and incredulous. Lizzie swallowed and searched her friend's eyes.

Doubts battered her. She shouldn't have said anything.

She had never spoken of it before. What if Maybelle didn't understand? What if she thought Lizzie had deserved the beating from Papa Jude?

Instead of the censure she expected, Maybelle's shock gave way to compassion and a righteous anger. She gave Lizzie a quick hug. "I'm so sorry. How could he do that? You were just a child."

"My behavior wasn't supposed to reflect ill on him. That night, it did."

"I'm sorry, Lizzie. What an awful man." She added fiercely, "I'm not sorry he's dead."

Lizzie smiled wanly. "Would you please not tell anyone, Maybelle? Not even Hank. He means well, but—"

"He has a big mouth." Maybelle patted her hand. "I promise I won't tell anyone."

"Thank you." A sudden warmth crept through Lizzie, along with a sense of being freed. It felt good to tell someone.

"Lizzie?"

"Yes."

"That was a long time ago. Do you still blame C. J. for leaving you that night?"

She hesitated. "Blame him? I don't think so."

"But you resent it?"

"Yes." But her usual conviction was missing. What *did* she feel toward C. J.? "I guess so."

"Even though you were children? And he came back for you?"

"I know all that, Maybelle. It's just—" She broke off. She did resent C. J. for leaving her on her own, didn't she? Yet she couldn't erase the picture of his face, concerned and angry on her behalf last night when he'd learned of Jude's ultimatum.

"C. J.'s a good man, Lizzie."

"I suppose he is." She glanced down at her hand again. The hawk hadn't scratched her on purpose; he'd simply been startled. In a way, that paralleled C. J.'s actions. He hadn't deliberately left her to fend for herself that long-ago night.

Remembering that night brought back the feelings of desperate fear and utter loneliness, but the anger was gone. "All right, maybe I don't resent him anymore. You're right; it was a long time ago. But that doesn't mean I'm . . . I don't want anything to do with him. I'm not interested in him. At least not the way you mean." She refused to acknowledge the disappointment of that.

"But, Lizzie—"

"I don't mean to be harsh, Maybelle, but you can't change my mind."

"I'm sure if he's coming around, it must mean he's interested."

"What woman *doesn't* interest him?"

"Oh, all right, you have a point. But he's a good man. He wouldn't hurt you."

"No, he won't." Lizzie wouldn't dwell on these new feelings that he stirred—not the friendship, not the acceptance, not the illusion of caring. She said fiercely, "I won't let him."

The last strains of "Amazing Grace" faded away and Lizzie automatically bowed her head for the closing prayer. She squeezed her eyes tight and refused to acknowledge C. J.'s gaze on her.

He had stared at her all during the church service. Even if she hadn't been able to see him out of the corner of her eye, she would've known. Her skin tingled with unfamiliar heat; her body and mind grew soft at the thought of him. He made her feel on the verge of something new and exciting, eliciting a hope she hadn't felt in years.

She battled the feelings, knowing that all he felt for her was pity. He'd admitted as much after the dance. And she'd seen it in his eyes after she'd told him about Jude.

She had no intention of giving in to the warmth and sense

of belonging that C. J. had resurrected by renewing their acquaintance.

The prayer ended and the circuit preacher, Reverend Timmons, dismissed services. She rose slowly, looping the cord of her drawstring purse over her wrist. Maybelle and Hank filed out ahead of her. In honor of Reverend Timmons's arrival, the town had decided to have a picnic. Lizzie had agreed last night to go with Maybelle and Hank. She hoped C. J. wasn't going.

She stepped onto the porch and nodded to Reverend Timmons. He was a short man, only a few inches taller than Lizzie, with a round face that was gentle and guileless. She moved down the steps while Maybelle stayed to talk.

"Good morning, Lizzie." C. J.'s voice caressed her like the spring breeze.

She spun, swallowing hard when she saw him standing behind her. Her gaze traveled up lean, muscular thighs encased in black britches. Under a dark blue coat, he wore a snowy white shirt with a black string tie, and he held a black hat in his hand. Noon sunshine fingered through his gold hair, picking out strands the color of sunshine and wheat and the deep gold of an autumn sunset.

His mouth curved in an inviting smile and she fought her own smile. His blue eyes were somber, with a hint of pity.

Her spine stiffened; her shoulders braced as though for a blow. "Good morning." She turned, determined to escape the compassion in his eyes. She ignored the weightless feeling in her legs and walked toward her house.

"Hope to see you at the picnic," he called after her.

"Come on, C. J. We're supposed to help Ma." That was C. J.'s brother Atlas.

Behind him, their sister Allie protested that she was not carrying any dumb old basket, even if it was full of food.

Drat and blast! He was going to the picnic as well. For an instant Lizzie considered staying home. But knowing C. J., he'd think it was because of him and pester her further.

There was nothing to do but go.

She would simply ignore him.

Several minutes later, Lizzie stood in the shade of a monstrous oak and deliberately forced her gaze to slide over C. J. without lingering. It shouldn't be so difficult. He certainly hadn't paid a whit of attention to her since she'd arrived.

But her gaze kept returning to him. He sat in the back of the Daltry wagon, powerful legs outstretched, boot heels digging into the red Texas earth. He'd discarded his blue coat and rolled up the sleeves of his shirt. Next to the white cloth, his skin gleamed like polished oak.

His hat was pushed back on his head, giving him a jaunty, reckless look; his arms were folded across his wide chest. Strong forearms corded with each movement and the shirt pulled tight at his shoulders, hinting at their breadth.

A sigh eased out of her. She grimaced in disgust when she heard herself. Why was she admiring him? His ego certainly didn't need boosting.

Emma Samuels, Ann Marie Hardin, and Colleen and Maris Thornton were gathered around him. He tilted his head back, revealing the strong tanned column of his throat. The whistle of a mockingbird floated on the air, and Lizzie looked up, searching, until she realized it had come from C. J.

When she looked again, a lazy, sensual smile curved his lips and his gaze seemed directed straight at her. Her breath hitched. She could hear the low tenor of his voice and the answering giggles of the women around him. An emptiness filled her. She pulled her gaze away and opened the hamper she had packed.

She became aware of a man standing several feet away. He was a shade over six feet, not as tall as C. J., and was dressed in a brown Sunday suit. He held a brown bowler loosely in his hand. The sun glinted off his sable-dark hair. She didn't remember having seen him before. His gaze caught hers and she looked away.

Under a tree on a small rise, C. J.'s sister Venus held court just as he did. Lizzie couldn't help but notice Venus. She sat in an old straight-backed chair under one of the few shade trees. Three men surrounded her. She was beautiful and confident and Lizzie watched her admiringly.

"May I help you with that?"

Lizzie whipped around. The man she'd noticed earlier stood in front of her, smiling pleasantly. Up close, she could see his eyes were light brown, flecked with green and gold. He smiled and his eyes crinkled at the corners. His gaze never shifted or slid to her scar.

"Ma'am?" The word rolled from his tongue in a slow drawl, reminding Lizzie of a warm, soothing bath.

She faced him, curious about the accent and the man. He smiled and extended his hand to take the hamper from her.

Who was he? She tightened her grip on the basket. "I'm fine. I don't need any help."

"Yes, ma'am." A faint flush suffused his neck just above the collar of his white shirt, and he quickly turned away.

She released the breath she'd been holding.

He pivoted, a look of determination crossing his pleasant features. He cleared his throat and ran a finger under his collar. "The truth is, I was hoping to introduce myself."

"To me?" She couldn't keep the shock from her voice. Why wasn't he with Venus or one of the others? Surprise and a sudden self-consciousness crept through her. She glanced over her shoulder.

He grinned and revealed a deep dimple in his left cheek. "I'm new in town and I just thought—" He shook his head. "Please forgive me if I was too forward."

She narrowed her gaze at him. "I guess I haven't seen you before." She realized how suspicious she sounded and felt a blush creep up her neck. "I'm Lizzie. Colepepper."

"Hi. I'm Tom English." He bowed at the waist and Lizzie grinned.

"Yes, you are definitely new." No one else in Paradise

Plains had ever bowed to her. She studied him, feeling a bloom of kinship. He looked as though he felt out of place, and she knew that feeling well. "Where are you from, Tom English?"

"Alabama. Just arrived." He reached for the basket and smiled expectantly.

She hesitated, then relinquished it to him. "Alabama? That's a long way."

"Yes, ma'am." He knelt on the blanket she had already spread and opened the hamper. "I just bought a place north of town. Past the Circle D."

"You're a cattle rancher." In her mind, she was hardly aware of her polite conversation. She was actually talking to a handsome man. She felt like Venus . . . almost.

He grinned up at her as he removed the platter of chicken and the pecan pie from the basket and deposited the food on the blanket. "Yes, ma'am."

"Lands, Lizzie, who's this you're hidin' over here?"

Venus Daltry breezed up and Lizzie's eyes widened, shocked that she knew someone Venus didn't. And a man, at that. "Venus, this is Tom English. He's new to town. Tom, this is Venus Daltry. Her family owns the Circle D."

"So you're our new neighbor." Venus gave a dimpled smile, and her blue eyes sparkled warmly at Tom.

He grinned, though Lizzie thought he looked a trifle sheepish. "Nice to meet you—"

"I declare, I knew you had to be new. I would remember if I'd seen such a handsome man before." Her words were tinged with the same slow accent as Tom's. "Lizzie, you must introduce Mr. English around."

"Oh, no, you go ahead." No sense starting him off on the wrong foot.

"Mr. English?" Venus smiled expectantly, a dazzling combination of command and request.

Tom dragged his gaze from her to Lizzie. He looked dazed. "Lizzie, will you excuse me for a minute?"

"Of course." She smiled. "It was nice to meet you." Fascinated, she watched Venus lead Tom from group to group, introducing him, before maneuvering him into walking her back to her chair under the shade tree.

Lizzie stared, unable to help it. How could Venus be so at ease with everyone? Especially men.

"If there's a man in sight, Venus must have him. I hope she didn't hurt your feelings."

At C. J.'s voice, she turned. The underlying compassion in his voice was meant to soothe, she knew. Instead, it annoyed her. It didn't help her composure that he looked so handsome, standing there gilded by the glow of the sun. His voice stirred a spark of heat deep inside her.

"She didn't steal my toy, C. J.," Lizzie answered coolly. "I certainly have no claim on Tom."

"Is that his name?" His glance flicked over her shoulder to the man with his sister.

"Yes. Tom English. He's new."

"How do you know him?" C. J.'s eyes darkened; his jaw tensed. "Where is he from? I've never seen him before."

Probably because he's not a woman. The possessiveness in his questions spurred a flash of anger. "I just met him. He's from Alabama. Have you been taking busybody lessons from Hank?"

His gaze shifted back to hers and his lips twitched. "Sorry." His gaze moved to the blanket. "Your chicken looks good."

"It's for me and Hank and Maybelle." Why didn't he just go away? She didn't want him here. Last night he'd made her feel an instant of warmth and belonging, coaxed her into believing that she mattered to him when she knew she didn't.

She looked up, startled to find his gaze on her, speculative and sad. Reflexively her hand went to her cheek. "What are you looking at?"

"No." C. J. reached out and pulled her hand away. His

hand was warm on her wrist. When he released her, a tingle shot up her arm and the heat from his touch lingered. "Don't let Venus discourage you."

"Discourage me? From what?"

"Tom, if you're interested." He watched her closely, an unsettling intensity in his blue eyes.

"Oh, bother, I just met the man." She felt as if his gaze could bore into her soul and know her deepest secrets. She turned away. "Venus is a beautiful girl. It's only natural men would want to be around her. You certainly don't have to apologize to me for that."

"That's very gracious of you."

Sympathy resonated in his gentle words and Lizzie gritted her teeth. "I'm fine, really. There's no need to concern yourself." She gestured to the wagon where C. J.'s entire family was gathered. "I think your family might be ready to eat."

"Trying to get rid of me?" he asked softly, a teasing light warming his eyes.

She said flatly, "Yes. Why can't you take a hint?"

He threw back his head and laughed, a mellow, throaty sound that made her lips twitch. He gave her a wink and strolled off toward the Daltry clan.

Frustration filled her and she refused to smile. She hadn't ignored him at all. In fact, she seemed more aware of him today than she had last night.

A disturbing realization surfaced. She didn't want him to ignore her, either. She wanted him to see her as a woman. A desirable, beautiful woman.

She groaned and turned back to the picnic hamper. C. J. felt only pity or some misplaced sense of responsibility toward her. What she felt was new and unfamiliar, but it was neither of those things.

She realized then she might never be able to ignore C. J.

Six

C. J. WATCHED LIZZIE WITHOUT BEING OBVIOUS. HE FELT concern and a headiness he was coming to recognize after a challenging exchange with her, but today there was something else.

Was he seeing her differently, or did she look exceptionally pretty? Sunlight threaded through her jet hair, making it shimmer like spun silk. Her sky blue calico dress was faded. It rounded over her full breasts as though smoothed by a lover's hand. The scoop neck of the bodice bared delicate collarbones and creamy skin. Awareness of her physical charms shifted through him.

She took her plate and sat with Maybelle and Will on the blanket she'd brought. C. J. didn't know what he'd done to make her so prickly, but he kind of liked it. When she was annoyed, her eyes shot blue fire and a faint flush tinted her skin.

Protectiveness stirred again. He hadn't been able to escape that feeling since Friday night, when he'd learned about Jude. But deep down he knew that wasn't the only reason he wanted to spend time with her.

Had he ever noticed the way she blushed when he looked at her? How gracefully she moved? Even now, he could remember how light she felt in his arms at the dance, and he was still haunted by the scent of roses. Curiosity gnawed at him—about her life with Jude, her life before, what she thought about him.

There was something new and provocative and tantalizing about Lizzie.

C. J. shook his head and brought his thoughts back to the picnic. There were several eligible bachelors here today. He had to find one for her.

His gaze slanted to Venus and the admirers crowded around her. Tom English, the new man who'd been talking with Lizzie earlier, stood at Venus's right elbow. He seemed as taken with C. J.'s sister as did Henry Taylor, Ben Hogan, and Ted Lacy. Seeing that Tom was still occupied by Venus, C. J. felt a flare of relief. He didn't particularly care for the man to seek out Lizzie.

A long table that had been set up under an oak sagged under the weight of chicken, beef, beans, vegetables, bread and desserts. Roasted meat scents hung on the air and mixed with those of fresh bread. George stood at one end of the table, waiting behind Atlas to fill his plate.

C. J. wandered over. "You with Lily today, George?"

"Yes. She's waiting for me."

"Did you apologize to Lizzie?"

George flushed. "Not yet."

C. J. inclined his head toward her. "She's right over there."

"I can see," George grumbled. He glanced around and saw Lily waving to him. "I'll do it later."

He walked off and Atlas shuffled up beside C. J. "What are you going to do about finding someone for Lizzie? The whole town saw George leave her at the dance."

"Bates isn't the only bachelor in Paradise Plains. There're plenty of men I haven't talked to yet," C. J. said with a nonchalance he didn't feel.

82 DEBRA S. COWAN

A smile crept across Atlas's face. "Why don't you go ask some of 'em?"

"Mind your own business." C. J. thumped his brother's ear and walked off toward a circle of single men eating lunch.

The twins stood quietly, wolfing down heaping platefuls of food. Harvey Crandall and Jed Bostick stood beside them. C. J. figured all of them would treat Lizzie politely.

"Hey, fellas."

They all nodded, mouths full.

"I woulda thought you fellas would want to eat lunch with a pretty girl."

"They're all taken," Harvey said around a mouthful of corn.

C. J. slapped Harvey on the back. "Not all of them. Haven't you seen Lizzie Colepepper today?"

"Lizzie?" Jed glanced over his shoulder, then shrugged. "Don't she look the same as she does every day?"

"Why don't one of you ask her to eat with you?"

Each twin's eyes grew big and both shook their heads, looking as horrified as if he'd asked them to shoot a kitten. C. J. should've known both of them would be too shy.

Jed turned, considering Lizzie for a long minute. "I don't think so."

"Oh, come on, Jed." C. J. edged closer and lowered his voice. "It'd be worth ten dollars."

Jed frowned, his gaze slicing to C. J.

He slid the gold piece from his pocket, holding it between two fingers so the sun winked off the coin. "Look at her hair. You ever seen hair like that, all shiny and thick and black as the ace of spades?"

"Her hair wasn't what I was noticin'." Jed turned to get a better look. "She fills out that bodice pretty nice."

"Watch your mouth, Bostick," C. J. growled. "She's a lady." He turned to Harvey. "What about it, Harv? I think you two would get on pretty well."

"Not me, Daltry." He wiped a sleeve across his mouth. "Why don't you go eat with her?"

"Looks like she don't need *nobody* eatin' with her." Jed jabbed his fork in her direction. "Who's that?"

C. J. jammed the money back into his pocket and turned toward Lizzie. Tom English had left Venus's side and made his way back to Lizzie. As C. J. watched, a sudden dread clutched at his stomach, but he didn't understand it. He wished he could hear what Tom was saying to her.

She held up a hand to shield her face from the sun. She nodded, and Tom held out a hand to her, helping her to her feet. C. J. took a step, an unfamiliar burning sensation in his chest.

Lizzie smiled, the first smile C. J. had ever seen from her that was not tinged with bitterness or sadness. He lifted his chin, his instincts pricking. Her face softened and glowed. Even though he couldn't see them from here, he knew her eyes would be liquid and dark sapphire blue. Why hadn't she ever smiled like that before? Why hadn't she ever smiled at *him* like that?

Tom and Lizzie turned and began walking in his direction. Where were they going? He forgot the men he stood with and walked toward a cottonwood tree in the couple's path. He leaned against the tree, his heart hammering, curiosity coursing through him.

Lizzie and Tom passed, hardly sparing him a glance. What was the matter with her? He noticed her hand was tucked in the crook of Tom's arm and he frowned. Suddenly he had an urge to smash Tom English in the nose. "Where y'all off to?"

Lizzie's smile faded as she met his gaze. Irritation burned in her eyes.

Tom glanced from her to C. J., then smiled. "We're going to take a walk by the river."

Walk by the river! In broad daylight? Panic shot through him. C. J. had taken plenty of girls to "walk by the river." He glanced at Lizzie's picnic spot and saw Hank and Maybelle packing up the blanket. "Uh, Lizzie, it looks like Hank and Maybelle are leaving."

She tilted her chin at him, her gaze angry and defiant. "As you know, I can see myself home."

"Nonsense!" Tom said, patting her hand. "I'll see you home."

"Thank you." She smiled at him, that same gentle smile she'd never used on C. J. "Shall we?"

"Have a good time." C. J.'s voice was gruff, almost harsh.

Tom and Lizzie walked past him and he straightened, watching them disappear over the hill. Anger churned inside him. Damn. *Damn.*

"Where are they going?" Atlas spoke at C. J.'s elbow.

"For a walk by the river," C. J. snapped. "I can't believe she's doing that. Doesn't she know what that means?"

Atlas frowned up at him. "It's only a walk."

"I know what 'a walk by the river' means." C. J. planted his hands on his hips, staring after them. "You're just a kid. You don't know nothin'."

Atlas scratched his head. "Is it one of those boy-girl things?"

"Yes," C. J. bit out. He should be glad Lizzie was with someone, but he didn't know this Tom English. That had to be the reason for this restless churning inside him, this urge to charge after them and see her home himself.

"I'm glad Lizzie's having a good time," Atlas broke into C. J.'s thoughts. "But you didn't pick out that fella."

"No." He couldn't stop the images that sprang into his mind—Tom touching Lizzie, Tom kissing Lizzie. Atlas was still talking, and his words finally penetrated C. J.'s unsettling thoughts. He dragged his gaze to his brother. "What did you say?"

Atlas eyed C. J. speculatively. "I said Grandma might not think that counts. Since you didn't have anything to do with it."

"That's dumb. It shouldn't matter *how* Lizzie gets a husband, as long as she gets one." He frowned, suddenly uncertain. His gaze swung to the hill, where Lizzie and Tom had disappeared. "You might be right."

He hesitated. If he went after them, every fella here would think he was staking claim to her. His gaze swung to Venus, who still sat surrounded by her beaux. He started for his sister.

Atlas hurried after him. "Where are you going?"

"To get Venus."

"But what about Lizzie?"

"This is about Lizzie."

"I don't understand."

C. J. shoved aside the branches of an oak tree, his strides twice as long as those of his brother. "I'm sending Venus after Tom. There's not a man alive who can resist her."

"Is that fair?" Atlas huffed beside him.

"I don't know. I've got to do something. I can't let Tom English—" C. J. bit off the rest of the words. Venus would distract Tom, then C. J. could find someone appropriate for Lizzie.

He walked up behind Ted Lacy and caught his sister's gaze. "Excuse me, Venus. Can I talk to you?"

Venus rose, as did Ted, Henry Taylor, and Ben Hogan. She smiled sweetly at each of them. Ted made a sweeping bow and kissed her hand. Venus dimpled and fluttered her eyes.

She followed C. J. to a spot a few feet away, but her gaze stayed on the men next to her chair. "What is it? You look positively tortured."

"I need you to go find Tom English."

"That new man?" Her gaze snapped to C. J.'s, then she gazed out over the other picnickers. "I don't see him."

"He's at the river. With Lizzie." C. J. added the last to stir Venus's competitive streak.

She looked startled. "I don't want to interrupt—"

"I want you to."

Her gaze returned to the men waiting for her, and she wriggled her fingers in a wave.

"C. J. didn't have anything to do with that fella asking Lizzie to go walking," Atlas threw in.

Venus turned her gaze to C. J. and frowned.

"It might not count with Grandma," Atlas prodded, looking from Venus to C. J.

"All right." Venus glanced longingly toward her waiting beaux. She poked C. J. in the chest. "But I'll want something in return for this."

"Fine." He took her by the shoulders and steered her toward the river. "Whatever you want. Just come back with Tom English."

"What about Lizzie? You can't just leave her down there."

"I'll take care of her." C. J. stroked his chin. He would walk her home himself. Guilt surged at ruining her outing with Tom, but he justified it. The man was probably no different than George. C. J. was saving her from another heartache. He wanted to feel good about that; instead he felt cheap and sneaky.

Venus disappeared over the rise and he folded his arms to wait, tamping down his impatience. Atlas moved from C. J.'s left to his right, then back again. Back and forth. Back and forth. Like a damn pendulum, grating across C. J.'s nerves.

The fourth time Atlas moved, C. J. thumped him. "Be still."

"Uh-oh."

C. J.'s head snapped up. Venus was walking up the hill, alone and looking dazed. He hurried toward her. "What the—"

She shook her head, a puzzled look in her blue eyes.

"Well?" C. J. demanded.

"Somethin's wrong with him."

"What do you mean? What's going on?" Alarm kicked at C. J.'s gut. If English had hurt Lizzie—

"He would hardly look at me." Venus sounded confused rather than hurt. Her brow pleated in a frown.

C. J. stared, his jaw going slack. "He wouldn't walk you back?"

"No." She glanced back over her shoulder. "He said he was obligated to walk with Lizzie, but that he'd enjoyed meeting me."

"Was he impolite? There's no telling what he'll do to Liz—"

"No, he was courtesy itself." A bemused look crossed Venus's perfect features. "Very honorable. He was determined to stay with her."

"Honorable?" C. J. scowled. "What does she want with a guy like that?"

"You'd rather he wasn't honorable?" Atlas put in.

C. J. glared at his younger brother.

Atlas thrust out his chin. "You're just mad because she went with him."

C. J. exhaled and leaned against the tree, one booted foot propped on the trunk behind him. "Was he touching her? Doing anything? Taking liberties?"

"I hardly think so," Venus answered, glancing over her shoulder to wave to the men still waiting at her chair. "She acted as if she were enjoying herself."

"Damn." C. J. stared at the horizon. What was he going to do?

Atlas crossed his arms. "I think you've got a problem."

"I think you do, too," Venus said.

"Are you sure you wouldn't rather go with Venus?" Lizzie stared at the rise where C. J.'s sister had disappeared. "I would certainly understand."

"I'd rather walk you home." Tom grinned and leaned

back against an old cottonwood tree. "Besides, I gave my word."

Disbelief jostled with surprised pleasure; she narrowed her gaze at him.

"What?"

"I find it hard to believe that you turned Venus down. Men generally don't."

"She's awful pretty," he agreed wistfully. He dragged his hat from his head and tapped it against his thigh. "May I confess something to you?"

"If you would like," she said stiffly. She liked Tom, but sharing confidences with a man, with anyone, was new to her.

A flush crept up his neck. "She makes me nervous."

Lizzie laughed, at ease again. "Your stomach flutters and your palms sweat? You feel there's something going on you can't control? I understand perfectly. C. J. makes me feel the same way."

Tom pushed away from the tree. "Are you and he—"

"Heavens, no!" She was stunned at what she'd revealed, and to a stranger. "It's nothing like that. We're just friends." Disappointment stabbed as she realized how very true her statement was. "We've known each other a long time."

Tom glanced over his shoulder, his features reflective. "Do you think it's a family trait?"

"Probably."

"I like Venus, don't misunderstand me." He turned to Lizzie and grinned. "But she makes me feel like I'm in the middle of a twister."

"Exactly." She smiled. "I think all the Daltrys have that effect."

"Ooooh, the dastardly Daltrys," Tom whispered in an ominous tone, then wiggled his eyebrows.

Lizzie laughed.

*   *   *

"Tell me all about him. He's so handsome. He hardly had eyes for anyone but you."

"Maybelle, Tom and I are just friends." The next morning, Lizzie stood with her friend in the back room of the store, opening crates. "He's new in town and I enjoyed meeting him."

"And?" Maybelle unwrapped a new dress form for Miss Lavender.

Lizzie sighed. "There is no 'and.' He's a nice man. I think he liked me the same way I liked him. There's no romance going on. We have an understanding." *A "Daltry" kind of understanding.* She smiled at the thought.

"So is C. J. your friend, too?"

"Haven't I said that all along?" Her heart tilted at the mention of his name. Despite talking about Tom since she'd arrived at work this morning, she hadn't been able to stop thinking about C. J. Her feelings for him were changing and she didn't understand it.

Maybelle crumpled the brown paper into a ball and tossed it into the corner. "C. J. sees a lot of women, but never gets involved. He's more involved with you than he's ever been with anyone else. Do you still insist you're just friends?"

"We are." Lizzie felt trapped by Maybelle's persistence. After talking with Tom yesterday, Lizzie knew that she felt more than friendship for C. J., but what was it exactly? Judging from the pity and compassion in his eyes at the picnic, he saw her not as an enticing woman, but as someone to be helped.

If she ever let on that she wanted more than friendship with him, C. J. would disappear faster than a shooting star.

". . . and I think maybe you could fall in love with him."

"Maybelle, that's ridiculous," Lizzie's voice rose in frustration. "C. J. and I are friends. That's all we'll ever be."

Maybelle folded her arms across her breasts and grinned. "I was talking about Tom."

"Oh." A flush heated her cheeks. "Well, it doesn't matter who you were talking about. Don't you ever give up?"

"No." The other woman patted Lizzie's cheek. "Neither should you. There are plenty of unmarried men in this town, and you're just starting to blossom."

"I'm twenty years old and I've never been courted," she reminded mildly. "You saw what happened with George at the dance. You and Hank are the best friends I have. Where do you get all this hope for romance?"

"Do you think it's because of your scar?" her friend asked gently.

Lizzie's gaze skittered away as she lifted a box of scissors from the crate. "Partly, maybe. It just doesn't matter. Some people see only the scar; others see only how I got it."

"Others—like C. J., you mean?"

She nodded. "He feels responsible. That's the only reason he's coming around."

"I think it's more than that," Maybelle said stubbornly.

Lizzie smiled. "I can see I won't be able to change your mind."

"No. And I'm right about C. J. I know you have feelings for him—"

"Maybelle, Lizzie? You back here?" Hank poked his head through the curtain of the back room. "Lizzie, Henry Taylor's here to see you."

Lizzie's gaze shot to Maybelle, who raised her eyebrows. "Well, go on out there."

"What does he want, Hank?" Lizzie whispered.

"He wants to see you, girl." He dropped the curtain and disappeared.

Lizzie frowned and set the box of scissors on the floor before going to the front of the store. She stopped behind the counter and Maybelle eased up next to her. Hank climbed a ladder in front of the window to stock a shelf.

Lizzie studied Henry, suddenly wary. "Hello, Henry."

"Hi, Lizzie. How ya doing today?"

"Fine." She knew she sounded cool, but she couldn't help it. What was he doing here?

His gaze roamed over the cans and jars of fruits and vegetables on the shelf behind Lizzie. "Say, I was wonderin' if you'd like to have dinner tomorrow night?"

Maybelle elbowed her in the ribs. Hank turned, jostling a watering can, and a noisy clang broke the silence.

"Dinner?" Lizzie echoed, trying not to look stunned.

"Sure. I thought I'd take you to The Buc."

"Well, I don't know." What if he left her, as George had done?

"Are you otherwise engaged?" He frowned, then his eyes widened. "If it's that new fella in town—"

"No! Nothing like that." Her stomach fluttered and Lizzie wished it were C. J. asking her. She pushed the thought away and considered the man in front of her.

He stood a couple of inches under six feet and had a slender build. His features were regular and pleasant. Sandy brown hair was cut neatly at his neck and blue-gray eyes peered hopefully out at her from behind his spectacles.

He was nice enough—at least he'd never called her names after she'd gotten the scar. But why was he suddenly interested in *her?* There was only one way to find out. "I accept, Henry. Thank you."

"Really?" Pleasure lightened his gray eyes.

She nodded, smiling at his excitement. Her unease lifted somewhat.

"I'll call for you at six-thirty. Does that give you enough time to get home from the store?"

"Yes."

"I'll see you tomorrow night." He grinned, a crooked tilt of his lips that highlighted a small dimple at the corner of his mouth.

She gave a shy smile in return. "All right."

He saluted Hank and Maybelle, then walked out.

"Oh, Lizzie, I told you!" Maybelle squealed and clapped

her hands together. "What will you wear? If we start right now, we can make up that white-and-rose stripe."

"Maybelle, please—"

"Well, you must've been the hit of the picnic," Hank drawled, climbing down from the ladder.

"Nonsense." Lizzie blushed, her mind racing with thoughts of Henry and his invitation. She moved out from behind the counter and watched as Henry walked up Main Street. "I just can't figure it out."

"What's that?" Maybelle rushed over to the fabric table and pulled out the bolt of white-and-rose-striped fabric.

Lizzie shook her head. "I've never had so much attention paid to me in my entire life. Do you think it's because Jude is gone?"

"Could be, honey." Maybelle smiled. She unrolled a length of fabric and brought it over to drape across Lizzie's shoulder. "You are working at making new friends."

"Could be because I'm such stimulating company," Lizzie said dryly, thinking of the way George had left her at the dance.

Hank squeezed her shoulder. "Could be because you're so beautiful."

"You're the only one who thinks so, Hank," she corrected fondly.

Maybelle clucked her tongue and took the fabric to the cutting table.

Lizzie stared out into the street, her churning thoughts punctuated by the rattle of wagon wheels, the clip-clop of horses' hooves, the ring of the blacksmith's hammer.

Why were these men suddenly so interested in her? It had all started when C. J. began coming around again.

Lizzie didn't like the suspicion that wormed its way into her thoughts, but she couldn't prevent it. Did C. J. have something to do with her sudden popularity? No matter what Hank and Maybelle said, Lizzie knew that most people in town thought her aloof and unneighborly, especially the people her age. Why were they now treating her differently?

She would find out, starting with Henry.

"It looked like you enjoyed yourself, Henry." The next evening, C. J. stood behind the livery, paying Henry for his dinner with Lizzie.

He watched his friend closely, trying to tamp down the churning inside him. All through dinner and dessert, he had watched Lizzie and Henry. She had been stunningly demure in a white-and-rose-striped dress and appeared to be captivated by the quiet-spoken Henry. A slow burn inched through C. J., but he told himself it was curiosity. Nothing more.

"Yeah. I like Lizzie." Henry watched closely as C. J. counted the remainder of the money into his hand. "I don't feel right taking this money, C. J. I had a real good time."

The surge of hope that C. J. expected to feel was replaced by an unreasonable irritation, and he frowned. "Will you be calling for Lizzie again?"

"I'm not sure."

He didn't question the relief that washed through him, but pushed the money into Henry's hands. "We had a deal. The money's yours."

"Well, this'll come in handy."

"I bet she'd go if you called for her again." C. J. tried to sound unconcerned, but he knotted his fists at his sides. Both Lizzie and Henry had seemed to enjoy the dinner. Henry had seen her home a few minutes ago and there seemed to be no problems. C. J.'s task might soon be over, but again, instead of relief, all he felt was irritation.

"Ah, well, I don't know." Henry stuffed the money in his pocket and shifted from one foot to the other. He wouldn't meet C. J.'s gaze. "She's a nice girl, but—"

"You didn't take liberties with her?" C. J. shot at him.

"No! Nothin' like that."

"Well, what then?" Frustration sawed at him. He had noticed that Lizzie hadn't taken her eyes off Henry all during supper. Hell, C. J. could barely get her to look at *him* more than once in the course of conversation.

"I like Lizzie, but it's more friendly-like. You know? She's a good listener."

"She seemed to be listening to you, all right," C. J. muttered.

"She understands about Daisy."

"You told her about Daisy? Hell, Henry." C. J. clapped a hand to his forehead. Concern for Lizzie wiped out his unexplained annoyance. "Don't ask her anywhere again. Ever."

Henry squared his shoulders. "I guess I will if I want."

"Don't. She needs someone who wants her for herself." C. J. looked across the field that separated the town from Lizzie's house. "Not someone who's makin' eyes at another girl."

How was Lizzie feeling? First George and Lily; now Henry and his talk of Daisy. *Grandma, what have we done?*

"You're actin' mighty strange, Daltry. And don't think I haven't noticed," Henry said belligerently. "If you're so all-fired taken with her, call for her yourself."

C. J. snorted and walked off. Though he would never admit it to anyone but himself, all through dinner he'd had this overwhelming urge to join Henry and Lizzie, to eavesdrop on their conversation and learn how Henry could hold her so enthralled. And the whole time Henry had been talking about Daisy?

C. J. had to see Lizzie. Was she all right? What had he done wrong? How could this have happened to her twice?

He started across the field, then rocked to a halt about fifty yards from her house, frozen by a sudden thought. What if she didn't want to see anyone? What if she didn't want to see *him?* How would it look for him to come charging over, demanding to know if she was all right?

Then he saw her. Light flowed from the windows of her small house and painted her in a golden haze. She stood on the porch, one arm curved around the square support post, her face tilted up to the moon.

Longing pulled tight in his chest. She looked tiny and achingly vulnerable, a beautiful midnight angel. Beads of sweat dappled his palms. He might not be welcome. He remembered how she had wanted to be alone after George had abandoned her at the dance.

But he couldn't sleep tonight without knowing how she was. Had Henry hurt her? Had C. J.'s machinations done more harm than good?

He told himself to walk away, to wait and talk to her tomorrow. But he couldn't. He had to know. He would check on her and leave. That was all.

Seven

HE WALKED OUT OF THE MOONLIGHT LIKE SOME CONJURED mythical illusion. Lizzie's stomach fluttered and one hand crept to her cheek. In that instant, all her questions about Henry and George and C. J.'s involvement disappeared. She was aware only of C. J. as he walked toward her.

Stories and legends of ancient gods, men more than mortals, sprang to her mind. She told herself it was a trick of the moonlight and his animal-sleek grace. She blinked, thinking to make him disappear, but he materialized in front of her.

Hesitation stamped his features. For a long moment, they simply stared at each other. Lizzie's heart rushed in her ears. Around her the wind whispered gently; locusts groaned a lazy song. The night sounds magnified and she imagined she could hear the slight rasp of C. J.'s breath as well.

What did he want? Her heart swelled with an unfamiliar warmth, and a sudden sweetness washed through her, leaving a tingle in her arms. She couldn't feel this way about C. J. Responsibility and pity were all he felt for her. Her throat was dry as she forced out the words, "Taking in the night air?"

Her voice sounded low and husky, alien to her. He stepped into the wedge of lamplight coming from the house. His blue eyes darkened as they rested on her face.

He swallowed hard, his lean features predatory and intense. "Yes. How about you?"

"The same." She looked away from him, suddenly feeling vulnerable and uncertain. She wanted to know if he was involved with the invitations from George and Henry. She *had* to know—but what if he was? She had tried to steer her conversation with Henry around to his invitation, but he wanted only to talk about his lost love.

C. J. stepped closer, resting his elbow on the waist-high porch rail. He stood so close that she could touch his hand, if she was brave, and his heat tangled with hers. A clean, masculine scent mingled with that of dust and horse and the hint of cigar smoke from the restaurant. "I saw you at dinner tonight. With Henry."

Her gaze met his. A sense of expectation stirred through her and seemed to hover in the air between them. "Yes."

C. J. muttered something noncommittal. "Did you enjoy yourself?"

She rested her cheek against the rough wood of the post and studied him. She wanted to ask C. J. why he was there, if he'd had anything to do with her sudden invitations. "Yes, I did."

"Really? I mean, you looked like you did, but—"

"I've been wondering about all my sudden invitations."

He stiffened and his gaze held hers.

She could read nothing in the blue depths. "You don't have anything to do with them, do you?"

"What do you mean?" His gaze bored into her, wary and intense.

She swallowed, surprised at the fierceness of his question. She wanted to know if he was involved, but then again she didn't. After a moment, she said, "No one in this town has ever paid much attention to me. Except you. I know you feel badly about my—face—and I thought you might be trying to make up for it."

She watched him, apprehension curling through her.

Disappointment raced across his features. "Lizzie—"

"It's okay." She realized she had hurt him by reminding him of the past, questioning his friendship. "At least I know Tom's asking because he likes *me.*"

"Tom?" The word was sharp and explosive. "The new fella?"

"Yes." She frowned.

"You're going somewhere with him?"

"Lunch," she answered coolly.

C. J. scowled. "You don't even know him! You don't know anything about him!"

"I like him and he likes me," she said, confused and annoyed at C. J.'s sudden vehemence.

"You'd better be careful." He pushed away from the porch and planted his hands on his hips. Raw energy vibrated from him.

"At least he won't abandon me or talk about someone else all night," Lizzie muttered.

"That might make him more dangerous."

"Dangerous? What are you talking about?" She stepped off the porch to stand in front of him.

C. J. frowned. "What do you mean, talk about someone else all night?"

"Tell me what you mean about Tom being dangerous."

"Are you that naive?" He huffed out a loud breath and leaned into her face. "He might want something from you," he said pointedly. "He might want *you.*"

For a moment she stared, trying to piece together what he meant. Then a flush heated her body. "Do you mean he might try to—with me—" She broke off and angled her chin at C. J. "So what if he does?"

"You don't mean that, Lizzie. He's not some little boy you can chase off with a switch."

"Do you know something about him I don't know?" she demanded.

Reluctance shifted across his features. "No," he admitted grudgingly. "I'm just trying to warn you. I wish I knew him better. Why don't you wait until—"

"He doesn't have to pass anyone's approval," she pointed out quietly. "Except mine."

"I guess not." He raked a hand through his hair. "What did you mean about him not talking about someone else? Did something happen with Henry?"

Lizzie looked away, cursing herself for having alluded to her earlier dinner with Henry. "I just can't figure it out."

"What's that? Tell me," he coaxed, his voice trickling over her like a tentative caress.

Suddenly she felt bared, all her emotions laid open to him. She felt vulnerable in a way she never had with anyone else. "Why men take *me* somewhere when they want to take someone else."

C. J. was silent for a long moment. A muscle twitched in his jaw. "What happened, Lizzie?"

"Nothing dreadful. Nothing like George." She bit at her lip, wondering at C. J.'s stillness. "Henry is in love with Daisy. She moved away over a year ago and he's still pining for her."

"Henry's a fool," C. J. said tightly.

Lizzie angled her head toward him. "Because he loves Daisy? No, C. J., Henry's mistake is that he hasn't gone after her."

"But he took *you* to dinner."

"And we had a nice time. It doesn't mean I'm going to marry him."

C. J.'s eyes widened. "No. I guess it doesn't." He sounded choked.

Lizzie's nerves tingled with his nearness. His features were shadowed by moonlight, his eyes searing with blue heat. They stood on the porch, bathed in a soft breeze that carried the scent of earth and dark, masculine secrets. She let herself imagine doing this every night with C. J., then pushed the thought away. But this time it didn't leave so easily.

"You never do that," she said shyly.

"Do what?" His voice was low and lazy. He eased back against the porch rail and slanted a look at her.

A shiver tiptoed across her spine. Suddenly self-conscious, her voice dropped. "Talk about other women."

"And who would I talk about?"

"Diana Whitlaw?" Lizzie hesitated, uncertain about continuing. "I know she hurt you, C. J."

He looked away quickly, but she saw his lips flatten, a muscle flex in his jaw. Still, he kept his voice light. "Now, Lizzie, how do you know she did the hurting? You know I can't be tied down."

She did know that, but she also knew Diana had broken the engagement . . . although Lizzie didn't know why. She heard the shadows of pain and regret in his words. Perhaps she shouldn't have asked, but she ached for him to share something with her after he'd witnessed her own vulnerability. "What did she do?"

His gaze sliced to her. "I'd think you would be tired of men talking about other women."

He lifted his head, staring up at the moon. His profile was rugged in the washed light, carved from darkness and pain. He stroked his mustache. Lizzie thought he wouldn't speak, but his voice threaded through the night.

"I thought she was perfect for me. She was the most beautiful girl I'd ever seen. Even her name was perfect. Diana, goddess of the moon. It had to be the Fates, right? Considering my family." He gave a bitter laugh.

Lizzie held her breath, her chest burning for the hurt she detected beneath his words.

"I'd always had my pick of girls. I could have any one of them." There was no triumph or arrogance, just bitterness.

He crossed his arms over his chest and looked down at the ground. "But I'd never been in love until her."

"What happened?" Lizzie's fingers gripped the rough wood of the post.

He jammed his hands into the pockets of his denims. "I asked her to marry me and she agreed. Then she changed her mind a few weeks before the wedding." He gave a short laugh and ducked his head as though embarrassed. "I've never talked about this with a woman before."

"I'm so sorry," she said hoarsely. "Why wouldn't she marry you?"

"Said she wasn't ready to settle down and . . ." The words trailed off and a muscle rippled along his jaw. "She said I didn't look like the fella she'd fallen in love with."

Lizzie's eyes widened and a sharp arrow of pain pierced her. "Because of your accident?"

She hadn't seen him after it had happened, but she had heard. Never had she imagined that Diana had broken off her engagement with C. J. because of that.

His features hardened as though a mask had slipped into place. "Yes. My face was pretty torn up and she thought my looks would be ruined."

"I can't tell a thing." Lizzie stepped in front of him, searching his features. His aquiline nose was unmarked; his cheekbones high in a rugged face. He had a strong jaw with a stubborn chin and beautiful features that still managed to be blatantly male. "Your nose doesn't even have a bump in it."

"My pa built a special contraption for my face. It was a box that held the bones in place so they could heal."

"Like a splint?" she asked, amazed at the concept.

"Exactly."

"How ingenious," she murmured.

C. J.'s gaze locked on hers for a moment and she glimpsed the pain in his eyes, along with a deep vulnerability.

Then his features closed against her. "Anyway, I can see now I wasn't ready for marriage either. Never will be."

She willed away the ache in her breast. "Don't you ever hope to find someone?"

"Why? I have plenty of . . . companionship, plus the ranch and my family to keep me busy."

"The ranch is yours?" She felt a stab of envy that he had already obtained his goal and secured his future, but she willed it away. Someday she would have a percentage of the store and it would be solely hers, she reminded herself.

C. J. hesitated briefly. "Actually, it belongs to Grandma. When she passes on, we all figured Lee would get it. But he's never loved it like I do," he added fiercely, his eyes gleaming. "The land isn't in his blood like it's in mine.

"I'm like my grandfather in that respect. He started the Circle D, and I'm trying to convince Grandma that it's as much a part of me as it was of him. That I have his vision."

"And is she swayed?" Lizzie was fascinated by the play of shadow and hunger on his face.

He looked away, a grim determination tightening his features. "I don't know yet. But she does know how much I want it. I'd do just about anything to get it."

"Yes," she answered emphatically. "I know what you mean. It's something that drives you, that completes you and still challenges you."

His eyes widened and he shifted closer. "Yes."

She smiled, feeling a new, different connection with him. "I feel that way about the store."

"What? The mercantile?" C. J.'s gaze fastened on her.

Lizzie hesitated. She had never told anyone but Hank and Maybelle of her dream. "I'm saving my money to buy a partnership with Hank."

"Well, I'll be. I had no idea you loved the idea of being a merchant." Admiration shaded his voice.

A flush of pleasure warmed her. "It's interesting to me,

but mainly I want something for the future, something secure that I can build."

"Yes, I feel that way about the ranch."

She wondered if Diana had known of his passion. "Don't you think you might want someone to share it with?"

"No." His voice was flat, his eyes turning as hard as obsidian.

The defiance and ruthlessness in his gaze stopped her. He'd been hurt badly and Lizzie knew now that he'd never given his heart to any of the women he'd squired around town. Would he ever?

"No one will ever do that to me again. If I hadn't been so stupid over her, I would've seen the signs that her feelings weren't as deep as mine. I don't think she ever really loved me."

Lizzie wanted to remind him that no one could see into the future. And Diana was at fault for being so cruel and shallow. "At least you found out before you married. That would've been—"

"Hopeless," C. J. finished for her. He straightened and pushed away from the porch rail, a new energy vibrating from him. He was once again self-assured and teasing, pulling back from the intimacy created by their conversation and the darkness. A gleam lit his eyes. "There are too many women to settle for just one. Mind you don't go falling in love with me."

He grinned and winked, but she heard the vulnerability under his words and wished she could be the one woman to make him forget what Diana Whitlaw had done.

"Don't worry." She felt *something* for him, but not love.

He wouldn't have confided in her if he thought they were anything other than friends. And they *were* just friends, Lizzie reminded herself.

He stepped backward, fading into the darkness. "I'm sorry about Henry."

She watched him go, stunned by the sudden sense of loss she felt, the sharp stab of loneliness.

"Take care, Lizzie."

She waited on the porch, listening as his footsteps faded into the night.

In the course of their conversation, George's and Henry's invitations had been forgotten. She still didn't know if C. J. was responsible for them or not. At the moment she didn't care.

She had seen a side to him she had never known existed—he could be vulnerable, uncertain, wary. It tore at her, making her long for him even while she knew she mustn't.

Her feelings were jumbled, a heated mix of desire, impatience, and resentment. What exactly did she feel for C. J. Daltry?

I've been wondering about all my sudden invitations. You don't have anything to do with them, do you?

Frustration and regret scissored through him and he reined Goliath to a halt just up the hill from the house. He hadn't been able to walk away. By Thor, he never should've gone to check on her. Not only had he spilled his guts about Diana, he had flat-out lied to Lizzie.

The knowledge stung like a new splinter.

And now he felt a new elemental connection to her. She understood exactly the depth of his feelings about the ranch, his tie to the land. Because she had a fierce desire for something, too.

Thoughts of the ranch triggered a reminder of the task. He had wanted to tell Lizzie about it, every last bloody detail, but he had resisted the urge—partly because he couldn't bring himself to jeopardize the task, and therefore the prize.

She had nearly guessed his part in her outings, anyway. If she hadn't changed the subject, C. J. thought he really might have told her.

And ruined their friendship in the process. The thought brought with it a sudden sense of loss.

Holding the stallion to a walk, C. J. guided him to the barn. He turned over their conversation in his mind. Guilt bit at him, nipping sharper and deeper as he unsaddled his horse by the light of the lantern and brushed him down, but there was something else.

A lingering sense of want, a heat that wouldn't fade. In his mind, he could still see her on the porch, bathed in the alabaster light of the moon. She beckoned to him like a siren's song; he wanted to touch her creamy skin, inhale the essence of her. He remembered her dark, limpid eyes and felt a rush of heat as his mind taunted him with the picture of her lips.

He didn't understand these feelings and certainly didn't welcome them.

He had to talk to Grandma and convince her to release him from this task. They couldn't continue this maneuvering of other people's lives. Lizzie would be hurt, if she wasn't already.

A few minutes later he stood in the library, his hat in his hands as he watched his grandmother. She sat on the edge of the divan in front of the fireplace, her eyes closed and her breaths coming deep and even.

Floor-to-ceiling shelves lined the opposite wall. They were filled with books. On a small desk in the corner was an unrolled map of Europe and Odie's latest drawing for a new architectural project. A small lamp on the table next to Grandma spread a pool of gold around her.

"I'm not asleep, C. J. Come on in." Her gray eyes targeted him like a hawk would a mouse, making him wonder if she knew why he was there.

He hung his hat on the hat tree and walked into the room, skirting the wing chair and halting in front of Minerva.

"What is it?"

Lizzie's words rang in his ears. *Why do they ask me when*

they want to be with someone else? "Grandma, you've got to give me another task. This one—I can't—this isn't right."

"C. J., we've been through this. What's wrong? Surely you aren't out of possibilities?"

"It's not that at all!" He struggled to control the flash of temper that surged through him. "It's Lizzie. This isn't right. It will hurt her."

"I don't see how finding a husband for the girl can hurt her," Minerva returned, watching him speculatively.

He rubbed the back of his neck where the muscles corded tightly. "Didn't you hear what happened at the dance?"

"You didn't exhibit very good judgment by picking George. Everyone knows he's been sweet on Lily for years."

"Well, what about Henry, then?" C. J. demanded hotly.

"Henry Taylor?" Minerva frowned. "What about him? He's nice."

"He took Lizzie to dinner tonight."

"And?"

"And . . ." Would his grandmother understand? She hadn't seen the loss in Lizzie's eyes or heard the longing in her voice.

"Did he take liberties?"

"No, nothing like that." C. J. shoved a hand into his hair. Remembering how Lizzie had watched Henry so intently, that odd combination of desire and anger assaulted C. J. again, but he quickly buried it. He couldn't be feeling desire for Lizzie. "Henry talked all night about Daisy Myers."

"I don't know her—didn't she used to live in Paradise Plains?"

"The point is, Henry was crying on Lizzie's shoulder when he should've been paying attention to her. She was hurt, Grandma."

"Oh," Minerva murmured, her eyes softening. "I'm so sorry. Perhaps this wasn't the thing to do at all."

C. J. nodded. "That's what I've been trying to tell you. I

mean, it was bad enough for George to abandon her in front of the whole town—"

"I hope you spoke with him about that," she said sharply.

"I knocked the holy hell—er, heck—out of him." C. J. paced in front of the massive fireplace, warmed by anger and the hope that Minerva finally understood. "We can't play with her life like this, Grandma. I'll do anything you say, even wait until Atlas has had his turn, but—"

"What did you do about Henry?"

"I told him not to see Lizzie anymore. She's the one who told me, and I—" He broke off, remembering the lonely ache in her voice, the powerful urge he'd had to hold her. "Of course, I can't very well stop Henry from calling on her or from talking about Daisy."

"You told him to leave her alone?" Minerva's brisk tone had changed to curiosity, but C. J. didn't stop to ponder it.

"He's not right for her. I told him she needed someone who would love her for herself. She's bright and funny, beautiful, even charming when she wants to be. And brave." His voice trailed off as he thought again of her scar and how she'd obtained it. "Very brave."

Minerva rose from the couch, leaning heavily on her cane. Her gaze pierced him and a frown marred her papery skin. "I think you need to carry on with the task."

"I knew you'd understand. She's just going to get hurt again and—*what* did you say?"

"In the end, Lizzie will thank you. And you, I think, will thank *me*," she added cryptically.

C. J. frowned, trying to tamp down the sudden flash of panic. "But Grandma—"

"No *but's*, C. J. You've presented your case very nicely, but I think a little more effort on your part will see better results."

"But—but what about Lizzie?"

"You're learning to weed out the bad ones, like George. Pick more carefully next time."

"Grandma, you can't mean this. She's going to be hurt. You didn't see her eyes tonight."

"You can always forfeit, but as I said, there will be no other chances."

Fury erupted inside him. "I never thought you could be so heartless. This isn't fair."

Minerva gazed at him with an expression of fondness and compassion. "I know you don't understand now, my boy."

"You're damn right I don't." C. J. spun and strode for the door, yanking his hat from the hat tree. "I hope I never do."

"But you will. And I hope then you can forgive me."

Her words were faint and he wasn't even sure he'd heard her correctly, but he wasn't about to return. He slammed out the door and headed for the barn.

Frustration and a sense of urgency clawed at C. J. He wanted to forfeit, but he had the uncomfortable feeling that if he quit, it wouldn't be fair to Lizzie.

She needed a family. And there was *someone* out there who needed her. He just had to find that someone. She'd never said that she wanted a family, but he had heard the loneliness, the wistfulness in her voice when they'd talked about her stepfather.

A little more effort on your part. His grandmother's words pounded through his head. With a sigh of resignation, C. J. knew she was right. He had approached his task half-heartedly. If he had done his best, he wouldn't have picked George. The whole town knew George didn't have eyes for anyone except Lily.

He wouldn't forfeit until he'd at least given an honest effort. Perhaps he could find someone for her, and it might, in part, make up for his responsibility for her scar.

He couldn't abandon his dream of having the ranch. And, C. J. admitted to himself ruefully, his pride wouldn't let him back down. Lee's task hadn't been easy, yet he hadn't given up. Neither had Persy.

He would do better by Lizzie. Determination took root in his mind and spawned a new sense of urgency. The one man he could trust with her, besides Lee, who was already taken, was Webb Callaway, his hired hand and a true gentleman.

The next morning, C. J. stood at the corral fence, waiting his turn on Hades. The ebony stallion had already thrown Roper and now thrashed and bucked, slinging Webb as if he weighed no more than an empty burlap sack.

Usually C. J. itched to try his hand at taming the wild ones, but today a restlessness worked through him. He needed to talk to Webb. In private.

Lizzie was going to lunch with Tom, so C. J. needed to convince Webb to take her to dinner.

Roper, one of the best horse handlers C. J. had ever seen, stood next to him at the fence. The older man's coarse-textured work shirt and denims were embedded with red dirt. Scratches and bruises marred one side of his ruddy face. He grinned and glanced at C. J. "He's a devil, ain't he? Take the tar out of that black devil, Webb," he yelled.

C. J. rested his elbows atop the fence post. "Dig in your heels!"

Around him, the other ranch hands whooped and hollered commands. Webb's body jerked and snapped, the muscles in his neck cording as he struggled to hold on.

C. J. ran a hand over his face, his eyes gritty from lack of sleep. Gradually Hades slowed. Though his bucking became more infrequent, tension coiled in the sleek muscles of his body. C. J. watched as Webb dismounted, speaking in a low voice to the animal.

Webb Callaway was the only eligible man among the Circle D ranch hands. The others were either married, like Roper, or old enough to be Lizzie's father. And there was Clayton Turner, but he was downright mean, and C. J. wouldn't sic him on Lizzie for anything.

Webb stroked the stallion's head. Hades remained still,

but his black eyes were wild and wary. His sides heaved and sweat sheened his dark coat.

Under Webb's touch, the stallion stomped and snorted, but didn't move away. The cowboy grinned and gave the animal a last pat before walking toward C. J.

The cowhand was lean and lanky, with the wiry strength of a tempered rope. A scar, a trophy from a wild mustang, ran from the outer end of his left eyebrow to the crest of his cheek, bracketing his dark eye. C. J. didn't think Lizzie would mind. The other women in town certainly didn't.

He hadn't realized it before, but the scar was something Webb and Lizzie had in common. That thought gave him hope. "Good ridin', Webb."

"Way to stick like a burr, boy." Roper grinned.

Webb acknowledged the compliments with a wry smile. He tugged off his gloves and eased his body between the fence posts, straightening to stand next to C. J. "What'd ya think, boss?"

"I swear, Webb, you're part horse."

"Sometimes I wish I were." Webb grinned and grasped Roper's extended hand, giving it a quick shake.

The older wrangler shook his head and ducked through the fence into the corral to lead the stallion out.

C. J. motioned Webb a short distance away. "Got a minute?"

"Sure. What is it?" He stuffed his gloves into the waistband of his denims.

Roper walked by with the stallion and several of the hands. C. J. waited until they were out of earshot.

"I've got a proposition for you."

Webb wiped the sweat from his forehead with his shirtsleeve. "What kind of proposition?"

"You know Lizzie Colepepper?"

"Heard of her. Can't say I know what she looks like, though." Recognition flared in his eyes. "That the girl with the scar on her face?"

"There's more to her than that," C. J. returned sharply.

Webb regarded him curiously. "Figured there was."

"Sorry." C. J.'s jaw tightened and he glanced away. Was he doing the right thing? He would trust Webb with his life. And had. "I'd, uh, like you to take her to dinner tonight."

Surprise flared in the other man's eyes. "You playing matchmaker, boss? Can't picture it."

"Never mind why." C. J. lowered his voice and leveled a steely gaze on his ranch hand. "I'll make it worth your while. A day off with pay."

"You're givin' me a day off to take some lady—all right." Webb held up a hand at C. J.'s glare. "No questions. Sure, I'll take her. Does it matter where?"

"I thought The Buc."

The ranch hand shrugged.

"You'll need to go on to town and ask her." C. J. shifted from one foot to the other, unable to stem the restlessness crowding through him. "I hope it's not too late."

Webb shook his head. "I can't do it tonight."

"What do you mean? It has to be tonight."

"Can't, boss. I've already got plans."

"You're not courtin' anybody! I would've heard."

"No, sir, but that don't mean I'm gonna turn my back on the one I'm seein' tonight. It wouldn't be gentlemanly."

C. J. couldn't argue, considering Webb's manners were one of the reasons he had wanted the man to call for Lizzie.

"How about tomorrow night? I'm free then."

"No, it's got to be tonight." Urgency tripped through him again. If he didn't hurry up, Tom English might ask Lizzie to dinner himself.

"Sorry, boss. It ain't because I don't want to. She's right pretty, if I recall, and a day off with pay—"

"It's all right, Webb."

"You're sure?"

"Yeah." Frustration boiled in him. There were no other

prospects here. And he'd be damned if he'd ask Jed Bostick, after his comment at the picnic.

"Okay." Webb started for the barn, then turned. "Any other time, boss. I'd be happy to."

"Right." C. J. caught the man's eye. "Hey, Webb, let's keep this to ourselves, all right?"

"Whatever you say."

Webb disappeared into the barn, and C. J. tamped down the panic that threatened. Determination surged through him. Lizzie *would* go to dinner tonight with someone besides Tom English.

C. J. would take her himself.

Eight

IT'S NOT DIFFICULT. C. J. HAD ASKED DOZENS OF WOMEN TO
dinner. To lunch. Hell, even to "walk by the river." So why
was Lizzie different?

Because last night he'd shared a part of himself
he'd never shared with anyone. An unfamiliar vulnerability
stole through him, and he shrugged restlessly against the
feeling.

He remembered, too, how she had asked if he'd had anything to do with her invitations, and the unexpected rage
he'd felt at Henry. Doubts pelted him, sharp points of fire
that pricked his conscience as well. Had she learned of his
task?

In a way, he wished she would. He hadn't lied to her, but
neither had he told the truth.

He had ridden into town an hour ago, and now he hesitated outside the mercantile. The sun warmed him, causing
him to perspire. His white work shirt clung, suddenly confin-
ing. Behind him, a wagon creaked and small whorls of red
dust settled around his boots. A steady breeze flowed from
the southwest, stringing along fecund odors of the livery and
the burnt-toast smell of coal.

Clay Masterson's press clacked busily away, in time with

the doubts that pelted C. J. Would Lizzie see through him, know why he was asking her?

Stop. He strangled the uncertainty and stepped up on the porch. He would take her to dinner tonight, then approach Webb again.

Maybelle glided outside with a broom. "Good morning, C. J."

"Morning." He tipped his hat to her and smiled, walking through the door.

Hank stood behind the counter, scribbling on a piece of paper and muttering under his breath. His bald head gleamed.

"Hey, Hank. How are you?" C. J.'s gaze wandered around the store, searching for Lizzie, though he didn't really expect to find her out front.

"Fine, just fine." Hank raised his head and eyed C. J. speculatively. "What can I do for you today? I don't think I have an order in for you."

"I came to see Lizzie." C. J.'s nervousness subsided and he hooked his thumb in the waist of his denims. After all, escorting women was one of his gifts.

The store owner's eyebrows climbed a notch, but he merely nodded and went through the curtain to the back of the store.

C. J. heard the low drone of voices. Outside, shoes tapped the planked boardwalk, and the rhythmic swish of Maybelle's broom filtered in from the street.

Hank stepped out and Lizzie followed.

C. J. studied her. There were no shadows beneath her blue eyes to show she'd lost any sleep. She looked fine after her night with Henry, and relief edged in.

"Hello." Her voice was pleasant, but he saw the curiosity in her eyes.

"Morning." His voice sounded rusty and he cleared his throat.

She smiled and C. J.'s gut knotted. Desire inched through

his belly. He straightened to his full six feet four, trying to banish the same sensual awareness that had broadsided him last night.

He noted Hank's watchful gaze. "Can you go outside for a minute?"

"All right."

They stepped out the door onto the porch. C. J. relaxed somewhat, but the heat still lapped at him, gently insistent, stroking his nerves. He knew the feeling, but he'd never experienced it with Lizzie, and for an instant he felt disoriented. Caution flared. He shouldn't feel these things for her, and didn't understand why he was.

Maybelle stood at one end of the porch talking to Clay Masterson. C. J. and Lizzie moved to the opposite end. In the uncompromising daylight, he judged the magnolia smoothness of her skin and noted that there were truly no circles of fatigue under her dark blue eyes. "You slept well."

"Of course." Her brows arched. "Somehow, I don't think you came here to find out how I slept."

Her tone was wry, but hunger fired her blue eyes. C. J.'s gaze locked on hers. He wanted to drown in those liquid blue pools, lose himself in the newness of this feeling, even though she knew things about him that no one else did.

One corner of her mouth quirked up. "Oh, you thought I didn't sleep because of Henry?"

He nodded, his original reason for coming now a jumble in his mind.

Pleasure and surprise eased across her features. "Thank you. I'm fine."

"Good." His chest loosened and his breath came easier. Her scent, a hint of roses, tiptoed around him, and he resisted the startling urge to take her arm and draw her closer. "I came to see if you'd like to go to supper tonight."

The light in her eyes dimmed. "I'm not your responsibility."

"I'm asking to take you to supper, not be your guardian."

"It's because of last night. You feel sorry for me," she challenged, blue eyes blazing at him, her chin angled.

She was right and his conscience pricked. But there was something else—a subtle heat and excitement stirring. "It's because I want to." He wasn't lying, he realized. Without thinking, he reached for her hand and squeezed it. "I'd enjoy it. I had hoped you might, too."

She hesitated, searching his eyes as if to judge whether he told the truth.

Heat spun between them, webbing him in an invisible velvet rope. Abruptly, he released her hand. His gaze never faltered, but uncertainty drummed inside him. "I'd ask you to lunch, but I know you're going with . . . someone."

Speculation narrowed her eyes. "Yes."

He wanted to squirm under her steady gaze, but he forced a smile instead. "So how about supper?"

She pursed her lips. "I'd like to, but I'm already obligated."

It was Tom English. C. J. knew it by the defiance in her face, the even tone that practically dared him to ask if he was right. The minx! He folded his arms across his chest and snorted. "That guy sure spends a lot of time in town for somebody who just bought a ranch."

Lizzie's eyebrows arched. "What guy?"

"You know who." C. J. scowled. Was English already courting her? A strange sharp emotion sliced through him.

She smiled sweetly, though her eyes blazed. "Maybe y'all have something in common. Since you also spend a lot of time in town."

Touché. "I have ranch hands."

"Maybe he does, too."

Again, she eyed him with resentment and suspicion.

Her lips flattened. "Thank you for the offer."

"You're welcome," C. J. said grudgingly, his mind racing. There had to be somewhere he could take her.

She stepped around him to go back inside.

He cupped her elbow and felt that strange jolt of heat funnel through him again. He heard himself asking, "What about Saturday? Will you be able to come to the barbecue?"

"What barbecue?" She half turned to face him, her hair brushing his knuckles.

Her floral scent drifted to him, and his palm itched to touch her. "Uh, we have one at the ranch, before spring roundup every year." *Where had that come from?* The Circle D had *never* had a barbecue before roundup.

Hesitation marked her features and he knew she was about to refuse.

"The whole town's invited."

"I haven't heard anything about it," she said warily.

That's because I just made it up. "You're the first one I've told—asked."

She measured him, blue eyes somber and probing.

"Everyone will be there," he encouraged.

Her eyes turned the pewter blue of steel. *"Everyone?"*

He realized she was asking if Tom English would be included. Irritation spun through him. "Yes."

"All right."

He blinked, then frowned. "See you Saturday."

She nodded and disappeared inside the store.

Frustration burned through C. J.'s gut. He hadn't been able to get Webb to call for her tonight. He hadn't been able to secure her permission for dinner.

And now he'd made a whole passel of work and trouble by inviting her to some barbecue that was as much a myth as the ones his grandmother loved.

Irritation flared. Part of him wanted to forget her, forget the task, everything. But C. J. knew he wouldn't.

He kicked at a clump of dirt and walked over to Maybelle and Clay, issuing an invitation to the barbecue he was now giving.

*   *   *

I'm not having supper with Tom. It had been on the tip of Lizzie's tongue to tell C. J., but anger held her back. What she was doing and with whom was none of his business. She could easily have told him her plans that evening were with Hank and Maybelle, but she refused.

White-hot fury blazed through Lizzie. How *dare* he!

Had C. J. asked her to dinner and that blasted barbecue because he didn't like that she was having lunch with Tom? Or was it that he felt pity for her?

She tended to believe the second reason. After last night, she was certain he felt some misguided need to protect her. She wanted to tell him that his protectiveness was neither wanted nor needed.

But she hadn't. Their conversation last night was too fresh in her mind. She had seen a completely unexpected side of him, a vulnerable side that brought out her own insecurities. She understood too well what it meant to be hurt, to be rejected on any level.

Last night she had learned that C. J., for all his glorious looks and money and charm, had been rejected, too.

It was a bond she hadn't expected to share with him. The new connection spawned another feeling, a shivery sense of expectancy that she didn't want to dwell on. Something more than friendship, something she wasn't willing to name.

Despite their newly re-formed friendship, she wasn't some child to be guarded. Fuming, she picked up the ledger and sat down, trying to balance last month's numbers.

But irritation drove her out of the chair to pace the back room. All morning she'd carried disturbing, haunting visions of him. Images of his mouth on hers, his bare skin against hers, his hands running over her breasts.

She thrust the thoughts away, wishing she understood this crush of new emotion. They were friends, and yet . . .

Did friends experience this rush of giddiness like she did when he walked into a room? The sight of his dark blond good looks and lean, muscular power caused her heart to triple its beat. Her palms became damp. Heat licked at her from the inside out, making her wish for time alone with him and dream about what his kiss would be like.

It was silly. Ridiculous, she told herself. C. J. Daltry could've been named Adonis. He was a perfect physical specimen, a charming blend of cockiness and gentleness, packaged in taut, gorgeous sinew and muscle.

She was flawed by the scar, brusque with people, and clumsy. But all that didn't stop her from wondering.

"Lizzie, you all right?" Maybelle poked her head through the door.

She turned, trying to forget the insecurities she couldn't shake and calm her anger. "Of course."

Maybelle stepped inside, doubt clouding her green eyes. "You're pacing."

"Oh."

The petite woman studied her with a tentative smile on her face. "Are you going to the Daltrys' barbecue?"

"I said I would, but . . ."

"I can see you're upset," Maybelle said quietly. "Is it C. J.?"

"Not exactly."

"Do you want to talk about it?"

Lizzie hesitated only briefly, then the words tumbled out. "C. J. wanted to take me to supper tonight."

"And?"

Lizzie frowned, pacing to a wall of shelves, then back to the desk. "That's all."

"That made you mad?" Maybelle's eyes widened.

She pushed aside a stack of sales tickets. "He only asked because he knows I'm going to lunch with Tom today."

"Why would he do that?"

"He doesn't like Tom, or for some reason doesn't want me spending any time with him."

"But why?"

"He says it's because he doesn't know Tom and neither do I. That I should be careful."

Maybelle regarded her warily. "Is that so bad?"

"It's none of C. J.'s business, which he seems determined to make it."

"If he's not courting you, why is he so interested?" Maybelle's eyes widened and her mouth formed a perfect *O*. "Do you think it's because of your scar?"

Lizzie nodded, thinking of her talk with C. J. last night. "He feels somehow responsible for me. I don't want to go to the barbecue just so he can watch over me. It's starting to annoy me."

A chuckle escaped Maybelle. "Why don't you go and let him watch while you show him you don't need his protection?"

"Oh, I couldn't—how could I do that?" Lizzie shoved the ledger to the side and leaned toward her friend.

Maybelle eased down onto the corner of the desk. "You go and have a good time. The rest will take care of itself."

"Is it that easy?"

"Of course it is. Hank and I will be there to make sure you have fun." She grinned. "As will Tom."

Lizzie smiled at the thought of proving to C. J. that she didn't need his pity. "This might really work."

"Of course it will."

It had to work. On Saturday, Lizzie stood under a budding pecan tree at the Daltry spread. Despite C. J.'s constant gaze, determination surged through her.

Under his watchful eye, she had seen the stable and the house with Tom and Henry. The house, a two-story frame affair that looked like something out of a picture book, commanded instant attention. Its gingerbread trim and fresh white paint seemed almost out of place on the rugged landscape.

Around her were rolling hills, covered with buffalo grass

and dotted with scrub oaks, pines, and pecan trees. The smell of roasting meat jostled with the scent of greening trees and sunshine.

The day was perfect. Spring had shed its winter coat to reveal a clear blue sky with faint wisps of clouds. The sun pulsed a mild heat and brilliant patches of blue, red, and yellow wildflowers showered the hill beyond the roasting pit. Tables were set up around the gazebo—whoever had thought of that?—and groaned from the weight of food.

True to C. J.'s word, it appeared that every person from town was in attendance. Lizzie had ridden with Hank and Maybelle in their wagon. They had been greeted at the entrance to the Circle D by Atlas, C. J.'s youngest brother.

Lizzie had stared, mouth agape, as they drove under the massive wooden arch that proclaimed the beginning of the property. At the center of the arch, a "D" was carved into the middle of a circle. The land rolled with winter wheat and thigh-high grass, dipping and curving over the hills like a green tide, only to disappear into a flat horizon.

She had never been to the ranch and was amazed at the amount of property. Maybelle had laughingly called the huge place Mount Olympus, and Lizzie could understand why. Then she had seen the house. And C. J.

He stood with his mother at his side. Jane Daltry had been charming and gracious, and not once did her gaze flicker to Lizzie's scar.

Lizzie wore her new rose-and-white stripe at Maybelle's suggestion and was glad she had. C. J.'s gaze lingered on her, hot and arrogant. "I'm glad you came."

"I wouldn't have missed it," she said airily and walked off with Maybelle, conscious of his eyes on her.

Just as Maybelle had predicted, Lizzie enjoyed herself. Surprising to her had been the number of people who'd said hello. George and Lily had chatted for a few minutes. Henry and Tom had eaten lunch with her. Even Jed Bostick, whom

Lizzie barely knew at all, had asked if he could get her dessert.

When she noticed how C. J. was glaring, she had smiled and said certainly.

Now, stuffed with beef and ribs cooked in a dark, spicy sauce, she sat in a chair under a tree.

Tom had disappeared with Venus some time ago. Henry had joined C. J. and his brothers to look at a new stallion. Voices hummed in a lazy cadence. Allie Daltry and Hal Anderson raced past, disappearing behind a scrub oak. Lizzie sighed in contentment as she watched Maybelle play with Will and Jimmy, Lee and Meredith Daltry's adopted son.

The entire time, she felt C. J.'s gaze on her like a caress. It heated her skin, recalled those disturbing visions she'd had of him, but also served to remind her why she was here.

"Are you enjoying yourself?"

Minerva Daltry appeared at Lizzie's elbow.

Lizzie bolted from her chair, knocking it over in her haste. "Yes, ma'am."

"I didn't mean to startle you. I just want to chat."

"Yes, ma'am." Lizzie groped behind her for the chair, then turned and set it upright.

"Sit down, child. I'm not so old I need the chair."

"Yes, ma'am." Obediently Lizzie sank back down into the chair, her face heating. From the corner of her eye, she saw C. J. watching them.

Mrs. Daltry moved in front of her and blocked Lizzie's view. Gray eyes pierced her. "You're Lizzie Colepepper."

"Yes, ma'am."

A ghost of a smile hovered around the older woman's mouth. "You're one of Cupid's friends."

She nodded, unable to control the nervous flutter in her stomach, the caged feeling at the way those gray eyes sharpened on her.

"Don't scare her away, Grandma." C. J. walked up behind

Minerva and draped an arm across her shoulders. He leaned down and brushed a kiss across her cheek.

"Save that flirting for the young ones, my boy." Minerva turned her attention to Lizzie. "You seem much too sensible to be taken in by this one's pretty face."

"I hope so, ma'am." A sense of happiness tripped through her at the obvious closeness grandmother and grandson shared, but also a sudden flash of envy.

The gray eyes turned dark. "You're a polite one."

"Yes—"

Minerva waved a hand, cutting her off. "It's all right, child. I won't bite."

Lizzie flushed. "I didn't think you would."

C. J. grinned.

Minerva chuckled and the warm sound eased Lizzie's discomfort. "I'm glad to meet you, Lizzie."

"Likewise, ma'am."

"I'll leave the two of you. Best see to the other guests."

"Hello, Miz Daltry." Jed walked up and removed his hat, bowing to Minerva.

Minerva extended her hand. "Hello, Jed. You keeping company with this pretty girl today?"

"Yes, ma'am, I sure am."

C. J. frowned at that, but Lizzie blithely ignored him.

He watched Minerva's retreating back. "Jed, there's a horseshoe toss going on by the barn."

"I thought me and Lizzie would go for a walk," he said firmly, holding C. J.'s steely gaze. He turned to Lizzie with a smile. "If you'd like."

C. J.'s gaze sliced to her and she saw an angry warning in his eyes.

Irritation rippled through her. She rose and placed her hand on Jed's offered arm. "Thank you. I'd like to."

She walked off without a backward glance. She did not need C. J.'s protection. Hadn't she just proven it?

* * *

He would not go after them. C. J. watched Lizzie and Jed disappear behind a cluster of scrub oaks and head for the river that ran in front of Lee and Meredith's house.

Frustration churned in his gut. She had seen the warning in his eyes and determinedly ignored it.

He pivoted and stalked toward the horseshoe game.

Thirty minutes later, Lizzie and Jed were still gone. C. J. had lost three games of horseshoes and couldn't stifle the prickle of alarm that crept along his neck. Lizzie should've been back by now.

He'd been uneasy about her walking off with Jed, especially after what the man had said at the picnic about Lizzie filling out her bodice. But she had ignored C. J. and he couldn't very well have ordered her not to accompany the man.

Unease mingled with frustration, and C. J. threw down his horseshoe.

"Where ya going?" Atlas called.

"I'm out." He turned and walked toward the river.

He'd said he wasn't going, but he couldn't help it. Even if it angered Lizzie, he had to see that she was all right.

"Jed, stop that. This instant!" Lizzie pulled away, her irritation growing into alarm.

They stood on the bank of the river in a small cleared spot where grass had been washed away. Water inched by, a transparent wash of red, gray, and brown. Pieces of chalk rock and pebbles studded the ground and the incline leading back to the barbecue.

For a while they had stood on the banks of the river and talked. But Jed had moved closer and closer.

First he had touched her hair. Just now he had tried to kiss her. She turned and started up the bank, struggling to find her footing on the hard red earth, which was gouged with crevices from the rise and fall of the river.

A large hand closed over her arm, bruising it. "Not so fast, girl. It wouldn't hurt you to be a little nice to me."

"I was a *little* nice, Jed." She jerked away and started for the hill again. "It doesn't mean you can paw me."

"That's no way to treat me, Lizzie." His hands clamped around her waist and he hauled her back against him. His breath burned her ear; he smelled of sweat and wood smoke.

A sliver of fear inched up her spine. "Jed, I'm sorry. I wasn't trying to be mean. Let me go so I can turn around." She instinctively resorted to the same calming manner she'd used in her years of dealing with Jude.

Jed pulled her tighter against him, his massive hands splaying across her stomach. Against the clean rose-and-white stripe, his hands were dirty and menacing.

"Jed, please—oh!" He squeezed her hard and cut off her breath. Her mind raced.

With his other hand, he lifted the shining strands of hair that flowed over her left shoulder. "You got pretty hair, Lizzie. What's under here?"

"Don't, please!" Panic shuddered through her. He was going to look at her scar. Or worse.

"Now, I just want to see your pretty face." His finger caressed the crest of her cheekbone, then traveled to her jaw, pushing aside her hair to reveal the scar. "Well, it don't look so pretty under here, does it?"

"Don't do this." Lizzie tried to make her voice even and firm, but it shook. "Stop."

He shoved the heavy mass over her shoulder and it rippled down her back. His hand crept higher on her rib cage and caressed the underside of her breast. Hysteria surfaced. *Think, Lizzie. Think.*

"You got a nice long scar all the way down your face. How'd you do that? Some man get ahold of you?"

"Stop it this instant." Fury flooded in, drowning out the fear. She stomped his foot with her heel and pulled away.

He grabbed her hair and tightened his fist around it, pulling until her scalp smarted. "Come here and give me a kiss."

"I will not, you disgusting pig." She reached up, trying to tug her hair from his grasp. All the years of abuse from Jude and all the promises she'd made herself never to succumb again kicked in and released her determination like water through a dam.

She glared at him. "Let me go. Now."

"Or you'll what?"

"Kick you in your most valued spot."

Doubt crept into the hard eyes and his gaze skated over her, judging. She held his gaze, anger boiling inside her. His hold slackened just a fraction and Lizzie jerked away from him.

"Don't ever touch me—"

"Get your damn hands off her!" C. J. launched himself through the air and crashed into Jed.

"C. J.!" Lizzie cried, startled.

He and Jed rolled to the edge of the water. C. J. dragged Jed up by the neck of his shirt, landing a stinging punch to the man's nose. Jed's head flopped backward and blood spurted.

"I give, Daltry. I give. I wasn't doing nothing."

C. J. landed another punch. Lizzie frowned, momentarily stunned into silence by his vehemence.

"Daltry—hell, man—let me up." Jed coughed, blood streaming from his nose and now one eye.

C. J. drew back his arm to land another punch. And another.

Lizzie rushed up behind him. "No, C. J. Let him up!"

He didn't seem to hear her, focused as he was on some private rage. His face was hard, no trace of softness or his ready smile.

She saw he meant to strike again and she grabbed his arm, shocked at the power vibrating through his body. "No, C. J. No!"

He paused, arm poised, fist drawn. His chest heaved and his features were distorted into a savage mask. He stared at Lizzie, uncomprehending.

"No, C. J.," she said softly, her heart pounding in her chest. "No more."

Slowly, the rage melted from his features. He blinked and stared down at his knuckles, bruised and stained with blood.

"Let me up!" Under him, Jed lay with blood smeared all over his face and shirt. "It'll never happen again."

"It better not." C. J. dropped his arm and moved cautiously off Jed, his body poised to strike.

Tension coiled in his lean muscles and Lizzie shivered. She had never seen C. J. angry.

Jed propped himself up on one elbow and wiped at the blood flowing out of his nose. "Damn. If she was yours, why didn't you say so?"

"She's not mine." C. J.'s voice was unfamiliar, flint-hard and cold. "And she's not yours either."

Lizzie felt a stab of disappointment at his declaration, but worry and an unfathomable anger were stronger.

Jed pulled a kerchief out of his britches pocket and grabbed his nose, cursing under his breath. He passed Lizzie without a glance and limped his way up the incline to the grass beyond.

Lizzie turned to C. J., shocked by the blood on his shirt, the flush of rage on his face. Her hands shook, but whether it was from her own anger or just a reaction to his she didn't know. "Are you all right?"

He nodded. "He didn't get in a punch."

Her heartbeat slowed to normal, but her stomach still fluttered nervously. "I'm glad you were—"

"Why in the hell did you come down here with him?" he exploded. "You knew I didn't want you to!"

"I thought he wanted to walk. There seemed to be no harm—"

"That was a stupid, irresponsible thing to do. It's lucky for you I came along when I did." He brushed dirt and bits of grass from his shirt.

Lizzie's eyes narrowed and rage pinched at her. "Now, hold on just a minute, C. J. Daltry. I was handling him just fine."

"Ha! 'I'll kick you in your most valued spot,' " C. J. mimicked roughly. "Oh, that was good. He was so scared, he went hightailin' it right outta here."

Lizzie flushed, as much from anger as from embarrassment. "I did not ask you to come charging down here like some ridiculous Sir Galahad and beat him to a bloody pulp."

"Lucky for you I did," he yelled. "Do you realize what could've happened?"

"I'm not totally naive!" she yelled back. "And I was perfectly capable of handling him on my own."

C. J. dusted off his denims, making a dismissive sound. "You were gettin' ready to handle somethin', all right," he muttered.

She glared at him and turned in a whirl of skirts. Humiliation battered her. She had tried to prove she didn't need C. J.'s protection, then Jed had tried to hurt her! The whole incident inflamed her, inciting her pride and anger.

"Yes, you better get on back before people start to wonder—hey, where are you going?"

"Mind your own business." Lizzie grabbed up her skirts and charged up the incline, heading through the trees for town.

C. J. scrambled up the hill after her. "Wait a minute. What are you doing? Where are you going?"

Lizzie strode through the tall grass, her skirts still clutched in her hands, grass pricking her legs through her cotton stockings.

Anger swirled through her. Of all the nerve! Had C. J. been spying on her, waiting for just such an opportunity? Her earlier fear of Jed was destroyed in the wake of anger.

She stalked through the trees, looking for the road that led back to town.

"Lizzie, damn it, I said wait."

"You can go to Hades." She sniffed, pleased that she had managed to throw in a mythological choice of words. There! He should have no problem understanding that.

"Elizabeth Colepepper, get back here."

He growled instead of yelling, and it was the use of her full name that caused Lizzie to falter for just an instant. But she didn't stop. She would not listen to him. She wouldn't.

She had so wanted to prove she didn't need his pity or his interference. Instead she had proven just the opposite.

Nine

HE HAD TO GET TO LIZZIE.

C. J. raced through the grove, where most of the towns-people were still enjoying dessert. He skirted groups of people standing gathered in clusters of fours and tens. He dodged an oak tree and shot past his grandmother and parents.

Laughter threaded through the gentle spring air. Several people called to him as he rushed by, but he didn't stop.

He vaulted over the corral fence and into the barn for Goliath. He didn't take time to saddle the horse, just slipped a bit in the palomino's mouth and leaped on.

He had hurt her, he knew. But he'd gone crazy when he'd seen Bostick holding her that way. C. J. hadn't been able to hear what was said, but the look of fear on Lizzie's face had strangled his breath.

He had reacted instinctively. For some reason, she was now angry. But so was he.

He urged Goliath to a flat-out run, leaning low over the horse's neck and tightening his thighs to keep his seat. He passed Atlas and Lee, who jumped out of his way and yelled.

Pastel stripes and ginghams and men's dark pants blurred as he headed for the road to town.

He cut across the east pasture and cleared a wood fence with no effort. **Goliath responded to C. J.'s silent commands.**

They cleared the next fence, the one marking the entrance to the Circle D, and C. J. saw her walking down the road.

He slowed Goliath as they neared, moving the horse in front of her and halting in Lizzie's path. She didn't even look up, just edged around him and kept marching.

Her face was flushed an angry red; her lips were pinched and tight. She still gripped her skirts, giving C. J. a full view of shapely calves encased in white stockings. He swallowed, unwilling to be distracted. "Lizzie, hold up."

She kept walking.

"Elizabeth," he growled.

She didn't even glance back.

He reined Goliath up beside her. "Where are you going?"

She stared straight ahead, her shoulders as stiff as a pump handle. Anger vibrated from her trim body.

He took a deep breath and gentled his voice. "Lizzie, are you hurt?"

There seemed to be a tiny hesitation in her step, but she walked on, chin thrust out stubbornly, head held high.

"Lizzie," he coaxed.

"Go away, C. J. I don't want or need your pity."

"Pity!" he sputtered. Damn fool woman! "Get up on this horse right now. You can't walk all the way back to town."

"I certainly can. And I intend to."

"No, you're not." Fueled by a new surge of anger, he reined Goliath to a halt and leaped down from the saddle.

Tears of anger sheened her eyes and she sidestepped him. "Don't you lay a hand on me."

"Get up on this horse." He towered over her; he was not

in the least contrite about his threatening stance. "Or, by Thor, I'll put you up there."

"No one asked you to come after me. I don't want you here."

"Lizzie, get on that horse."

"No, I—oomph!"

C. J. hooked an arm around her waist and whistled to Goliath. The stallion trotted up and eyed them balefully, switching his tail as though impatient.

"Put me down this instant," she gritted out.

Her body heat soaked into him and he inhaled the soft rose scent of her. Her breasts teased his arm where it wrapped around her waist. He again saw Jed with his arm wrapped around her like this and he felt a sudden softening in his heart. "I'm going to take you home."

Her body was tight and uncompromising in his arms, but she made no move to escape. He hoisted her onto Goliath's back and mounted himself.

She said not a word all the way back to town. C. J. searched his brain. What had he done wrong? Why was she so angry?

Since he hadn't taken the time to saddle the horse, Lizzie's body was melded to his. Her breasts flattened against his back; her belly pressed low against his hips. C. J.'s thoughts scattered and his body focused on the sensation of her fitted so closely to him.

Moist heat shimmered between them. He could smell her roses and a softer, sweeter scent that was her. Though she tried to hold herself away from him, the horse's motion and its sleek hide conspired against her. With every step, she sank closer to his body. He hadn't been aware that he had put her on astride, but he was painfully aware now.

She straddled his hips from behind and he found himself imagining the feel of her beneath him, naked, her hips rising up to meet his. He clamped down on that thought, but the tantalizing ebb and flow of her touch incited his musings, flaming a fire that had sprung to secret life inside him.

They reached her house and she slid off without waiting for him to give her a hand.

He swung down from Goliath and followed her onto the porch. "Won't you at least tell me why you're so upset?"

"As if you didn't know," she muttered.

"I don't." He stepped closer, dropping the reins and trying to catch her gaze. Anger and desire and concern clashed.

She huffed out a breath. "I did not need your help. Everything was fine. Now I look like an idiot and everyone probably thinks you've got some kind of claim on me."

His mouth fell open. She was worried about being humiliated? For the first time, he wondered if he'd handled Jed wrong, but stubborn pride won out. He snorted. "That's just like a woman. I probably saved you from being ravished."

"Why did I think you would understand?" She leveled a flat stare on him and turned to go.

"All right, I'm sorry."

When she opened the door to her house, he stepped in front of her. He couldn't leave like this. "I'm sorry. Lizzie, please—"

"I'm sick of your pity, C. J."

"I don't understand why you keep saying that."

"I know that's what you feel for me."

Pity was not what he felt at all, but you didn't follow through on these kinds of feelings with a woman like Lizzie. He'd practically killed Jed for trying it. He couldn't do it himself. "You're wrong," C. J. said quietly. "What I feel is . . . friendship."

"Well, you can keep your friendship. I don't need another guardian." She pushed past him and sailed inside her small house.

His anger flared and C. J. followed her inside, incredulous. "You're saying you don't want to be friends because I made Jed Bostick leave you alone?"

"I didn't need your help. I didn't ask for your help." She tossed her reticule on the table and whirled. "Were you spying on us?"

"Of course not!" C. J. roared, then shoved a hand into his hair, trying to control his temper. "I care what happens to you—"

"I was handling Jed Bostick just fine without your interference. There's probably not a man alive now who will have anything to do with me because you had to act like some—some conquering hero."

Good! C. J. wanted to yell, but instead he gritted out, "I won't apologize for hitting him. He was taking advantage of you! He could've become dangerous if I hadn't gotten there when I did."

"First Tom, now Jed. Are you planning to disapprove of every man I see? Frankly, it is none of your business, and I want *you* to leave me alone. Stop coming around here and trying to butt into my life."

Her words speared a raw place inside him, but it was the mention of Tom that snapped the rein on his temper. C. J. knew he would regret it, knew he might drive Lizzie away forever, but caution dissolved along with common sense. He advanced on her, wearing a deliberately suggestive leer.

Her chin came up, but alarm flickered in her eyes. She backed up a step. "Get that look off your face."

"Isn't this what you wanted? For Tom to look at you this way? Do you know what a man wants when he looks this way, Lizzie?"

Uncertainty flared in her eyes. "Tom would never—"

He grabbed her arm, cutting off her words. She stared up at him, wariness and a hint of fear in her eyes. He hated himself for pushing her, but didn't she realize how close she'd come with Bostick? He eased his body up to hers, pushing her against the wall in the process.

"C. J., stop it." She shoved at him, but he planted his feet.

He pressed against her, hating the anger that wouldn't let go, that even now turned to heat at the feel of her breasts crushed into his chest, her thighs quivering against his. His hand tangled in her hair. "Is this what you want?"

"So what if it is?" Her words defied him, but he read the panic in her eyes, the confused awareness. She bucked against him and her knee nudged between his legs.

C. J. tightened his legs around hers, increasing the pressure against his arousal. Anger and hot power shot through him. "Ah, yes, you said so once before. How much do you want, Lizzie?"

"Why are you doing this?" Her voice shook and hurt flared in her eyes.

Intoxicated by her nearness, a quiver ripped through his body. He noted with surprise and detachment that his arms were shaking. He leaned closer, so he could feel her breath mingle with his.

"Is this what you want from Tom?" he said harshly.

"No." She arched against the wall, bringing her pelvis into contact with his.

Flames cinched his gut. "For him to touch you?" His free hand stroked her waist and slid up to the curve of her breast.

"No," she choked. Alarm and bewildered passion quickened in her eyes.

C. J.'s body tightened and lust clawed through his belly. She had to know what kind of trouble she courted. Didn't she understand?

"For him to taste you?" He kissed her, harsh and quick, sliding his lips across hers, getting so much of her sweet heat that his purpose wavered.

She bit his lip and he tasted the salt of blood. He kissed her again, harder, trying to make the raging lust for her go away. It multiplied, steepling in his belly like a caged thing.

He pulled away from her, his world spinning. Something shifted between them, a conscious awareness that turned to hunger. Her eyes were glazed with fear. And a burgeoning passion. Her gaze locked on his mouth and she licked her lips as if tasting him there.

His knees wobbled. He knew he should resist the urge to kiss her with persuasive gentleness, and peel the clothes from her body. But her eyes drew him in, pleading silently with him, and he realized he didn't give a damn about what he *should* do. He had to kiss her.

Slowly he lowered his head, wanting to be gentle, wanting to show her the way.

Their lips touched and C. J.'s reason disappeared. His free arm went around her slender waist and hauled her up to his chest. Her breasts flattened against him, her swollen nipples burning him through her dress. She twined her arms around his neck, meeting his open mouth with her own.

When he dipped his tongue inside, she stiffened slightly, then relaxed. Her tongue stroked his and his arousal strained against his denims.

C. J. was barely aware of where they were. His senses were flooded with the dark satin of her mouth, the sweet curve of her breast nestled in his palm. Never, in all his joinings with women, had he felt this sense of oneness, of . . . inevitability. Only with Lizzie. *Lizzie!*

He jerked away and backed off, his chest heaving. The words ripped from his throat. "By Thor!"

Lizzie opened her eyes slowly, looking dazed. Her eyes glimmered, dark and smoky with promise, and her voice rasped out, raking fire along his belly. "Oh my gosh."

"That was a mistake." His stunned mind struggled to accept what had just happened.

A mistake.

He saw the devastation in her eyes, the slash of pain across her features, and realized he'd chosen the wrong words. He didn't want her to think that he regretted the kiss because he didn't find her attractive or worthy. "I'm sorry,

Lizzie. It's nothing to do with you. I took liberties I shouldn't have."

Before he weakened and reached for her again, he bolted out the door.

His body throbbed with want. He needed to sink into her body, feel her pulsing around him, and ease the talons of desire hooking into him. But this was Lizzie. He was supposed to find her a husband, not take advantage of her.

C. J. hated himself. He was no different than Jed, except he *had* taken advantage of her. He threw himself onto Goliath and spurred the massive horse toward home.

As if the hounds of hell were chasing him.

A *mistake?* He'd said that the kiss was a mistake.

Anger razored through her. Of all the nerve! She hadn't even liked it!

She grimaced at the lie. Heat still shimmered low in her belly, taunting, potent, weakening. Frustration shifted through her. C. J.'s kiss had possessed her, consumed her with its heat.

He had wanted her. As a man wants a woman. The realization was too unfamiliar to make her smile, but her body quivered in response.

She had despaired of anyone ever wanting her that way, and certainly never imagined that C. J. would. She tried to bring up her anger at his interference with Jed, but couldn't. The concept that C. J. might want her was foreign, but utterly beguiling. Her dreams were filtered with images of him beside her, naked, kissing and caressing, loving her.

Even the next day, as she readied herself for church, she couldn't deny the memory. She even forced herself to think of Jude.

It's just as well you're scarred, Lizzie. No one would take you to wife anyway.

Her fingers moved over her scar and she closed her eyes, wishing she couldn't feel the raised ridge of skin.

C. J.'s kiss had shaken her to her core. He had wanted her, yes, but it was no more than that. And he'd been just as shocked as she had.

There had also been revulsion in his eyes when he'd pulled away. He'd labeled it a mistake and he was right. Best to remember that.

She tried. She really did.

Lizzie dreaded going to church. She knew everyone in town would be talking about the incident with Jed. No doubt they would point at her and whisper and speculate as to whether she had invited trouble.

For an instant she considered not going. But she had endured worse as a child after she had gotten the scar. No longer would she hide away from the people of this town. She had done nothing wrong, just as she had done nothing wrong all those years ago.

The one person she could not face was C. J., and she prayed he wouldn't attend. She draped her hair over her left shoulder and angled her dark blue hat on her head. Usually the hat made her feel pretty; today its familiarness reassured her.

A knock at the door startled her. *C. J.?*

She immediately dismissed the possibility and peered through the window next to the door. Tom stood outside.

"Lizzie, you home?" He knocked again, gripping his brushed brown bowler by the top and smashing it.

She cracked the door wide enough to speak to him. "I'm here, getting ready for church."

"Can I walk you?" His hazel eyes met hers, his testing and uncertain.

She frowned. "Is that why you came?"

His gaze flickered away.

Heat rose in her face. He'd heard about C. J. and Jed.

"Are you all right?" His voice came husky and low.

She sighed and opened the door for him, turning to pluck her hat pin from the table. "I look all right, don't I?"

"What happened at the picnic yesterday?" His voice was low and concerned.

"Tom, I don't really want to talk about it."

"Hank and Maybelle are worried about you."

"Does the whole town know?" She turned away, resisting the urge to bury her face in her hands. How could they not?

"Well . . . C. J. did go tearing through the party, hell-bent. Then Jed Bostick showed up with a broken nose and jaw. After a while I noticed you were gone. So did C. J.'s mother and grandmother. I put it together and . . ."

Lizzie groaned and hid her face in her hands. "What a mess! I was trying to prove to C. J. that I didn't need his stupid interference."

"Did Jed hurt you?"

"No. Not really." She shuddered, thinking of Jed's hands on her, his cruel words. She explained to Tom, ending with, "I could've handled Jed Bostick. I had everything under control when C. J. charged over the hill like an offended bull and attacked him."

Tom was silent for a long moment. Lizzie looked up to find an angry flush on his face. "Are you sure you're all right?"

"Yes. I just feel a fool. And now the whole town knows."

"I would've done the same thing if I'd been the one to find you."

"Somehow I wouldn't have minded if *you'd* done it."

Tom regarded her curiously. "Did C. J. see you home? When he took off on that monstrous stallion—"

"Yes." Lizzie cut him off. She didn't want to talk, or think, about what had happened when they had arrived at her house.

He grinned. "I imagine you gave C. J. a piece of your mind."

"Yes, I did," she said hotly, then flushed. She didn't want to tell Tom what else she had given C. J. last night.

Tom squeezed her elbow. "Hey, he thought he was helping. Don't be so hard on him."

"I don't know why he thinks I'm his responsibility."

"Maybe he cares."

"No," she answered quickly, annoyed that she had started to wonder if maybe he did. "He doesn't."

"But, Lizzie—"

"Tom, I appreciate what you're trying to do, but it's over now and I'd like to forget it."

He eyed her speculatively. "Did something else happen?"

"Mercy, no!" She turned away before he could see the blush heating her cheeks. But Tom's sharp observation forced her to examine her feelings for C. J. Feelings she thought she had understood. "No," she said again, more firmly.

"Are you sure?"

"Yes." She turned back to him, managing to keep her gaze on his. "Thank you for asking."

"I wanted to come by and check on you." His gaze narrowed on her, probing.

"I'm fine. Really."

He hesitated for a moment more, then nodded. "All right. So, do you want to walk to church with me?"

"Thanks. I'd like that." She smiled, feeling suddenly drained of energy. She didn't want to think about C. J. anymore. Church would definitely take her mind off the sinful feelings he'd provoked.

Tom stayed close, but didn't hover. He didn't refer to C. J. during their walk to church, and Lizzie found herself grateful to have made such a friend. He offered support without preaching or lecturing or judging.

Maybelle and Hank stood at the front door with Reverend Timmons. When she and Tom walked up, they stopped talking.

For an instant, her heart clenched. Then she lifted her

chin and walked to the top of the church steps. "Good morning."

"Hello, Lizzie." Reverend Timmons clasped her hand in his and smiled warmly into her eyes. "You're looking well this morning. I'm glad to see you're all right after that business with Jed Bostick yesterday."

Lizzie gaped, then remembered herself and thanked him. Beside her, Maybelle beamed and Hank wore a fiercely protective scowl. What was going on?

They walked inside, and the churchgoers already seated turned toward her of one accord. She forced herself to scan the room for C. J. and sighed in relief when she saw he wasn't sitting with his family.

She could feel the gaze of every person burning into her. It was all she could do not to turn and run. Tom broke the tension by ushering her into a seat and leaning up to speak to Miss Lavender.

Despite her best effort, during the service her thoughts were riddled with C. J.

Snatches of "I'll Meet My Jesus" and "Soldiers of Christ Arise" were jumbled with memories of the stark craving C. J. had aroused in her. The sermon, entitled "How to Live a Gracious, Charitable Life" was invaded by memories of his tongue stroking hers, making her want to feel it in other places on her body. Underlining it all was a building curiosity. About him. About her. About the possibility of *them*.

She sat ramrod stiff in the pew between Tom and Maybelle, her skin prickling as she felt the weighted gazes of people behind her.

After the closing prayer, Tom made his way down the aisle to speak with Reverend Timmons. She leaned down to get her reticule, stalling until most people had left.

"Lizzie?" Miss Lavender's chirpy voice sounded above her and she raised her head.

The tiny woman patted Lizzie on the shoulder and whispered. "I'm so glad you're all right, dear. I say they should horsewhip that young man."

"Th–thank you, Miss Lavender." Though stunned, Lizzie managed a smile as the older woman tottered off.

She glanced at Maybelle, who smiled triumphantly and reached over to squeeze her hand. Lizzie rose and stepped into the aisle.

"Miss Colepepper?"

She turned to see Odie and Jane Daltry standing before her. Nervousness fluttered. Were they angry? Would they blame her for disrupting the barbecue?

"We wanted to make sure you're all right, dear." Jane Daltry stepped forward and took Lizzie's hand in hers. "I hope you'll let us know if there's anything we can do to help."

"I'm perfectly fine." The words sounded stiff and heat climbed into her cheeks. She forced herself to relax and added shyly, by way of apology, "Thank you for asking."

"Certainly."

"Jane, Odie, you're embarrassing the girl." Minerva Daltry pushed through, her gray eyes—sharp yet concerned—on Lizzie's face. "You look well to me."

"Yes, ma'am."

Minerva grinned. "My grandson can be quite helpful at times, can't he?" She didn't wait for an answer, but walked off with her son and daughter-in-law.

Lizzie stared after them, wonder coursing through her. These people actually cared! She smiled at Maybelle and felt tears sting her eyes. How long had she waited for this? And why was it happening now? Was it because *she* had finally made an effort, an effort Jude had forever discouraged? Or was it because of C. J.?

Outside, there were more well-wishers: Fritz and Rosy from The Buc, Clay Masterson, Sally Louise Orndorft, and even Sheriff Sampson.

For the first time since she had moved here at the age of

ten, Lizzie felt she truly belonged in the town of Paradise Plains.

Though a wayward part of her longed to see C. J., to gauge his reaction to what had happened between them last night, she was glad he wasn't here.

Her irreverent musings during church had made one thing glaringly clear. Friendship was not what she felt for C. J. And last night, when he'd kissed her, friendship wasn't what he'd felt either.

It had happened slowly, over a period of time since she'd gotten to know him again. And seen the vulnerability, the doubt beneath the charm he showed to the world.

With a sinking heart, she realized she cared for him. But she refused to believe it could be more than that.

Ten

HER MOUTH OPENED TENTATIVELY UNDER HIS, INVITING HIM IN,
then opening wider to his coaxing tongue. Heat spiraled
through him, driving him to push her into the wall and plunge
his tongue deeper into her mouth.

C. J. swore and banished the thought. Two days later, he
was still thinking about that kiss with Lizzie. He stood in the
barn, the pitchfork forgotten in his hand. Sweat itched his
bare shoulders and frustration churned in his gut. He had
worked all morning, cleaning stables, hauling in fresh wood
for the new troughs, and still the memory persisted.

The kiss haunted him. It had invaded his sleep with memories of the way she melted into him, the way her tongue
touched his tentatively, then more boldly, as she became
swept up in a whirl of heat and passion and promise. He
pulled on his gloves, feeling again the weight of her breast in
his hand, and fire raked through his belly.

He closed his eyes, trying to forget, wishing he could explain it away as anger, but he couldn't. He'd known what he
was doing every step of the way.

What had started out as determination to show her how
foolish she'd been by going off with Bostick had become a
dark, driving need to infuse his soul with hers, to possess her
in a way he'd never cared to possess anyone or anything
since Diana.

That need had obliterated common sense—a first for him, and a last, he vowed.

Not that he hadn't enjoyed it. Hell, he'd never been so in tune with a woman, so frustratingly aware of moans that beckoned him to stroke her tongue with his, of the tiny sound coming from the back of her throat that matched his.

Why Lizzie? He didn't understand.

He'd wanted her for a while now, but he had figured that was only because he couldn't have her. He was responsible for finding her a husband, not giving her pleasure. At least not the kind of pleasure they had shared Saturday after the party.

If he'd only wanted her because he couldn't have her, then why did he want her still? Why hadn't the honey-sweet taste of her left his lips? Why hadn't the feel of her faded from his body? Why was his gut still gnarled into knots?

He'd never experienced that kind of driving need, the kind that damned everything else and shoved him toward a blind completion. But neither had he ever experienced anything like he'd felt when he'd seen her with Jed Bostick.

An unfamiliar rage had rocked him, a raw power he couldn't refute. And he had reacted purely on instinct. He was still stunned.

Even with Diana he had never been prone to jealousy, and it was ridiculous to be thus with Lizzie because they were nothing more than friends.

Friends. The word echoed with doubt, uncertainty, and gut-twisting frustration.

He stabbed the pitchfork into the pile of hay and tossed a load into the stall. His muscles burned and sweat sleeked his chest and back. He welcomed the fatigue, the ache of work. He needed it, needed to be here in the barn where he could think.

He'd sent all the hands out to the pasture today and his younger siblings were in school. He was alone, just as he preferred. So he could forget.

But the want still throbbed low in his belly and anger flashed through him. He wasn't supposed to feel this for her, of all people. He couldn't feel this way. He was supposed to find her a husband, not make her a woman.

Every detail of that night haunted him. Vague flashes of her house tripped through his memory. His senses had seemed more acute that night. He could recall the scent of beeswax, a white lace doily on the small dining table, the threadbare curtains—but something nagged at him. Something was missing. Some part of her—

He stilled. *There were no mirrors in her house.* The realization caused a twisting in his insides. Was she unable to look at herself? Was the omission her doing or Jude's?

A full-blown picture of her sprang into his mind. And the images taunted him again, shadowy pictures of her taut thighs twined around his, her smooth ivory breasts teasing the golden darkness of his chest.

And she thought all he felt for her was pity. Ha! If he weren't straining against the fly of his denims, he might laugh. Maybe he'd felt pity for her once, a long time ago, but that had changed when he'd seen how she had survived Jude and his treatment of her.

She was strong, although sometimes her strength was hidden beneath sharp words. He knew that was just a form of protection. She'd been an outsider in this town for a long time.

It seemed everything had changed. He looked closer at her now, understood things he had never considered before. At first he had felt responsibility about her scar and the desire to complete the task to ease his guilt, but that too had changed.

Pity for her? He was more apt to feel sorry for *himself,* the way he was knotted up over this woman, a woman for whom he had never expected to feel such conflicting, confusing emotions.

And lust? He felt that, just as he'd felt it for several eligible females he'd known over the years.

But there was something else. Caring, maybe—but pity? No!

The image of her blue eyes, smoky with passion and wonder, was etched in his mind. His gut clenched and he tightened his hold on the pitchfork, stabbing at the mound of hay, wishing he could destroy the image of her.

How had she reacted to his abrupt departure? He had been shocked by that kiss, and for the first time, completely uneasy with a woman. She drew feelings out of him he'd never experienced, never even realized he had.

He could still see the hurt in her eyes and he wanted to go to her and explain, but he couldn't without revealing his task and looking more a fool. Besides, he didn't understand what was happening himself.

Frustration and restlessness clawed through him. He had to forget what had happened between them. He would just blank his mind and concentrate on physical labor.

"Anybody out here? Daltry?"

The voice penetrated C. J.'s teeming thoughts. He raised his head and looked over the gate of the back stall. Tom English stood inside the doors. Surprise held C. J. immobile for an instant. What the hell did English want?

C. J. leaned the pitchfork against the slatted wall and stepped out in the middle aisle of the stable. "What can I do for you?"

The other man squinted against the sudden dimness of the barn and halted in front of C. J., extending his hand. "How ya doin'?"

"Fine." C. J. shook Tom's hand, frowning. Was the man here because of Lizzie? "Everything okay?" he asked warily.

Tom grinned and pushed his dark hat back on his head. "I, uh, saw Bostick's face. And heard about what happened."

C. J.'s shoulders tightened. "And?"

"I'd like to thank you for taking up for her."

He studied the man, trying to determine if Tom had another motive for coming to the ranch. But the other man's eyes were serious and sincere. "Lizzie didn't think it was such a good thing."

"I heard that, too." Tom laughed. "She's a pretty independent sort, but that incident could've turned nasty. I'm glad you were there and helped out."

English acted as though he were here as Lizzie's champion. "Why *wouldn't* I help her? I care about—she's a lady, after all."

The other man's hazel gaze weighed him. "Yes. She is. A very special lady."

What is she to you? C. J. bit back the words. That odd anger spun through him again, suspiciously like jealousy. How could that be? He didn't have that type of relationship with Lizzie. Suddenly he wanted to know what kind of relationship Tom shared with her. "You've been seeing a lot of her."

"Yes, I have. She's gracious, kind, fun, not to mention beautiful." He stared off, a distant look stealing across his features. "You ever seen eyes like that? Her eyes remind me of the sky at dusk back home." He looked at C. J. "She's been good to me since I came to Paradise Plains."

Hearing Tom list Lizzie's attributes unseamed C. J.'s self-control. Tension coiled through his body and that strange anger returned, hammering at his conscience, his heart. "You have intentions toward her?"

Tom's eyes sharpened, though his face gave away nothing. "Are you her guardian?"

"Now, see here, English—"

"Just askin'." Tom held up a hand. "I thought maybe if you were or if you were somehow related . . ."

"You know I'm not."

"No offense intended." The other man smiled as though he knew of C. J.'s frustrations and enjoyed watching him squirm. "But I think my intentions toward Lizzie are between me and her."

Irritation spurted through C. J., but he couldn't deny the logic of what Tom said. And if he pursued it, Tom would think C. J. wanted to lay claim to her. "We're friends," he said quietly. "She has nobody to watch out for her."

"I don't think Lizzie would like knowing that we think she needs someone to watch out for her."

"A woman alone?"

"You don't have to convince me. I figure to keep an eye on her myself."

"I'll watch out for her," C. J. growled, squashing the urge to smash his fist into Tom's nose the way he'd done to Jed.

"I'd like to be there when you tell Lizzie that." The other man grinned and walked out.

C. J. stood in the barn door and watched English ride away on a strawberry roan mare.

Friends. He was supposed to be her friend, but friendliness was not what he'd felt during that kiss.

The thought of Tom English spending time with Lizzie, taking care of her, made C. J.'s belly twist in a most unfriendlike way.

He'd wanted to forget about her and that kiss they'd shared. Besides pushing the memory in his face, Tom's visit had brought a sobering revelation.

Tom English cared for Lizzie already. Perhaps C. J. should back off, let nature take its true course. It suddenly didn't matter if Grandma awarded C. J. the ranch for finding Lizzie a husband, as long as she found one.

He wanted to keep an eye on her, but after Saturday he didn't trust himself to keep his hands off her.

He would bow out, let Tom and Lizzie explore any feelings that might be budding. His heart lurched at the thought of staying away, but he'd botched things with her and *he* certainly wasn't the man for her. Though it galled him to admit it, Tom English probably was.

And if Tom wasn't good to her, C. J. would do to him what he'd done to Bostick.

C. J.'s resolve wavered over the next few days. He should go to her, apologize for what he'd done and said.

No, he should give her room. She was probably just as stunned as he had been, not to mention embarrassed.

He tried to forget her and couldn't. Tried to forget about the kiss and couldn't. In the end, he gave up.

As he worked the ranch, breaking horses or branding steers or taking Goliath over to George Bates for breeding, his mind stayed occupied. But in quiet moments or during a lull in the day, memories of that kiss surfaced.

Frustration filled him, flicking like the stroke of a lash that gradually cut through layers of conscience and his will.

And the want built. His groin ached. His mind conjured up images of her bare skin pressed to his, her tongue gliding tentatively into his mouth. And always was the misty reminder of her passion-glazed eyes.

He was right to step aside and see what, if anything, developed between Lizzie and Tom English. He repeated that over and over, trying to hammer his flaccid resolve into steel.

On Thursday, C. J. headed into town. A mare had died earlier in the week, leaving a brand-new foal who would neither eat nor drink. Roper had been working with the little filly, but to no avail. C. J. hoped one of the twins at the livery might be able to help him come up with a way to get the foal to eat.

And it gave him an excuse to check on Lizzie.

The fact that he needed an excuse caused him to grimace, but after what had happened Saturday night, he wasn't sure how to approach her. Or if they were still friends.

Later, he left the livery, armed with a mental list from the twins, and headed to the mercantile. Though the sun pulsed a gentle heat across town, the early spring day was crisp.

Sunlight gilded the whitewashed front of the mercantile and gleamed off the polished windows of the newspaper office.

Scents of fresh grass and animals chased the toasty smell of baking bread from The Buc and the stale odors of cigars from the saloon.

His step quickened as he neared the store and anticipation skidded along his nerves. While he placed his order, he could check on Lizzie.

C. J. stepped inside and scanned the stacked crates, the open barrels that boasted nails and pickles and city-made soap. Hank stood on a ladder, reaching for a pair of black work boots. Fritz, from The Buc, stood next to the ladder. Maybelle worked behind the counter, tallying Miss Lavender's bill.

His sister-in-law, Meredith, stood in the corner with their adopted son, Jimmy. Lee and Meredith loved children so much that C. J. knew they wanted to have more on their own, although Meredith wasn't in the family way yet. Jimmy shifted from one foot to the other while Meredith measured the width of his shoulders against a shirt she held in her hand. She saw C. J. and waved.

He smiled, glancing around for Lizzie. There was no sign of her.

Jimmy hollered. "Hey, C. J.!"

"Hey, kid! How's it goin'?"

Jimmy wrinkled up his nose and cut his eyes at Meredith. C. J. laughed.

Miss Lavender passed C. J. and headed for the door, carrying a brown-wrapped package. Her red felt hat, crowned with a sweeping scarlet feather, was set at a jaunty angle. She wore a red skirt and shirtwaist with a flounce of red and yellow lace at the collar. With the weight of her petticoats and the rows of ruffles on her skirt, C. J. thought she might tip over.

"May I help you with that, Miss Lavender?"

"What? Oh." She peered over the top of her package,

then smiled. "No, thank you. I'm only going across the street, you know."

"Have a good day, ma'am." He touched his hat, then slid his list of supplies across to Maybelle.

Maybelle smiled, a speculative gleam in her eye. "Haven't seen you in a few days, C. J."

He gave a noncommittal reply.

She walked out from behind the counter to fetch the small pail he wanted.

He edged back to peer under the curtain that hid the back room. Was Lizzie back there? He couldn't hear anything or see her small pair of black shoes.

"Lizzie's not here right now."

He looked up to find Maybelle's smiling gaze on him. He cleared his throat. "Been busy at the ranch. Getting ready for roundup."

"We had a wonderful time at your barbecue. Are you thinking of making it an annual affair?"

His gaze sliced to hers. He was glad Lizzie couldn't hear Maybelle, or she would know he'd made up that party out of thin air. "Thought I might, yeah."

Maybelle returned to the counter with the pail and a length of linen. She studied him for a minute. "She told me about Jed and what you did. I'm glad you were there."

"Yeah," he snorted, thinking of the visit Tom had paid him. Though it didn't sit well, he'd been grudgingly impressed with the Alabaman and his concern for Lizzie. "Everybody seems glad, except Lizzie."

A secret smile curved Maybelle's lip. C. J. itched to ask her what that meant, but just then he heard Lizzie's voice outside. He turned.

She stood at the edge of the porch, the wind plucking at her hair and skirt. Sunlight pooled around her feet and glistened on the ebony silk of her hair. Her purple sprigged day dress was crisp and edged with a white collar and cuffs.

It sleeked down her body like a second skin. C. J. swallowed, remembering the feel of her against him.

Don't think about that, he cautioned his mind, but his body responded anyway. He tried to focus on the relief that sliced through him at the sight of her. She was all right. Her voice was light and chipper; she looked none the worse for wear, and—

By Thor, she was talking to Webb Callaway.

C. J. frowned, moving closer to hear what was said. But the wind carried away their low words. Webb said something and Lizzie blushed. Just like she had after C. J. had kissed her.

A knot settled in his chest. What was Webb doing here? What did he want with Lizzie? Surely he wasn't going to ask her to dinner after C. J. had told him it wasn't necessary.

His gaze traced her delicate profile, slid over that black curtain of silky hair, and lingered on her high breasts. A familiar burn started in his groin. It inched to his belly, pounding, throbbing like a distant thunder that moved ever closer.

"Have you heard a word I've said?"

He became aware that Maybelle was speaking to him and turned his head slightly, trying to keep Lizzie in his vision from the corner of his eye.

"I said I think Lizzie could've handled Jed, but I'm glad you were there. He surely won't try anything like that again."

"Oh, yeah, sure."

Webb took Lizzie's hand and kissed it. And on the wind, C. J. heard something he'd heard too infrequently—the throaty sound of her laughter. His eyes narrowed and he took a step forward. Maybelle's hand closed on his arm.

"Webb Callaway is one of the nicest men in town, don't you agree?"

C. J. glanced at her, suddenly reminded of his earlier vow to let things concerning Lizzie take a natural course. A warning sounded in his head.

Damn, hadn't he been telling himself this was exactly

what Lizzie needed? Hadn't he himself tried to get Webb to call for her? C. J. had expected to see her with Tom, if anyone, but Webb was completely trustworthy.

So why was his blood churning? He fought back feelings of protectiveness and jealousy, telling himself that seeing Webb with Lizzie was good. This was what he'd hoped for. She was a beautiful, intelligent woman, and men were bound to finally see her as he did.

"They make a striking couple, don't they?" Maybelle mused beside him.

His gaze moved to hers.

She smiled and walked through the curtain into the back room.

His gaze swiveled to the couple on the porch and talons of envy hooked into him. *He* wanted to be talking to her. *He* wanted to make her laugh, make her smile at him with no uncertainty or guardedness.

But *he* was supposed to be finding a husband for her.

C. J. clenched his fists against the urge to stroll casually outside and break up their conversation. He wanted to look into her eyes, see if he could read the same intense longing he'd felt since that kiss. But he had sworn to forget that, hadn't he?

He had no business marching out there to whisk her away from Webb. It was none of his affair. He owed it to Lizzie to let nature take its course. He'd vowed to give his grandmother an honest effort. And he would. Even if it killed him.

His mind battled with what he wanted and what he had sworn; his heart ached as though it were being pulled from his chest. In the end, he gathered his purchases and stepped outside.

"Good day, Lizzie. Webb." He touched his hat in a two-finger salute and strode off down the street, feeling as though the light had dimmed from his day.

*   *   *

Frustration raked through him. For two days, all C. J. had thought about was Lizzie and Webb. Lizzie eating with Webb, riding with him, *kissing* him!

It didn't help that Webb had seen fit to tell C. J. that he and Lizzie were going to dinner. He acted as if C. J. should've been pleased. And he tried. He really did.

But C. J.'s imagination held devastating pictures of her. First with Tom, then with Webb. Once he even imagined her with the twins!

He knew Lizzie wasn't the kind of woman to play fast and loose. What drove him crazy was not knowing what she was doing—and with whom.

His mind tortured him with too-real memories of her velvet tongue exploring the roughness of his, the trusting way her arms twined around his neck, giving him a sense of power and humility at the same time. Again and again, he pushed the thoughts away. Still his body yearned for her.

He was edgy, flirting with rage most of the day, short-tempered with the hands and even his family. Since seeing Lizzie with Webb, doubts had assailed him. He was indecisive about the ranch and filled with doubts.

Had that kiss been a result of the heat of anger, or something else? Had it affected her the way it had affected him? Had it affected her at all?

It had been a week since that kiss and he didn't understand this carnal urge to have her, over and over and over. He wanted to kiss her again, talk to her, just sit with her. He didn't trust himself to do any of those things.

But he could see her. Just a glimpse would take away this wicked craving for the taste of her, soothe this insatiable desire to know what she was doing.

The urge was relentless, finally driving him into town later in the day. Just as the sun dipped low in a fiery sky awash with red and gold light, he reined up at her house.

Eleven

C. J.'s BREATH CAUGHT AT THE SIGHT OF HER. SHE STOOD IN THE
glow of the sun, a lone figure silhouetted against the sky
where the red-gold sunset met the flat blackness of the horizon. The hawk was perched on her outstretched arm.

The sight of her seeped into him like air long denied,
pumping awareness and life and heat like a bellows through
his veins. Arousal, deep and intense, pulled at his gut and
hardened him in a rush.

Impatience gouged him. Had she thought of him as he'd
thought of her? Had she been affected as he had? He swallowed, suddenly uncertain and annoyed to realize his palms
were sweating.

When there was no answer at her door, he had gone
around back to check the shed. He had found her standing
several yards away, on a small rise.

The woman and the bird were dark images carved from
the night, and the sight struck him as majestic, proud. The
bird perched on her slender arm, power and beauty and
leashed strength in its compact body.

An impatient spirit yearning to be set free.

In that way, the bird and the woman were the same. He
frowned. Where had that thought come from? He wasn't

given to poetic gibberish. Slowly he walked toward her, past the washed gray walls of the shed, into taller yellow grass and prairie flowers in the beginning stages of bloom.

Sound magnified in the vastness of the prairie, the grass rustling against his denims, scratching against his boots. There was a serenity, a peace about the scene that merged wild with tame, spirit with soul.

The bird started, its head swiveling around, its wings shooting out in a rapid movement. Dark obsidian eyes studied C. J. and he halted, unwilling to disturb the hawk further.

Lizzie glanced over her shoulder. "No sudden moves, please."

"Sorry." He could tell nothing from her tone. Was she angry or not? "May I stay?"

She hesitated, then said grudgingly, "If you wish."

She turned her attention to the bird, and C. J. moved slowly yet fluidly through the grass, stopping several feet behind her. From this distance, he had a perfect view of her, yet he wouldn't break her concentration.

Etched against the twilight sky, her arm looked slight and fragile. The sun sank behind the hills and disappeared in a wash of gold and rose. Lizzie's voice filtered through the air, calm and soothing and striking a stillness in the animal as well as in C. J. The hawk cocked its head as though understanding.

C. J. caught only snatches of her words.

". . . where you belong . . . ever need a place . . . free . . . be happy."

She lifted her arm and the bird took flight. In the quietness, C. J. heard Lizzie catch her breath. The bird beat its wings frantically and C. J. silently urged it on.

Then the wings expanded and the hawk soared up. Up and up, becoming a dim speck in the twilight. C. J. tilted his head back to watch, filled with a burgeoning sense of freedom.

He kept his gaze focused there, though he was keenly aware of the woman in front of him. The bird came back into focus directly overhead and circled lower, then dipped in a graceful arc before shooting upward to disappear into the sky.

A fullness throbbed in C. J.'s chest, and he dragged his gaze from the sky to Lizzie. She stood unmoving, her face turned up, staring into a blueing sky and gilt-edged clouds.

The yearning on her face tugged at his heart. She stood there for long minutes, making C. J. feel like an intruder.

Had she forgotten him? Or did she resent that he'd interrupted the moment?

She glanced at him, then away, rubbing her hands over her arms.

He shifted, moved by the naked longing and exhilaration he'd seen on her face. "Thanks for letting me watch. He looked good as new."

"She."

"What?" He stepped toward her, trying to judge her eyes, her tone. "Oh, the hawk is a *she.*"

Silence filled the air between them. Lizzie held his gaze and he detected a flicker of irritation. She moved toward the shed, and C. J. fell into step beside her.

"Lizzie, I—" What could he say? *I can't stop thinking about that kiss. Can you?* "I just came by to check on you."

"I don't need checking on." Her tone was even, firm in a way he'd never heard.

Damn. "Are you still angry about the other night?"

Her gaze met his. "Now, why would I be angry?" The words flowed like silk, but stung like buckshot. "Just because you made a jackass of yourself and me, too."

Was she referring to the kiss—or Jed? Cautiously, C. J. said, "I didn't mean to hurt you."

"Well, you did." She walked inside the shed, then returned with a lantern.

"I don't want to leave things this way between us." He

hadn't been able to sleep or eat or concentrate. He wanted to know if she had experienced any of that, if she was angry about the kiss or what he'd done to Jed.

She lit the lantern and soft gold light pooled around them, bleeding into the shadows. His gaze fixed on her lips and he remembered their silky heat, her eager surrender. He dragged his gaze to her eyes, searching for a clue to her mood.

In the inky depths of her eyes was knowledge of the kiss. She remembered. And she had said he'd made a jackass of himself for doing it.

He didn't know whether to defend himself or kiss her again.

Once more, his gaze drifted to her lips. She turned away abruptly to close the shed door. "Jed has a broken nose, broken ribs, and a broken jaw," she said briskly. "Did you know that?"

He allowed her to change the subject, though he wished he could kiss her again and find out if there was as much heat without the anger. "He'll heal."

"You had no right—"

"I was only trying to help." C. J. bit back a sharper retort. "He would've had you on the ground with your skirts up around your ears in no time flat."

"I am perfectly capable of taking care of myself. I *was* taking care of myself when you charged over the hill like some ridiculous Sir Galahad."

"I'm not sorry for helping you."

Lizzie's features tightened. "Why did you come?"

To kiss you. To find out if I imagined your response the other night. To find out if I'm crazy for imagining it now.

"Oh, yes, to check on me. I've told you I don't want your pity and I don't want you to feel responsible for me."

Pity! Responsibility! What he wanted was to kiss her. "Don't be angry. I was only trying to help."

"C. J.—" She broke off and sighed, indecision creasing

her features. "Things have to change. I don't understand why you're acting this way, but I don't like it. I'm a grown woman. I don't want or need a guardian. I do need a friend."

She was offering him a chance to salvage their friendship. He felt this was some kind of test, a crossroads in their relationship, and he didn't want to pick the wrong route. Though it chafed, he relented. "I'm sorry. Not for caring," he added quickly. "But for . . . not trusting that you could handle Jed."

Her eyes widened. "Really?"

A soft light, different from what he'd seen before, glowed in her dark blue eyes. His heart caught. "Really."

They stared at each other, the night soft around them, the memory of the hawk still etched in his thoughts. An awkward silence built.

"Well," she finally said, shifting the lantern from one hand to the other.

He wanted to know if she felt the awareness as he did. Reluctant to leave, his thoughts circled again to the hawk and the other animals she tended. He realized something they had in common. "You should come out to the ranch tomorrow and see the new foal. You'd like her."

"I can't." Her voice was guarded. "I have to work."

"How about Saturday?" He wanted her to come, to prove that she trusted him again. Whatever these new feelings were, they were powerful and unexpected, and he felt that if he didn't explore them, he would miss out on something grand. "Can't you leave the store for a little while?"

"Probably." She regarded him warily, and he felt her slipping back inside herself. "I don't know if it's such a good idea."

"I thought you said there were no hard feelings." He kept his voice light, but locked his gaze on hers, looking for any clue to her true feelings. Was she still hurt? Annoyed?

She held his gaze, eyes clouded with uncertainty. "There aren't."

"So come." He wanted to take her hand, feel her warmth seep into him, but he kept his hands at his thighs. Tension wound through his body and coiled across his shoulders. "Please?"

Indecision clouded her face, and her gaze probed his features. "All right."

"When?" He sounded as eager as a boy, but he didn't care.

A tiny smile ghosted her lips. "Saturday morning."

"Good." He grinned. "I'll call for you about nine."

"No," she said quickly, her gaze skittering away. "I'll bring a buggy. I don't mind. Besides, I want to bring Domino."

"All right." For the first time since he'd arrived, he sensed an energy other than anger vibrating from her. She was nervous because of that kiss. That had to be it.

Though there was something else, too. She searched his eyes, judging, as if to discern if he meant to keep his word. Regret nipped that he'd nearly lost her trust. He didn't want to take that chance again.

But he'd also seen awareness in her eyes. After his apology, he'd managed to win a fresh start with her. He would take things slowly, figure out whatever this was between them.

But he had to know if she had reacted to that kiss the same way he had. His failure tonight to determine that only made his body burn with impatience. For her.

Was she crazy? Agreeing to go to C. J.'s might be the stupidest thing she'd ever done. But she was determined to forget about that kiss. And get him to forget, too.

She knew he'd been thinking about it. It was there in the slumberous heat of his eyes, the lazy way his gaze wandered over her, the slow curve of his lips. He looked at her with the same fascination of a man who'd found something he wanted to take apart and put back together. As if he had to figure out every nuance and curve and shadow.

Two nights ago, he'd apologized for interfering with Jed. Although he'd watched her closely, he'd done nothing untoward.

C. J.'s part in the incident with Jed had angered her, but the kiss afterward had triggered fantasies that startled her. She was determined to put it behind her. C. J. had apologized and she was more than willing to forget it.

He had readily agreed that they were just friends. So why was her stomach fluttering as though the buggy that carried her was rocking down a steep hill? Why was excitement shooting through her like a bullet? Why were her palms clammy?

She halted the buggy in front of the Daltry's barn and put on the brake. The older man who had met her at the entrance swung down from his chestnut mare and helped Lizzie down.

The sun's warmth tingled on her scalp. Already the morning air was stuffy. Domino sat on the floor, thumping his tail on the floorboard. His black gaze darted everywhere.

The ranch hand, Roper, walked around and reached inside for Domino. He set the dog gently on the ground and chuckled as the animal limped away on three legs toward the barn.

C. J. came to the door, tugging off a pair of tan gloves. "Roper led you in?"

"Saw her comin'," the older man said. He tipped his hat to her. "Gotta get back to it."

"Thank you, Mr. Roper."

"Just Roper, ma'am." He winked, then ambled around the corner of the barn.

C. J. bent to scratch behind Domino's ears. His blue gaze stayed trained on her. "Good morning."

His eyes shone like polished gems, and Lizzie smiled, her

nervousness receding somewhat. The gleam in his eye the other night had told her he'd known she didn't want to ride out with him, but this morning only pleasure flared in his eyes. Warmth surged through her. "Good morning."

He motioned her inside and her gaze cataloged every inch of him. It wasn't as if she'd never seen him before, but today he looked . . . different somehow.

The blue eyes tipped with dark blond lashes were the same. Her gaze traced down the aquiline nose, the chiseled lips, the sturdy jaw and chin. Even in harsh daylight, she could see no sign of the accident that had broken his jaw and nose, but she knew it had happened. Just as she knew how his lips molded to hers, the way his arms bound her like velvet ropes.

She shoved the thought away and followed him inside, her eyes on him rather than the barn. His jeans and boots were tinged with red dust. He wore a blue work shirt, sleeves rolled up to reveal tanned, corded forearms dusted with golden hair. Jeans stretched over lean, mile-long legs and molded to powerful thighs. Lizzie's throat dried as she attempted to school her thoughts.

He might be her friend, but she wasn't blind. C. J. Daltry was one handsome man. Or, as Maybelle would say, a cool drink of water. But nothing felt cool to Lizzie right now.

Her face was flushed; her skin tingled. A spurt of annoyance tripped through her and she focused on the dim, musty barn. Wedges of sunlight slanted through the doors, fingered through the wall to dip and swerve around her skirts as she walked. Domino hobbled alongside her, moving surprisingly well considering his injury.

C. J. stopped in front of a double-sized stall and she halted beside him. He motioned for her to be quiet and she inched closer to peer inside.

She didn't see the filly at first. Tucked in a corner and black as a shadow herself, the foal moved restlessly on a pile of hay. Lizzie could see the whites of her eyes and realized she was afraid.

She inched closer, her arm brushing C. J.'s. Heat surged between them, but she ignored it. "She's beautiful."

He nodded. "She's shy with people, though. Took Roper a while to get her used to him, and she'll come to me most times. Never seen a foal so people-shy."

"She's just lost her mother," Lizzie murmured, moving past C. J. and inside.

Domino followed, giving a loud bark. The foal scrambled up, backing further into the corner.

"Hush, Domino," Lizzie said firmly. "Hush."

The dog quieted, but limped inside the stall and circled the foal, sniffing. The foal watched warily. After a few seconds, Domino sat down and gazed up at Lizzie, thumping his tail on the dirt floor.

The filly watched, too, her nostrils flaring. Lizzie moved slowly, careful not to spook the horse. The odors of dusty hay and manure trickled through the air. The foal's eyes were wide with fear, and Lizzie could see the markings of two white socks on her back legs. She kept her voice low and soothing, talking to the foal as she neared.

"She can give a good kick, Liz. Watch out," C. J. warned.

She held out her hand so the foal could get her scent. "It's okay, baby. It's okay."

She reached the animal and sank down to her knees, extending her hand palm up. The foal stared, eyes wide with fear and burgeoning curiosity. Hay pricked Lizzie's knees through her day dress.

The foal's nostrils twitched, then she leaned forward and dipped her nose into Lizzie's palm. The moist heat tickled, but Lizzie stayed still, thrilled that the foal had shown such trust.

The filly took a step toward her and nudged her palm again. Lizzie smiled and reached out a gentle hand to stroke the velvety muzzle.

"I'll be darned." C. J. chuckled, sending a ripple of warmth across Lizzie's belly.

She turned, smiling, and caught her breath. His gaze, hot and intense, focused on her lips. Tension clicked between them. She turned back to the filly.

C. J. walked in and knelt beside Lizzie, his thigh brushing hers. Sensation rippled through her, but he didn't seem to notice. The filly sniffed him, then allowed him to scratch behind her ears.

C. J.'s hand was massive against the dainty dark head, and Lizzie's gaze traveled up to his. They shared a smile.

The filly pushed her head into Lizzie's chest, catching her attention, and she laughed, moving her hands to stroke the horse's neck.

C. J. sat down Indian fashion and ran a hand down the filly's back. "She got off to a rough start, but I think she'll make it."

"You're keeping her, then?" She let the filly nibble at her palm while she scratched the baby's ears.

"Sure."

"What's her name?" The foal smelled of hay and dirt and that sweet earthy scent peculiar to baby animals.

"Eterna, Grandma says. 'Cause she almost died but came back." C. J. grinned.

She smiled in return, stroking the foal's satiny head.

"You've really got a way about you. She took right to you," he said warmly.

"We're two girls on our own, aren't we?" Lizzie nuzzled the horse's nose with her own.

"I hadn't thought of that, but it's true," C. J. observed.

Silence draped the stall and tautened the air between them. She felt his gaze heavy on her, and she resisted the urge to look at him. Her lips tingled as though he'd touched them, and she knew that's where he was looking.

"Lizzie." His voice was hoarse.

Hearing the need in his voice, she turned reflexively. His

face was close enough that she could feel his heat, see the roughness of whiskers under the surface of his skin. She dragged her gaze to his and panic fluttered. Anticipation snagged her insides. He was going to kiss her again.

The thought had barely formed when he bent his head and his lips brushed hers.

The sound of children's voices erupted in the stillness of the barn. C. J. and Lizzie jerked apart.

"We can look, but we can't go in. Okay, Jimmy?"

"Atlas!" C. J. pushed himself to his feet and held out a hand to Lizzie.

Still feeling the brush of C. J.'s lips, the tickle of his mustache, she was barely aware of putting her hand in his. She rose on unsteady legs, her heart beating in a ragged rhythm.

"Hi, C. J.," the three children chorused.

Lizzie focused on the two boys and one girl who draped themselves over the stall gate. Lizzie knew Atlas, the tallest of the three.

"Allie, Jimmy, this is Lizzie," C. J. said, introducing the dark-haired girl and smaller boy.

"Hi," Allie said, her face open and friendly and curious. "Whatcha doin' in here?"

"Looking at Eterna." With a light touch to her elbow, C. J. guided Lizzie to the stall gate and through.

The foal stood uncertainly, watching the new arrivals. Domino hobbled out behind Lizzie and wagged his tail joyously, his eyes gleaming.

"Wow! This your dog?" Allie excitedly led Jimmy to the dog. "What's wrong with his leg?"

Lizzie explained about finding him with his leg caught in a trap. "I've been helping him get better."

"You're a doctor?" Allie looked up from petting Domino.

"No." She laughed. "I just know how to make a splint."

"She's real good at it," C. J. put in, smiling at her.

Lizzie flushed with pleasure.

Atlas and Jimmy knelt beside Domino to pet him. The dog licked Jimmy's hand until the little boy giggled.

Lizzie glanced at C. J. and saw his stare intensely focused on her. His blue eyes darkened with promise. She was again thankful the children had interrupted. "I'd better go," she remarked.

"Already?"

Lizzie wondered at the disappointment in his voice. "Hank and Maybelle expect me in today."

They walked outside and she showed the children how to hold Domino. Atlas gently lay the dog on the floorboard of the buggy while C. J. handed Lizzie inside.

She smiled at him, tamping down the nervous flutters in her stomach. "Thanks for inviting me. She's beautiful."

"I'm glad you came." His hand squeezed hers lightly, and the touch hummed along her skin.

Confusing, startling feelings bubbled through her. She wanted him to kiss her, to touch her the way he had that night after the barbecue. Suddenly she felt caged, trapped by his intense gaze. She didn't understand the heat coursing through her body. "I'd better go." Her gaze moved from him to the kids. "Nice to meet all of you."

"You, too," Atlas and Allie spoke in unison. Jimmy waved.

She clutched the reins and clucked to the mare she'd rented from the livery. In just a few minutes, she saw the distinctive arch of the ranch entrance and breathed a sigh of relief. She was several yards away from it when she heard pounding hooves behind her.

"Lizzie, wait!"

C. J.

She slowed the buggy and he reined up beside her. Goliath wore only a bridle, no saddle. C. J. sat easily on the horse's sleek, muscular back, his long legs guiding the stallion to a halt.

"I wanted to ask you—" The stallion danced sideways,

but C. J. brought him under control with little effort. "I wanted to ask if I could escort you to church tomorrow?"

"Church?" Something inside her stilled.

"I know you go."

"Yes, but—"

"We can go together," he declared.

Her gaze searched his and she became aware that he was nervous. Uncertainty clouded his blue eyes. Tension corded in his shoulders and the hand that gripped the reins.

Doubt, pleasure, apprehension shifted through her. Unable to look at the hope in his eyes, she tore her gaze away. "I don't understand what's going on," she said in a low voice. "What are you doing?"

"I don't know." His fist clenched on the reins, blanching his knuckles white. "I don't understand it, either, but you feel it, don't you? It's not just me?"

"Feel what?" she asked guardedly, unwilling to trust the giddiness she'd felt back in the barn.

"There's something between us, Liz. Something hot and fierce and—"

"Scary," she finished, her gaze going to his.

They sat in silence for a moment. The wind whistled through the grass. Goliath's tail swished, keeping time like a pendulum. Domino's panting echoed the rhythm of Lizzie's rapid heartbeat.

C. J. broke the quiet. "It's because I kissed you that night, isn't it?"

She shifted on the seat, feeling self-conscious. "You said that was a mistake. That it wouldn't happen again."

"I know." He looked down. "I don't know how to explain it, Lizzie."

"I thought we were friends."

"We are."

"I really don't understand," she said impatiently.

"I don't know. Don't you think it might be . . . something else?" he asked quietly. "Something *more?*"

He meant *romantic involvement.* Part of her thrilled at the thought, but caution edged in. "C. J., I don't want to hurt your feelings, but I'm not like the other girls you've seen. I don't want to be like them."

"I've never thought you were like anybody else, Lizzie." His gaze held hers, sober and earnest and seeking.

She stared back, uncertain in this territory, not sure she could trust the feelings he'd evoked. "Then let's just stay friends."

"You wanted to kiss me back there, Lizzie. Admit it."

"No. No, I didn't." She looked away, unable to meet his eyes. "Besides, what does that prove?"

He grinned as though he knew exactly how much she *had* wanted him to kiss her.

"We've known each other a long time," she felt compelled to add. "That's all it is."

"This is different. The way I feel is not about friendship, but something else."

"I don't understand."

"Neither do I." Frustration chased across his features. "All I know is I feel different about you. I haven't felt this way—"

"Since Diana," she finished ruefully.

"No! I've never felt this." He pushed his hat back on his head and stared out over the prairie. "I just know I like being with you and I don't see the harm in that."

"There is no harm in *that.*"

"If you don't like being with me, you can tell me."

She shook her head. "I do like being with you. I just don't want to make it more than it is."

"All right, we won't." His voice was even, but impatience snapped in his eyes. "So what about church?"

She hesitated. They should remain only friends. She should use her energy working for her part of the store. She could depend on those things. "No more kissing?"

His lips quirked. "Not until you ask me."

She shot him an exasperated look and picked up the reins to leave.

"Okay, okay," he amended. "Not *unless* you ask."

Pleasure and caution merged inside her. What harm could there be in going to church? "All right. I'll go with you."

He smiled and the smile melted through her, slow and sweet like candy on a hot summer day. "Good. You won't be sorry."

He saw her to the entrance and waved her on her way.

Excitement bubbled through her and she realized she was grinning. What could it hurt? She and Tom were friends. They'd gone to church together.

Though being with Tom had never felt like being with C. J. She had never felt this giddiness around Tom, or the uncertainty or the curiosity about his body, his kiss. She had certainly never longed for his kiss. Why was she feeling these things for C. J.?

Of all the bother! It was only church, not a proposal of marriage.

Twelve

HE'D PROMISED NOT TO KISS HER AGAIN, BUT C. J. WONDERED about the vow as soon as it left his lips. By Thor, he wanted her! He'd never followed rules with any other girl. But then Lizzie wasn't just any girl. Above all, she was his friend, and he didn't want to ruin that.

He meant to keep his promise, though it wouldn't be easy.

Being with her, C. J. felt anticipation, a deep pull, a bond, but there was also uncertainty. Yesterday he hadn't been sure she would accept his invitation. He'd never been unsure about any girl. While it made him uncomfortable, it also sparked a challenge in his veins.

He felt it the next morning as they sat together in church. Pleasure flushed her cheeks and something shifted in his chest. They sat two rows ahead of his family, who sat in their usual seats. He hadn't been to church in a while, and today everything seemed fresh and magnified. The whitewash looked more brilliant; the light flowed into the room like dazzling silver.

Beside him, Lizzie's voice rang out in a pure soprano. He let the words to "Amazing Grace" die on his tongue as he listened to her.

She glanced at him and he realized he was staring. He grinned, shifting his hymnal and picking up the words again.

Reverend Timmons's baritone rumbled through the small church, catching C. J.'s attention at odd intervals, but he couldn't remember a thing about the sermon. He'd been too focused on Lizzie, the way her hands were folded in her lap, the creamy whiteness of them compared to his nut-brown ones resting on his thighs.

The dark blue of her eyes, made more luminous by the indigo taffeta she wore, mesmerized him. Long cinder-black eyelashes curled enticingly at the tips. As usual her hair was pulled over to the side, curtaining her left shoulder and breast, exposing her slender neck. C. J. touched his tongue to his lips, wondering if her velvety flesh might taste like honeysuckle and cream.

After the closing prayer and announcements, they rose to go. He was careful to touch her elbow only lightly to guide her as they moved into the aisle. Hank and Maybelle met them.

Hank extended his hand. "Good morning, C. J."

"Morning, Hank."

Maybelle's eyes glinted. "We haven't seen you at church in a while, C. J."

Lizzie smiled at him, a flush pinkening her cheeks. She turned away to speak to Maybelle while Hank strode off toward Reverend Timmons.

C. J. felt the heat of someone's gaze and turned to encounter his grandmother's gray eyes narrowed in speculation. He experienced a pang of conscience, but shrugged it off. Going to church didn't interfere with Lizzie's chances of being courted by someone.

Smiling and speaking with the people who were walking past her, Minerva made her way down the aisle to stand in front of him.

"Good morning, all." She patted Lizzie's hand, then said something smart to Maybelle, which made her laugh.

Lizzie turned to speak with Maybelle. Minerva edged

closer to C. J., keeping her gaze on Lizzie and a smile pasted on her face. "What do you think you're doing?" she hissed.

He shifted from one foot to the other, feeling as if he'd been caught snitching. "I'm going to church with Lizzie. You didn't say I couldn't do that."

His grandmother stared, anger and indecision warring in her eyes. "You'd better think about what you're doing."

"It's just church, Grandma." Doubt twinged at this dismissal, but C. J. wasn't about to admit it. He nodded as Miss Lavender and Clay Masterson walked past.

Minerva inclined her head at the pair. "You're supposed to have her best interests at heart. Do you think you should be squiring her around?"

"Thank you for that confidence, Grandma." His voice hardened. "Being seen with me isn't going to ruin her reputation."

"I didn't mean that. Unless you're serious, you should stay away from her. What about the other young men who might be interested? What will they think if they see you two together?"

"That we're going to church?" he drawled, controlling his temper with an effort.

She cocked her head and pinned him with that steely gaze. "Are you interested in the girl? Tell me."

"There's nothing to tell." *At least not yet.* "What's the harm in seeing her? We are friends, after all."

His grandmother leveled a long stare on him. "Are you putting yourself forward as a suitor?"

"I might be." The words surprised him, but he held Minerva's gaze, determined to keep the uncertainty from his voice.

Her eyes darkened. "And are you considering marriage?"

"For crying out loud, it's just church!" he grated.

"And what happens if that girl decides she wants more from you?"

C. J. stared blankly at Minerva for a moment, then glanced at Lizzie. Suddenly the room squeezed in on him and the air seemed to thicken. "What do you mean?"

"I mean, if there's no husband for *her,* there's no prize for *you.* Since you haven't had much luck finding her a husband, I have to wonder about your motives. Remember that you can't marry her to get the prize."

Grandma glanced from him to Lizzie, then back, waggling her finger at him. "You mind yourself, do you hear?"

He fought the urge to tell her he knew what his prize was, and it had nothing to do with his wanting to spend time with Lizzie. His jaw tightened and he watched her walk away, irritation spiraling through him. Grandma made him sound calculating and cold. He felt neither of those things when he was with Lizzie.

And he resented the implication that he was using her. He wasn't certain if Grandma had just warned him away, insulted him, or if she was simply concerned about Lizzie.

His interest in Lizzie didn't stem from the ranch. He wanted to spend time with her, explore these exhilarating and curious feelings, but he wasn't using her. Was he?

"Everything okay?"

Lizzie's quiet voice interrupted his thoughts and he looked down into her midnight blue eyes. She regarded him curiously.

"Yes. Sure."

When she smiled, pleasure and a sense of completion flowed over him, but his grandmother's words hammered at the back of his mind.

What if he had to choose between the ranch and Lizzie? For the first time, the implications of being with her washed through him.

If he had to choose, which he *wouldn't,* he'd choose the ranch. Right?

Lizzie smiled, unguarded and sweet, then passed in front

of him and walked to the door. He stared after her, his gut twisting with desire.

Perhaps Grandma should've forbidden him to see Lizzie, after all.

They went to church together the next Sunday as well. C. J. didn't think about marriage, but whenever he thought of Lizzie, which was often, he found himself walking an invisible line between liking her and wanting her.

C. J. had chafed from Grandma's questions all week.

He was restless and frustrated. He worked longer hours at the ranch, trying to prove that he knew what he wanted. But thoughts of Lizzie wouldn't leave. He resented the doubts his grandmother had raised in him. He and Lizzie were just friends, nothing more.

He resented that they might not even have the chance to find out if there could be more, but he halted that line of thinking because he couldn't get from Lizzie what he usually got from other girls. And he wouldn't try.

After three days, he had convinced himself that his frustration had come mainly from Grandma's suspicious questions and not from his own feelings for Lizzie.

Late in the afternoon, after a day of branding, he rode into town. He had a drink at Lucky's saloon, then fueled by rebellion, walked over to the mercantile to say hello to Lizzie.

He stepped inside and found her next to the counter with Tom English and Will, Hank's son. She held the boy on the counter while Tom wadded a handkerchief into a ball and made it disappear.

Will's eyes grew wide. "Where? Where?" He grabbed for Tom's hand.

Lizzie laughed. "It's magic, Will. Tom made it disappear."

She exchanged a warm smile with Tom, and C. J. felt a pull of jealousy. Surprised, he shrugged it off and called, "Hello, everyone. Hey, Will."

Lizzie and Tom turned and Lizzie smiled warmly at C. J. "Hi." She sounded breathless and her cheeks were flushed.

He suddenly wanted to back her into the corner and kiss her.

Instead he shook hands with Tom. "How are things at your place?"

"Fine." Tom pulled the handkerchief from under his hat. "I'm trying to dig a new water well, but I broke my shovel and had to come in for a new one."

"Let me know if you need any help. I'll have some time tomorrow."

"Thanks, I'd appreciate that." Tom turned to Lizzie and stooped to pick up a coil of new rope. "I'll be back later this evening to fix your door."

"All right."

"What door?" C. J.'s gaze went to Lizzie, noting the smooth satin of her lips, the rosy color in her cheeks.

"The door to the shed. Tom offered to fix it."

"What's wrong with it?" The vague scent she wore tugged at him and he tried to keep his attention on her eyes.

"The hinge is broken and I can't fix it by myself."

C. J. hesitated only a split second. "I've got some time now."

"Oh, I couldn't ask you."

"You didn't," he said. "I offered. Besides, that way Tom won't have to ride back in later."

She glanced uncertainly at Tom.

He shrugged and said to C. J., "It's fine with me, if you don't mind."

"Not a bit." He relaxed somewhat. He hadn't felt the want curl through his belly since he had walked in. He would fix her door and be on his way.

Tom slung the rope over his shoulder and walked out. "See you later."

After Lizzie deposited Will with Maybelle, she and C. J.

walked over to her house. He had brought two hinges, and while he removed the door to the shed, she moved inside to tend the animals.

Domino hobbled to the doorway and sniffed at C. J. He scratched behind the dog's ears, then eased the door onto the ground. After removing the old hinge, he nailed in the new ones. Lizzie had been inside the entire time. Was she hiding from him in there?

She came to the door and offered a tentative smile. "I can help a little."

"I'm about finished." He handed her the hammer and their fingers brushed. Sensation jolted him.

His gaze met hers and her lips parted on a breath. Then she looked away.

In a rush, heat flooded him, pouring in like molten silk and igniting his nerve ends. He struggled against the feeling, fighting the urge to ask if she had felt it. He didn't need to ask. He could tell by the sultry smoke in her eyes that she had. Cursing inwardly, he rose and lifted the door back in place.

She moved close behind him, helping to hold it in position as he reattached it. He could feel the warmth from her body swirl around him, her sensuality tempting wicked thoughts. Lust tugged at his gut, but something sharp and deep pulled at his heart. He'd missed her.

The last three days without her had seemed like three years. How could that be? He didn't know and suddenly didn't care. In a heartbeat, he dismissed Grandma's warning and turned to Lizzie. "There, all finished."

"Thank you." She twined her fingers together and eyed the door. "Can you stay for supper?"

"No, thanks, they're waiting on me at home." He handed her the hammer.

Hesitation skittered through her eyes. "I'd like to do something to thank you. How about a pie? You can take that with you."

"It's not necessary. I was glad to do it, but if you're serious . . ."

"Yes?" She watched him, eyes guarded.

He smiled. "I really enjoyed church with you. How about dinner at The Buc sometime this week?"

"That seems one-sided to me." She smiled, as if testing him.

"I'll have the pleasure of your company, which is definitely the best of the bargain. What do you say?" His breath locked in his chest.

"I'd like to very much."

"Good. How about Friday evening?"

"All right," she said softly.

"That's real fine." He grinned and headed back to the mercantile for Goliath. Even Grandma couldn't find the harm in a dinner invitation. And perdition take her if she could.

During the next week, C. J. invited Lizzie to dinner twice at The Buc. The following week, he walked her home from work every evening.

Lizzie became more comfortable with their friendship. When she was with him, she enjoyed herself. But when she was alone again, she would brood.

She finally realized it was because he hadn't tried to kiss her again. Though she was disappointed, she knew it was for the best.

A tiny fringe of fear had haunted her after that near-kiss in the barn. She had wanted to surrender to him, to allow herself to be overwhelmed and swept away. That kind of thinking was dangerous.

Their time together, while enjoyable, was also laced with a latent tension, something that Lizzie couldn't quite finger, but it was there every time C. J. looked at her. He'd worn the same look in the barn, a combination of hunger and control that alternately thrilled and alarmed her.

One evening after work, they stood on her porch, talking about her animals. C. J. watched the sun sink lower in the sky, but Lizzie watched him. Bathed in red and gold and rose, his profile was fierce and commanding.

She studied him, though she could close her eyes and picture him perfectly from the warmth in his crystal blue eyes to the way his shirt veed open in the front to reveal a tuft of dark gold chest hair.

She was swept with the sudden urge to touch him, to run her hands over the sculpted sinew of his arms and shoulders, to measure the span of his hips.

He pushed his hat farther back on his head, then tugged it down again. He only fiddled with his hat when he was uncertain. What was bothering him?

They had developed an easy camaraderie, but always it was laced with this curious awareness, an intoxicating need that mushroomed inside her. He leaned against the porch, long legs crossed at the ankle.

He bent and picked up a rock, flinging it into the nearby field. "I'm leaving for Abilene tomorrow."

"Kansas?" she asked, startled.

"No. Abilene, Texas." He smiled easily. "Just to the west. That new town by the railroad. A man there is buying cattle for a drive."

"Tomorrow?" Her gaze swerved to his face. Loneliness rose inside her, but she tamped down the feeling. She tried to keep her voice neutral, but heard the hint of disappointment. "How long do you think you'll be gone?"

"Probably about a week." He tossed another stone. "Maybe less, if I can get the price I want."

She smiled, battling a sudden insecurity that things were about to change between them again. Nonsense. What could change? "Good luck. I hope things go well."

"Thanks."

They stood silently for a while and she savored the closeness. She was near enough to touch his shoulder with hers if she turned just a fraction, but she stayed where she was, tracing his profile with her gaze. She felt out of sorts and unsettled.

C. J. turned suddenly and his blue gaze captured hers. "Will you miss me?" His voice teased, but his eyes searched hers fervently. "I'll miss you."

"You won't have time for that, Mr. Cattle Rancher." She kept her voice light, trying to hide her disappointment and sense of loss. She *would* miss him. She hadn't realized how much time they had been spending together. Would this be the end of the closeness they'd shared over the last few weeks? She'd known it would have to end sometime. "You'll probably forget how to find your way back home."

"I won't forget. *Anything.*"

His gaze held hers and her breath hitched in her chest.

He shifted so that he faced her, his shoulders blocking out the glare of the setting sun. "Lizzie?" His gaze dropped to her lips.

She couldn't tear her gaze from his. Her mouth felt dry and fuzzy. Uncertainty, hunger, curiosity darkened his blue eyes.

He wanted to kiss her, she realized. And she wanted him to. Heat crawled over her skin at the realization, but she kept her gaze on his.

He lowered his head a fraction, his eyes blazing like heated cobalt. Shivers rippled through her. *Yes. Yes, C. J.*

Instead of kissing her, he reached out and snared her hand. His palm was warm and calloused against the silky smoothness of hers. Heat arrowed through her and her hand tightened on his. He leaned closer, his breath feathering her cheeks, then her lips.

An ache coiled in her belly and she swayed toward him, searching, reaching for a need she had only just glimpsed.

His eyes darkened; his hand squeezed hers. Then he lifted her hand to his lips. Moist breath and satin-smooth lips brushed her hand. Heat skipped up her arm. The silk of his mustache caressed her skin, spawning a tightness in her nipples.

Her legs were rubbery and she gripped his fingers for balance.

He bent over her hand, his gaze holding hers. "I'll see you when I get back," he rasped.

Fire scattered along her nerves. She nodded, her throat tight with need and a hunger she was only beginning to understand.

Kiss me. She wanted to say the words, but they wouldn't come, even though her body yearned to feel his hard length pressed against her. Her lips ached to feel his. "Take care." *And hurry back.*

His gaze dragged over her as though memorizing every detail. Then he mounted Goliath and rode off into the fading red rays of the sun.

Lizzie exhaled, feeling shivery and lost and restless. A knot of need tightened in her belly. She wanted him to kiss her—and much more.

Her emotions tangled in her throat. As she watched him disappear into the horizon, she realized why. She loved him.

Was it possible? Was there another explanation for the way her skin heated at his touch, the way her heart thundered when he merely looked at her, this ache at his absence that dug into her soul?

She fought it, unwilling to become one of his conquests. He hadn't even tried to kiss her, although she knew he wanted to.

Was he trying to seduce her with the outings to church, seeing her home each night?

Seduction. Yes, that's what it was. But her conscience argued. He had tried nothing untoward; he hadn't made her feel threatened.

She'd seen a part of him no one else had seen, a lonely

part that linked them and showed he was as vulnerable as she was.

There was a connection, a bond, but was it love? She cared for him. She couldn't deny that. But love?

She would have a week without C. J. clouding her thoughts. A week to figure out exactly what these churning emotions inside her meant.

Five days later, Lizzie hadn't been able to determine anything, except that she missed C. J. keenly enough to feel it as a gnawing ache deep in her belly. She kept remembering the heat in his eyes, the tender good-bye—those things meant *something,* didn't they?

"When do you expect C. J. to return?" Maybelle asked.

They stood in the back room of the store. Lizzie looked up from a newly arrived crate of spices and candy. "I don't expect anything."

Maybelle eyed her speculatively. "I see."

"He said he'd be gone about a week, but he wasn't sure." She stuck her head back inside the box, feeling as if she'd just revealed something she shouldn't have.

"You're still friends?"

"Of course." She marked a jar of cinnamon and set it aside.

"Not more than friends?" Maybelle's voice was casually cool.

Lizzie's gaze jerked to her friend. "No."

Maybelle planted one hand on her hip.

Lizzie walked past and cleared a space on the shelves for the new spices. She wasn't sure what she and C. J. shared. She'd been trying to figure that out all week. How could she explain it to Maybelle? A connection bonded them, but was it more than friendship? It felt that way to her.

"Don't you miss him?"

"I've hardly had time to think since he left." Lizzie gave a small laugh and knelt next to the opened crate. "I found a cat last week, with an injured tail—"

"That's not what I asked. You were spending a lot of time with him before he left. I just wondered."

Lizzie sat back on her heels and lifted her gaze to Maybelle's. "I do miss him." She shrugged. "It's funny. I hadn't realized how much we were together."

"So do you think he misses you, too?"

"I don't know. It doesn't matter, does it? We're just friends."

Maybelle leaned down and wriggled her eyebrows. "Tell me you don't want to kiss those luscious lips."

"Maybelle!"

"You can't be friends with a man like C. J." Green eyes took on a dreamy, faraway look. "He makes a woman think of forbidden things, sinful things. At least he does me, and I'm happily married."

Lizzie shook her head and rose to stack a jar of thyme on the shelf, grinning. "C. J. and I *can* be friends. We *are* friends."

The other woman swung around to hand Lizzie a bag of sugar. "Men and women can't be just friends. There's too much . . . play between them."

"What do you mean, 'play'?"

"The basic differences between men and women always come out, no matter what kind of relationship they start out with. Even if you haven't considered C. J. as more than a friend—and I don't for one minute believe you haven't—I bet he has considered you as something else. It's the way of men."

"Like a l–lover, you mean?" Lizzie wanted to toss out the word as if she said it every day, but she stumbled over it.

"Exactly! I've seen the way he looks at women. And he looks at you like that. All men are that way."

"Not Tom," she said emphatically. "Tom and I are friends. *Just* friends."

"I bet C. J. didn't see it that way," Maybelle put in slyly. "Besides, I've seen you with both of them, and you're different with C. J."

"They're two different men." She sighed impatiently, but a wayward thought taunted her. Was Maybelle right? Did Lizzie want C. J. as a lover? Her feelings certainly hadn't diminished in the week he'd been gone. If anything, they had become more intense.

"I think you have feelings for him. You're just too stubborn to admit it."

"C. J. has courted every woman in this town, Maybelle." Why couldn't she think of him as simply her friend?

"He's different with you."

Lizzie rolled her eyes and walked over to the crate.

"Admit it. You want him," Maybelle whispered, dangling the idea like a forbidden sweet.

Lizzie stared into the crate, rocked by memories of their kiss and the last night they'd shared before he left for Abilene. "All right, I admit I've thought about it, *but*"—she turned to Maybelle—"that doesn't mean anything will come of it. Or that he has to know."

"Why not?"

"I don't want to be like the other women he's seen. I mean, every eligible woman in this town has known him in that way," Lizzie said pointedly.

Maybelle responded with a shrug. "But what if he's the one? Like Hank was for me. I knew it right away."

"Well, I didn't."

"Give it a chance, Lizzie. Are you sure it's not love?"

She hesitated. "I like what we have now."

"Don't dismiss it. You could have so much more," Maybelle said as she swept through the curtain.

Her words echoed in the room as Lizzie let the realization unfold. Even if she loved C. J. Daltry, he didn't love her. He wanted her, she knew, and she could admit she wanted him. Through these last weeks the latent fire inside her had built, and his absence had only stoked it higher.

Now the flame simmered with a slow-building heat that burned away restraint and caution. Tempting, coaxing her to give herself over to it, even knowing he didn't love her.

When he returned, she didn't know if she would be able to resist. Or if she would want to.

Five days in Abilene, and finally the last day of the sale arrived. C. J. might have finished earlier if he had been able to keep his mind on business. But Lizzie had been in his thoughts the entire time.

He missed her like hell, like there was an empty place inside him crying out for her. Once again, he tried to forget that.

Incessant hammering and the rippling snap of tent canvas greeted C. J. on his last day, just as it had since the day of his arrival. A year ago, this section of the prairie had been just a sea of waving grass.

Now, due to the efforts of a few cattlemen and the expanding route of the Texas and Pacific Railroad, it was bustling and growing, even though it more closely resembled a camp than a town. An underlying sense of excitement and anticipation weighted the air.

Unlike the whistle stop in Paradise Plains, Abilene would have an honest-to-goodness depot on the railroad route. Right now, most businesses and churches operated out of tents. Even The Pickadilly, the hotel where C. J. was staying, was a tent. The rooms were partitioned with curtains and the room numbers penciled with charcoal.

Presently, only the post office and railroad operated out of something besides a tent. The post office had been the first to open a building and the railroad had placed a boxcar on a side rail for use as a ticket office.

One man in particular, Clabe Merchant, had been instrumental in establishing the site. He had named Abilene after the famous cattle shipping center in Kansas, in hopes that the fledgling town would become an equally important marketplace.

C. J. thought it might happen. There were plenty of interested cattle ranchers. Yesterday, he had concluded his business with John Simpson of the Hashknife ranch. Simpson had bought the two hundred head of Circle D stock that C. J. had offered, planning to drive them to Arizona.

Now C. J. stood in another tent, this one hosting a stock, feed, and tack sale. Outside there were enough pens to contain the livestock. The front flaps whipped against the canvas walls. In the center of the tent, the earth was packed hard from a frequent parade of stock and humans. The men formed a loose circle outside the center arena. One man roamed in the middle, conducting the sale.

Smoke hung heavy in the makeshift building. Roper stood next to C. J., and Webb stood a distance away, talking with a buyer from Dodge City. On C. J.'s other side stood Kenneth Rafferty, a rancher from north of Paradise Plains. Rafferty puffed on a stubby cigar.

A longhorn was prodded into the arena, led by a thick rope around the neck. C. J. tried to keep his attention on the stock, on the wiry frame and stringy body, the curve of wicked horns, but images of Lizzie crowded out everything else.

He kept reliving the feel of silky skin under his lips, her near-surrender that day in the barn. He wanted to lose himself in her midnight blue eyes, drown in the honeyed sweetness of her lips.

Roper's voice boomed in his ear. "Are you crazy?"

"What?" C. J. started, his gaze slicing to the older man.

Roper shook his head, his features creased in disgust. "You just bid seven hundred dollars for a hundred-and-fifty-dollar stock saddle."

C. J.'s gaze jerked to the arena. The longhorn was gone.

In its place stood a stock saddle, a roping saddle, and a sawhorse. He blinked. What the hell!

Outside in the pens, cattle lowed. The sound of shuffling hooves filtered into the tent. C. J. focused his attention on the animals being brought into the center area, a cow and her calf.

Good lines, healthy eyes, and the calf was shy but not skittish. Once again, thoughts of Lizzie trickled back. He could still feel her heat, her warmth circling him. If he closed his eyes, he could call her back into his dreams.

"Damn!"

C. J. glanced at Roper to find the man staring at him in disbelief. Several men who stood next to C. J. slowly moved away, frowning in confusion and shaking their heads.

"What?" He was almost afraid to ask.

Roper frowned, then peered closely into C. J.'s face. "You feelin' all right, boss?"

"Of course." C. J. risked a glance at the arena to see what was being offered. A paint gelding stood docilely in the center area, and C. J. breathed a sigh of relief. He *knew* he hadn't bought that horse.

Roper shifted from one foot to the other, looking uncomfortable and as if he wanted to swear a blue streak. He muttered something under his breath. "What's wrong with you?"

"Nothing." *Except a woman named Lizzie.*

Roper stared, as if C. J. had sprouted wings like his cherubic namesake. He leaned over and said very precisely, "You just asked if that gelding had been gelded."

C. J. laughed, hoping the cowhand was joking around. "Come on, Roper. That's ridiculous."

"No kiddin'," the old man muttered. "You been drinkin'?"

C. J. shifted his shoulders against a sudden unease. He could tell by Roper's expression and those of the men around him that he had indeed asked the dumbest question known to man. "Well, why didn't you stop me?" he growled.

"How was I supposed to know you wuz gonna up and say somethin' like that?" Roper stomped off toward Webb.

C. J. watched him go, aware of the speculative looks focused on him. When a woman, any woman, took precedence over ranching, something was definitely going on.

He quickly paid for the stock saddle and left the sale to walk back to The Picadilly. It was time to go home. He had to see Lizzie.

The words circled through his mind, igniting a fierce desire to see her, to touch her, to *claim* her.

He couldn't shake the image of her. Or thoughts of her. Obviously, he thought dryly. He'd just looked like a damn fool in front of every rancher in the county because of her.

Once inside his room, he pulled his saddlebags from under the wooden army cot and stuffed his clothes inside. His mind traveled back through the days he'd spent with her, the way her face glowed when she smiled, the way her eyes softened when she saw him.

He closed his eyes and imagined her naked, her bare skin gleaming like alabaster beneath his hands. Her breasts pouted ripe and creamy for him. He recalled their first kiss, openmouthed, hot, carnal. His body hardened, his manhood throbbing rapidly to life. It was only lust.

But the thought chafed his conscience, rang hollow in his mind.

It was more than lust. He wanted to probe her secrets and have her look at him with total trust. Never had he experienced this desire to keep himself only for one woman. Never had he realized that he wanted a deeper connection than just a physical one. He wanted more than sex; he wanted to make love.

It was something he hadn't wanted or ever done. Not with Diana. Not with anyone. But he wanted that with Lizzie.

He loved her.

He sat down on the bed. Hard. Stunned, he could only stare at the canvas of the makeshift wall, the dull wood of the bed. Something tight squeezed his chest. *Love?*

He shot up off the cot and grabbed his good Sunday coat, rolling it into a ball and stuffing it into the saddlebag.

He couldn't love her. She wasn't like any woman he'd ever wanted.

Which was exactly why he *did* love her.

No. C. J. shook his head, trying to erase thoughts of her. *How could he love her?* His mind cataloged everything about her, trying to come up with reasons he couldn't. But the answers only confirmed his newly realized feelings.

For the first time, his physical appearance was inconsequential. Lizzie didn't care about appearances. She cared about the inside, his character, his soul. Because of her scar, she had learned to judge people on factors other than physical. With a rising impatience, he realized that was what had drawn him to her.

For the first time since Diana, C. J. felt his heart open. The depth of his vulnerability alarmed him. If Lizzie felt the same way about him, she could change his world. He could do anything, conquer anything.

After Diana, C. J. had locked part of himself away. That part resisted the idea of loving anyone. He couldn't open himself up to that kind of hurt again. With a sinking feeling, he realized Lizzie could do worse damage. She could scar his soul.

He wanted to fight it, but another part of him, a part made stronger by his time with her, wanted a chance with her. The possibility of being without her made his future stretch before him in a bleak flat line.

Standing in that tent hotel with the stale odor of smoke and sweat clinging to the air, he realized what he wanted. He wanted Lizzie. Forever.

Despite Grandma's warnings, despite the threat of being without the ranch, he wanted her.

Impatience spurred him on. He grabbed his saddlebags and headed downstairs. He was going home. To Lizzie.

Thirteen

Urgency wound through him. He had to see Lizzie.

C. J. spurred Goliath to go faster. Restlessness, the same he'd carried all week, churned inside him. He wanted to see her, hold her hand, *kiss* her. He'd thought of her sweet lips the whole time he'd been gone, even though he'd promised not to kiss her until she asked. Mostly he wanted to tell her he loved her.

As he neared Paradise Plains, uncertainty twined with urgency. What would she say when he declared his feelings? Would she feel the same?

He headed straight for the mercantile instead of the ranch. Dust itched his skin and his shirt was damp with sweat, but impatience won over the desire to clean up. He *had* to see her.

Early afternoon sun spilled over the verdant green of prairie grass. Wildflowers grew in a jumbled mixture of reds, yellows, and oranges, a vivid slash of color woven into the hills. Scents of flowers and bruised grass floated to him.

The town bustled with activity as he rode in. Horses clip-clopped down the street and kids squealed, dodging in and out of alleyways. The smithy's hammer clanged, the sound diluted by the breeze and distance. Underneath the other sounds, the newspaper press clacked.

He reined up in front of Hank's mercantile and swung down from his horse, not bothering to loop the reins over the hitching post. Several older men sat on the porch in the rocking chairs Hank always had available. Dusty Roberts and Ed Pendergrass chewed on wads of tobacco, their jaws bulging. Sheriff Sampson stood next to them, one foot propped on a crate outside Hank's door as he whittled a new pipe.

"Howdy, C. J. How'd that sale go?" the sheriff asked, poking the pipe in his mouth for a test.

He grinned and extended his hand. "Fine. Just fine." He shook hands with Ed and Dusty. "You gentlemen excuse me. I've got a lady to see."

All three of the men arched their eyebrows and chuckled. C. J. grinned and walked inside Hank's, pulling off his hat. He wanted to tell the whole world how he felt about Lizzie Colepepper, but figured he should tell her first.

Hank looked up from his position behind the counter, where he and Tom English bent over a Sharpe rifle. "Hey, C. J. Didn't know you were back in town."

"Just got in." He shook Hank's hand, then turned to Tom. "Hello."

His neighbor's eyes gleamed. "You been at that sale over in Abilene?"

"Yep. Went real good." *Except for that damn saddle.* C. J. scanned the area, looking for Lizzie.

Tom rested both elbows on the counter and picked up a shell for the rifle. "Lizzie told me you were there."

"Where is she, by the way?" He moved behind the counter, intending to go through the curtain.

Hank grinned, jabbing his thumb toward the back room. "I reckon you know. She's back there."

"Thanks." C. J. pushed through the curtain and stopped. She sat at the desk, bent over a ledger book. Her hair rippled like a sleek black waterfall down her back. His gaze traveled over the trim curve of her back, her slender shoulders, and the quill flying over the paper.

"Hello, C. J." Maybelle's surprised voice pulled his attention from Lizzie.

"Hi."

Lizzie spun in her chair and bolted up. Pleasure flushed her features and warmed her blue eyes. C. J.'s chest ached. He'd known he missed her, but seeing her was like touching the light. She stepped toward him, then halted, uncertain. "Welcome home," she said softly.

He wanted to grab her and kiss her and thought he saw the same desire in her eyes. But he was frustratingly aware that they had an audience. Maybelle watched quietly from the corner, a slow smile curving her lips.

There was so much he wanted to tell Lizzie, to ask her.

"How was your trip?" she asked eagerly. Her gaze tracked over him, dark with hunger.

His gut clenched and he balled his hands into fists. "Fine." *I missed you like the devil.* "Took me a little longer than I expected."

She nodded. Silence draped the room, taut with a need that shimmered between them like summer heat.

He wanted to talk to her, but he couldn't do it here in front of Maybelle. His gaze flickered to her, then back to Lizzie. "Do you think you could talk for a little while?"

"Well . . ."

"Go ahead," Maybelle said, a smile in her voice. "I can finish up here."

Relief flooded through him and he stood back to hold open the curtain for Lizzie. Tom and Hank watched as C. J. followed her out the door. Her sweet scent tickled his nostrils and he was only peripherally aware of the men's gazes. All his attention centered on the woman in front of him.

"Where should we go?" She paused on the porch, glancing around.

There was something different about her, an openness, a vulnerability in her eyes he'd never seen. He wanted to blurt out his feelings, but reined them in, wanting privacy.

"We can ride to the river." He hoped she would accept. His throat tightened with determination and urgency.

She smiled at him, in a tentative but warm way, and his chest swelled with anticipation. He moved down the steps behind her to lift her up into the saddle. He swung up behind her and turned Goliath north toward the river.

Questions jumbled in his head. What had she done while he'd been away? Had she thought of him like he'd thought of her, unceasingly from daylight to dusk? Had she missed him?

They rode too fast to talk and he didn't mind. Instead he eased closer, his eyes closing briefly in tortured pleasure as her breasts brushed the arm he anchored around her waist. He pressed against her and clenched one fist around the reins. The faint rose scent of her crowded his nostrils, weaving tendrils of want through his belly.

Her heat soaked into him. He held her in the cradle of his thighs, her bottom fitted tightly against his arousal. He was hard and aching, throbbing with each stride of the horse. She had to be aware of him, yet she didn't move away.

He felt as though he were suspended in a net of heaven, all silk and rapture, bathed in a warm glow. Having her so close soothed something deep inside him, and the impatience that had clawed him all day subsided. The girl was in his arms; her name was on his heart.

Goliath stopped at the bank of the river, just under an old cottonwood tree. C. J. sat for a minute, inhaling her dark muskiness, which beckoned to a primal urge in him. His arm tightened around her waist.

There was warmth and desire, but also knowledge in her eyes. She wanted him. The realization slammed into C. J., sealing his breath in his chest for an instant. She wanted him, but did she love him? Did she feel as he did?

Reluctantly, he pulled his arm from around her waist, letting his hand glide over the taut flatness of her belly. He slid to the ground and held up his arms to help her down. When she braced her hands on his shoulders, he lifted her.

Her body skimmed his, a tantalizing play of thighs and breasts and arms. He wanted to crush her against him and never let her go, but warned himself to go easy.

She stepped away, smoothing down her skirts and glancing shyly at him over her shoulder. "I'm glad you're home."

The simple words sparked a soul-deep joy. He wanted to come home to her for the rest of his life. "Me, too."

His voice was hoarse with need and he saw a flush stain her neck and cheeks. She turned quickly away, but not before he saw her gaze linger on his lips, an answering flame in her eyes.

Bolstered by her response, he walked up behind her and they moved to the bank of the river. Dark red-brown water flowed lazily by, upstream it rushed over rocks and around a bend.

"How was your trip? Did you sell the cattle for the price you wanted?"

"For the most part." He grinned, hoping Roper wouldn't tell her what a fool he'd made of himself at the sale. "And what did you do while I was gone?"

"I worked and I found an injured cat."

"Another stray." C. J. fixed his gaze on her lips, wanting to taste their deep wine once again, open himself up to the fire that her kiss sparked in his soul.

She stared back, awareness and uncertainty in her eyes. Abruptly she looked away, toward the river.

His skin heated and he cleared his throat, looked out over the water as well. "I missed you."

"Me, too," she said quietly.

He turned, silently urging her to look at him. After a long moment, she did. Her eyes were full of tenderness and warmth and that vulnerability he'd glimpsed earlier. His chest tightened.

She turned away quickly, as though she had shown him too much.

He moved behind her and cupped her shoulders, turning her to face him. "I want to kiss you somethin' fierce," he said hoarsely, "but I won't unless—"

"Yes," she whispered, swaying toward him. In her eyes was a sharp longing, a need that bordered on desperation.

The same desperation he felt. He crushed her to him and sought her lips with his. She tilted her head for him and opened her mouth.

He was gentle, trying to still the racing blood that thundered through his veins. His lips were tentative on hers. He breathed in her scent and caught the gasp she emitted at the heat that spun between them. He tasted her, reveling in the fact that she belonged to him. And he to her.

There were no barriers, no doubts. C. J. knew she saw inside him to the real person, not the outside. He struggled for control, lashed by a driving need that flamed to a frenzy.

"I want you." His hands framed her face and he bent, waiting for her to want it, too.

Her eyes darkened and she moistened her lips with her tongue. "Yes."

He tried to go slow for her, and to ease the frantic pounding of his blood.

Her hands gripped his wrists and she opened her mouth for him, like the delicate unfurling of a tiny bud. His tongue probed her mouth and she touched it shyly with her own. Tension jerked through him. He pulled her closer, caution overshadowed by the smoke in his blood, the urging lick of flames.

Want hooked into him with steel talons; his legs and arms quivered. He backed Lizzie against the cottonwood tree, trailing kisses over her cheeks and brow and eyelids.

She moaned softly, her hands clutching at him.

"You turn me inside out, Liz. I couldn't stop thinking about you, thinking about this."

"I know." She opened her eyes, smoky with passion, and the need there stabbed at his gut. "I know."

His hands itched to touch her, to drag a finger across her delicate collarbone, down the swell of her breasts. Fire licked at him and scattered common sense. He tried to temper his reaction, his want, but her hands curved around his waist and urged him closer.

With one hand, he cupped her jaw and tilted her face for another kiss. His tongue stroked hers in a rhythm he longed to make with their bodies. She held him tight, her fingernails dragging up his back. He wanted to feel her bare skin, touch it with his tongue, his hands.

His hands skimmed over her waist and to her breasts, then cupped their fullness through the fabric of her dress. She arched into his hands.

C. J.'s reason scattered. His hands kneaded her breasts and her nipples hardened in their wake. She moaned, dropping back her head to give him access to her neck.

"Oh, Lizzie, you are so beautiful. You are mine, truly mine. We belong to each other."

"C. J.," she breathed, her features tight with desire.

He wanted to touch all of her, know all of her. He kissed up her neck and over her chin, nipping at her lips. "I love you," he rasped against her mouth. "I love you."

She gripped his wrists and braced against the tree, pulling away. Panic clouded her eyes. "Don't say things like that."

Immediately he drew back. Alarm filled him, but his gaze held hers. "It's true," he said quietly. "I meant to tell you with softer words, but it's true all the same."

Stunned disbelief flitted across her features. She gave a nervous laugh. "You want me, but it's not the same as love. You don't have to say it is."

"It *is* love," he repeated firmly. "I couldn't stop thinking about you all week, wondering if you felt the same."

She hesitated, searching his eyes as though judging whether to believe him. "You missed me, that's all." She tried to pull away, but he held her fast. "That's part of friendship."

"There's that, too. Which is one of the reasons I love you." He smiled. "You're just about the best friend I've ever had, especially for a woman."

"Please don't say these things, C. J. We can't take them back."

"I don't want to," he said fiercely. Then his tone gentled and he stroked her cheek with one finger. "How could I not love you? You're smart, you're beautiful, you're perfect—"

"No, I'm not." Pain wrenched her features, but her gaze met his, unflinching and bright with tears. "I'm flawed and you know it."

"We all are, honey." He felt her withdrawing, pulling away from him and leaving his nerves as raw and exposed as if he'd been skinned. "No one's perfect in every sense, but you're perfect for me."

"I'm not talking about character flaws," she said impatiently. "I'm talking about *this.*" She pushed her hair away from her face and tilted her head so that the scar was revealed.

That damn scar. C. J. closed his eyes, his stomach in knots.

"You can't even look at it," she said softly, her voice thick with tears. "But this is why you started coming around. You felt guilty."

"Maybe in the beginning, but not anymore. I told you that." Panic gnawed at him. This wasn't how he'd imagined it. She was wrapping herself up in the past, in the hurt from Jude, and he couldn't reach her. "Why can't you believe me?"

"You're confusing your guilty feelings for something else." Her voice cracked and tears sheened her eyes. "Don't mock the friendship we have. I can accept that you feel something, but it's not love."

She started to walk away, leaving him bereft and lost, reeling from her disbelief. C. J. realized that he might not be able to convince her of the truth. But he would certainly try.

"You're wrong." The words exploded from him, desperate and pleading. He strode toward her, gripping her arm and turning her to face him. "I love you. Don't tell me you won't accept that."

She hated to see the pain that carved his features, but she couldn't bring herself to say the words. A thrill shot through her at his declaration, but doubts battered her. What if pity and responsibility were disguised by lust? What would make her different from any of the other women he'd had?

She wanted to surrender to the heat and promise in his eyes, but hesitated. Hadn't she seen a depth, a vulnerability, that no one else had? Hadn't he been honest from the beginning about their relationship?

"There's friendship, yes, but that's not the sum of my feelings." He added hotly, "And before you say it, it's not pity. It's not even want, though Thor knows I *do* want you, until I ache with it."

Her flesh heated at his words. She struggled to concentrate, to stand firm in the face of the temptation he offered.

His eyes darkened with desperation and longing. "Don't turn your back on it, Lizzie. It's deeper than friendship, and you know it. It's soft, yet it gives me strength." He tugged his hat from his head, looking uncertain and as if he were just as astounded by his words as she was. "I know there have been lots of women. I know I said I'd never open my heart for anyone again, but it's happened with you. Don't tell me I can't feel this, because I do. I love you."

Longing and panic and disbelief tumbled through her. Things had changed between them; she'd seen that clearly after he'd left Abilene. She loved him and trusted her feelings. But could she trust his? Very carefully she said, "How do you know? How can you be sure?"

"You feel something for me, too. You couldn't respond to me the way you do if you didn't love me."

"Women have . . . needs, too, C. J."

"Then deny you love me." Challenge fired his eyes, rippled in a steel line along his jaw. "Tell me it's only desire."

Reluctance sheared through her. Her feelings were much more than that, but were they enough to open her heart? Could a man like C. J. be happy with a woman like her, with all the doubts and regrets she carried from the past?

"It's love and you know it."

"C. J.—"

"Tell me it's not." His breath came in a rapid surge. Heat flushed his face and neck. "Tell me you don't feel wild and giddy and like you're about to go up in flames."

He described exactly how she felt about him, and her gaze locked on his. Did she want to consider C. J. as a regret in the future? No, she didn't. Could it be true? Did he really love her just as she loved him?

"I knew it," he said softly, moving toward her.

"C. J." Her voice shook. She didn't know whether the warning was meant for her or him.

He moved toward her, his eyes sapphire blue with promise. How could she tell him no when she wanted him so desperately? When he filled the dark void inside her with joy and sunshine. When she wanted to be convinced. *When she wanted to believe.*

They stared at each other, the wonder of something new and beautiful unfolding between them.

She gave a soft laugh. "I'm not sure. I can't understand all these feelings."

"All you have to understand is that my heart is yours." One hand cupped her jaw, not binding but capturing her with silken power. His lips skimmed over her cheek, her eyelids. She wavered, wanting to let go and give herself up to the melting persuasion of his hands. Her eyes fluttered shut.

Warm, moist breath kissed her temple, feathered down her left cheek, and moved ever closer to her scar.

She flinched, unable to make the final surrender. She wanted to be perfect for him. With her eyes closed, she could be that for him, but not like this. Not out in glaring daylight under the thoroughness of his gaze. Once again she felt shame and hurt and embarrassment, just as she had after Jude had struck her.

She gripped his wrists and pressed back into the tree. "C. J., don't."

Immediately he stopped. "Did I hurt you? What is it?"

Pain and disappointment bit at her. She glanced away, unable to meet his gaze. "You don't have to touch it," she said in a hoarse voice.

He was quiet for a long moment. "Your scar?"

She hesitated, then nodded, her gaze still averted.

One long finger caressed her jaw, forced her to turn and meet his eyes. Hunger and a desperate plea ravaged his features. "Lizzie, I want to touch you. All of you."

"But—"

"I love you. Everything you are. That scar is part of you. Don't deny me the chance to show you how I feel."

"I'm not saying I don't trust you or believe you, but it's not that easy." Frustration coiled through her and tears ached in her throat.

He slid his hands to her waist and held her loosely, looking earnestly into her eyes. "Lizzie, listen to me. What do you see when you look at me?"

She forced her gaze to his, searching anxiously for any sign of revulsion or hesitation or polite distance. She found love. Unconditional and infused with desire. Blue eyes pulling her in like a tempting summer sky. *Lose yourself in me,* they seemed to say. *Surrender.*

She wanted to, wanted to feel his soul merge with hers, but she couldn't make herself close the thin distance between them.

"Tell me, Lizzie," he whispered, fervent and demanding. "Tell me."

"I see . . . warmth and humor and love . . . a genuine, caring person."

"No," he dismissed her description impatiently. "Physically, what do you see?"

She frowned. "Blue eyes, blond hair, a stubborn chin—perfect features."

"When I look at you, I see perfect features, too."

She shook her head. "You know that scar is there."

"Yes," he admitted, frustration stamping his features. "But do you realize what you saw about me first?"

Slowly she shook her head.

He squeezed her. "You see the inside of me, what makes me a person. That's how I see you, too." He pulled her closer and his voice dropped to a husky pitch. "All my life, people have judged me on my physical appearance, and I used it to my advantage. Always had a girl, any girl I wanted. But after the accident, I pulled away from people."

She shook her head. "This isn't—"

"I had more to offer than just my looks, and I waited all my life for people to see that. You weren't impressed by outward appearance. It makes me feel honored and a little nervous to know that you know the real me and still want me anyway. You do want me, don't you?"

"Yes, but—"

"Shhh." He placed two fingers over her lips. "You see more to me than the physical, and I see you that way, too. When I look at you, I see beauty, grace, gentleness, a sharp tongue at times, but always your caring, your concern. And a strength that holds me in awe."

"C. J." She stared up at him, doubt warring with the warmth his words invoked. "I want to believe you. I do."

"Then trust me. Let me show you. Don't withhold any part of yourself from me."

She studied him for a long minute, struggling against the

love and determination in his eyes. She was staggered by a sense of inevitability and whispered shakily, "All right."

Joy flashed through his eyes, so acute it made Lizzie's chest hurt. "I've waited all my life for you, Lizzie."

In a heartbeat, all motion was suspended. As though from far away, she saw him bend toward her, heard her name on his lips.

His lips moved to her left temple, then dragged to her ear. She stiffened.

"Easy, honey. I won't hurt you."

His finger slid down her jaw. She felt its soft roughness trail along her scar. His touch was tentative and gentle, but to Lizzie it felt as if the scar were being reopened. And along with it, the secrets of her most private self.

She pulled away, breathing hard, unable to meet his eyes.

He stilled, his breathing ragged, his eyes blazing fiercely. "I love you, Lizzie."

She squeezed her eyes shut, reluctant to release to him the last hidden part of herself. "I can't," she moaned.

"It's okay," he soothed. "I want you to be as sure as I am. I won't do anything until you're ready."

"I'm ready for you to kiss me," she whispered.

She gasped as his tongue flicked at her lips, dipping in, then out, tracing her mouth with the taste of him. She opened her mouth wider for him, the ache in her belly arrowing down to coil between her legs. His mouth closed over hers.

Anticipation built. She could feel it, even though she did not fully understand what was happening. His hands stroked down her arms, around her shoulders, and hooked around her waist.

Her heart rushed so fast she thought it would give out. Tongues of fire pricked her from the inside of her thighs to her nipples, as though connected by some invisible bond.

While gentle, the kiss was demanding. And she gave. She

opened her mouth, yielding. Her heart pounded with the warmth of his breath.

Her hands gripped his wrists, feeling the echo of his pulse, the warmth of his skin, the crisp hair, the tempered strength. He pulled away to look at her. She touched her fingers to her lips and stared up at him, full of wonder and disbelief.

Hunger sharpened his features. In the gentle shadows of the tree, his crystal blue eyes glittered, feral and focused and sexual. Her heart ached, blooming with the heated savagery she felt vibrating from him.

The sudden rumble of hooves shattered their haven. With a jolt, she and C. J. drew apart. His skin was flushed and his breathing was as ragged as hers. She could still feel the imprint of his mouth on hers, his mustache tickling her skin.

Several Circle D ranch hands crested the rise and reined in their horses.

"Hey, boss. Miss Lizzie." Roger tipped his hat and grinned like a satisfied cat.

Webb shifted in his saddle and saluted. "Hey, Lizzie."

C. J. shot them a warning glare and squeezed Lizzie's arm, moving away to talk to the men. It gave her time to collect her scattered thoughts.

Roper's raspy voice carried to her. "Miz Minerva heard you wuz back and she wuz askin' about ya." The older man's face was grim, and Lizzie shot a glance at C. J.

His features tightened with determination and he waved the cowboys on their way.

He gathered her close and held her for a long moment, until Lizzie reminded him that she had to get back to the mercantile. Reluctantly he agreed.

In front of the mercantile, he lifted her down from the palomino, his gaze locked with hers. He couldn't kiss her; there were too many curious eyes on them. "I'll see you later," he whispered. "I love you."

"I love you, too." She smiled and moved around him to go inside.

He caught at her hand, stroking her palm with his thumb. Sensation skittered up her arm. "I'll see you tonight?"

"Yes." She smiled, still dazed and giddy from what had happened between them.

A woman's shoes tapped against the planked walk, jarring them, and C. J. dropped Lizzie's hand. Smiling, he vaulted into the saddle and rode off.

From behind Lizzie, Maybelle demanded, "Well, what happened?"

"You'll never believe it," she said softly.

Fourteen

C. J. RODE UP TO THE PORCH AND DISMOUNTED. FOR THE FIRST time in his life, he left Goliath in front of the house, not in the barn. He would unsaddle and rub down the stallion later. Right now, he wanted to see Grandma.

Just as she had predicted, he had found himself in the position of choosing between Lizzie and the prize. He had chosen Lizzie. There was a sense of loss for the property, but it was outweighed by his hope for the future, an excitement that he and Lizzie would face it together.

Silence wrapped around him as he stepped into the house. From the kitchen he heard a thud, then the scrape of a chair.

He walked in and found Grandma at the table, peeling apples. She glanced up as C. J. doffed his hat, tossing it on the table.

"Welcome home, boy." Her gray eyes glowed like soft, well-tended silver. She tilted her head for her customary kiss on the cheek.

C. J. obliged, then straightened, wiping suddenly sweaty palms on the legs of his britches. "You were asking the boys about me?"

"How was your trip?"

"Good." He chucked her under the chin and walked to the sink, picking up a towel, then replacing it before turning to face his grandmother. "I'd like to talk to you."

"By that smile on your face, I take it the trip was better than good."

"Yes." He leaned against the counter, crossing his feet at the ankles, trying to appear relaxed and confident. His nerves lashed into a knot and tension stretched across his shoulders. No one in his family had ever done what he was about to. He folded his arms across his chest. "I'm not going to find Lizzie a husband."

The knife clattered to the table and the apple followed, thumping hollowly. Minerva's eyes narrowed. "What's this you're saying?"

"It's true." His mouth went as dry as burlap, and apprehension streaked through him, but he faced her. "I'm through looking. I don't want her to be hurt anymore."

A look of impatience skated across Minerva's features. She leaned down and snatched up the apple and knife. "We've been over this before. If you can't find anyone, it's because you're not trying hard enough."

"Oh, I found someone, all right, Grandma."

His cryptic words brought her head up, eyes narrowed. This time she deliberately laid the knife and apple in the bowl. "Out with it, boy."

He took a deep breath, nervous and exhilarated at the same time. "I'm forfeiting the task."

For a long, dragging heartbeat, silence webbed the kitchen. C. J. could hear his heart thudding, the creak of wood from the floor upstairs, the tick of uncertainty rushing in his ears.

His grandmother stared at him as if he'd given up the equivalent of the English throne. "You'd best consider your words. I warned you."

"I've thought about everything, Grandma. I want Lizzie." His voice was hoarse, but the words strong.

She rose, shaking her head. "You don't know what you're giving up, boy. You have no idea—"

"I know it's the ranch, Grandma," he said gently.

She stiffened. "How?"

"I was in Wiley's office that day. Waiting to tell you I couldn't go through with the task."

Her gaze weighed him for a long time. "The ranch, Cupid. Think about it."

He met her gaze unflinchingly, shedding the uncertainty, the last hesitation. "I love her."

"There will be no other chance. I won't stand by and let you hurt her," she said crisply. "That was never my purpose."

"I don't want to hurt her. I want a life with her." He felt the strength of the simple words, the awe of the commitment he meant to make. Why couldn't Grandma?

She watched him as if she were a cat stalking a mouse, searching for any weakness or hesitation. But he didn't squirm or flinch. He'd never been more sure of anything in his life.

Finally she eased down in the chair, her voice amazed in the stillness of the room. "No one has ever done this. Ever."

"I know." Muscles corded across his shoulders. Would she accept his decision? He didn't want to go against her, but he would. He had suddenly discovered he would brave even Grandma's displeasure for Lizzie.

Minerva's eyes softened with love and pride. Then she smiled.

C. J. frowned at her unexpected reaction. "Grandma?"

"When you asked me to give you another task, you spoke so highly of her. I thought you were softening toward her."

"Is that why you wouldn't let me quit until I gave a better effort?"

"Yes. I was hoping you truly cared for her."

"And that's why you said I might thank you someday?"

"Yes."

"I do thank you, Grandma." C. J. drew in a ragged breath, still shaky with exhilaration. "I never thought I'd love anyone like I love Lizzie."

The bright sheen of tears glimmered in Minerva's eyes. "I didn't expect you to give up the prize, though. And certainly not if you had learned it was the ranch. I'm so proud of you."

"You are?" He pushed away from the counter, not certain he'd heard her correctly.

She rose and leaned up to kiss his cheek. "Yes, very proud. You've given up your greatest desire for something higher. I love you very much."

"I love you, too, Grandma." He felt disoriented and suddenly swamped by the urge to laugh. He'd done it. The future lay wide open, as brilliant with promise as the love he'd discovered. He caught Grandma around the waist and swung her into the air. "Whooooeee!"

"I'm about to bust." Maybelle dragged Lizzie to the back room. "Tell me."

Lizzie smiled and a knot of excitement and warmth unraveled deep inside. "C. J. loves me."

Maybelle's eyes widened, then filled with tears. "Oh, Lizzie." She brushed the tears away and planted her hands on her hips. "There! Didn't I tell you something was different?"

"I don't mind saying you were right this time." It felt strange to say the words, as if she'd walked into a familiar place only to find it changed. She felt restless and unsettled, impatient to see C. J. again. She wished she could have surrendered totally to him, but that would come.

Needing something to keep her hands and mind occupied, she reached into a long rectangular crate, newly arrived from New York.

He loved her.

She felt a combination of disbelief, anticipation, and the

thrill of having something she'd never expected. She felt a strange sense of peace and at the same time a shiver of excitement. The sun's warmth had nothing to do with the heat inside her.

She folded back the paper covering Hank's shipment. Undergarments. A soft lawn chemise lay on top and she picked it up. The undergarment was sheer and trimmed with delicate lace. Several more chemises, of practical cotton, followed. She opened a box inside the crate and found corsets.

Putting the corsets on a chair behind her, she again ran her fingers over the lawn chemise. She'd never had anything so fine, so . . . transparent. She stroked the fabric, pulling the veil-thin material over her hand. Closing her eyes, she imagined herself wearing it, imagined C. J.'s hands exploring her body, burning through the sheer covering.

She took a deep breath and put the chemise with the others.

Maybelle shot her a sideways glance and smiled knowingly. "Tell me everything." She pulled over Lizzie's chair from the desk and pushed her into it. "What did he say? Where did you go?"

"He said he missed me." Lizzie couldn't control the urge to grin. She dropped the undergarments, unpacking forgotten now. "We went to the river."

"And did you tell him you felt the same?"

"Yes," she admitted shyly. A burst of heat radiated around her heart. Hope blossomed at the future she had never let herself imagine before.

"Oh, this is wonderful! I can't wait to tell Hank." Maybelle twirled with a saucy smile. "Did he kiss you?"

"Maybelle!" A flush heated her cheeks.

"He did." Maybelle smiled triumphantly. "Was it as good as you thought?"

"It was better," Lizzie confided, relenting. She laughed, caught up in a camaraderie she had never thought to find.

Maybelle fluttered her eyelashes and fanned herself with one hand. "Oh, he is delicious."

"Wickedly." Lizzie giggled, enjoying their silliness. Her life had taken on a new dimension today, so different from yesterday. She was still dazed by C. J.'s admission, as well as by her own.

"Get out. *Now!*" Hank's voice bellowed through their laughter.

Maybelle's smile faded and she turned toward the curtain. Lizzie stilled, alarmed at Hank's harshness.

His voice rumbled out again. "I won't be having the likes of you in here."

A mumble floated through the curtain, but she couldn't make out the words or identify the voice.

"Now, I said!" Hank roared.

Lizzie started at the thunderous noise. She'd never heard Hank raise his voice. Maybelle rushed to the curtain that divided the front of the store from the back room, and Lizzie followed to peer over her friend's shoulder.

Her breath lodged in her throat. Jed Bostick stood in the center of the store, glaring at Hank. Hank, as tall as Jed but outweighing him by at least forty pounds, stiffened his shoulders. What was Jed doing here?

She exchanged a frown with Maybelle, who looked as confused as Lizzie felt.

"You get your no-account, lazy carcass outta here before I thrash you like C. J. did." Hank tucked his clenched fists against his sides, thrusting his chin at Jed.

The younger man glowered, his nose still swollen to twice its size. Black and purple bruises marred one side of his face and spread up under both eyes, making him look like a raccoon. "You're the only store in town. I gotta come in here sometime."

"Not after what you did to Lizzie."

"Hell!" Jed yelled, taking a reluctant step toward the door. "It ain't my fault. C. J. goes around trying to get somebody to notice the girl, then when I do, he beats the hell outta me."

Lizzie froze. A roaring invaded her ears. Maybelle's hand closed over her upper arm, squeezing hard.

"If C. J. didn't want any of us sniffin' around her, he shoulda said so," Jed snapped on his way through the door.

What had Jed meant by that? Battered by confusion and the deep rumble of Hank's voice, Lizzie stood quietly, unable to move for a second.

"Get out and stay out!" Hank hollered from the door.

An instinctive panic nudged her legs into motion and she pushed through the curtain. Even though caution screamed for her to let him go, she called, "Jed, wait!"

Hank turned, his features dark with concern. "There, he's gone. He won't be back."

"I need to talk to him."

"What!" Her employer's brows drew together. "What for?"

She moved past him and into the doorway. "Jed, wait. Stop. Please!"

Jed, already in the street, turned slowly. His gaze narrowed with distrust, then moved over her shoulder to Hank. "What do you want?"

"I want to know what you meant about C. J." Her heart hammered in her chest. Sweat surfaced on her palms and she tucked her hands into fists.

Jed's face darkened with hesitation and guilt, then his gaze skittered away. "I didn't mean nothin'."

"Lizzie, why do you want to talk to him?" Hank said quietly behind her. "After what he did . . ."

"I need to know, Hank. Please." Alarm pounded through her. A thick fog of expectancy, of dread, hung over her, but she met Jed's gaze. "Tell me."

His gaze slid from her to Hank, clearly weighing whether he should. He spun, sprinting down the street.

"Jed!" Lizzie bolted after him, as did Hank.

Hank reached him first and his grizzly-sized hand clamped onto Jed's shirt collar. He yanked the younger man to a stop and half dragged, half carried him back to Lizzie. "Tell her what she wants to know, boy."

A flush darkened Jed's neck and spread like a crimson stain onto his face and his swollen nose. He glared at Lizzie. "I don't know anything."

"Why would you think C. J. had any say about me at all?"

His jaw set in an obstinate line and his mouth worked for several seconds. Then he answered grudgingly, "He offered us money to sit with you and eat lunch."

"He offered you . . ." The words trailed off as she struggled to make sense of what he'd said.

"Hell's bells!" Hank's gaze shot to Lizzie. He shifted from one foot to the other, disbelief and speculation firing his eyes.

Jed claimed C. J. had offered money for someone to eat lunch with her? She stood motionless for a long, dragging instant. Her breath knotted in her chest. "Why? Why would he do that?"

"I don't know." Uncertainty replaced the anger on Jed's features. "But it was worth a ten-dollar gold piece that day."

"And why—why didn't anyone take him up on it?" A gnawing sickness crept through her and she felt a sudden chill. Blood drained in a dizzying rush from her head. *It was ridiculous! C. J. wouldn't pay someone to keep her company. Nobody would do that!*

Jed's eyes softened as he took in her stark features. "That Tom English was already sittin' with you." His gaze, now curious and apologetic, moved to Hank's.

"It's not true." She shook her head slowly, wishing she could strangle the suspicion that inched through her. "Why would he offer you money? Why should he care if I had someone to eat with at the picnic?"

Jed frowned, gingerly touching his nose. "I don't know." He eyed Hank warily, trying to twist away from the burly man's hold. "All I know is, he asked me and the twins if we wanted to sit with you and we said no. Then at the barbecue, when I asked you to go for a walk, he just about killed me."

Hank's gaze, concerned and baffled, rested on Lizzie.

No. No, it can't be. She backed away, unable to breathe the air that had suddenly turned thick. Her legs wobbled and denial coursed through her. "Thank you."

It wasn't true. It couldn't be. She felt trapped inside a glass jar. One false move and she would shatter. Pain and shock funneled through her mind, compounded by one bald question. *What if it was true?*

Had C. J. bribed men to pay attention to her *before* the picnic? Had he done it to others besides Jed? What about George? And Henry? Had they been paid to escort her to the dance, to dinner?

She closed her eyes, conjuring up C. J.'s face, the soft light in his eyes as he told her he loved her. No, it couldn't be true.

But doubts wormed in. With a sickening lurch of her stomach, she remembered her evening with Henry. She had asked C. J. then if he knew anything about her sudden invitations.

He hadn't answered her.

Angry determination kicked in, releasing the shock that had wrapped around her like a wet blanket. She would ask George and Henry. They would tell her Jed was lying, that he was still angry about what C. J. had done to him at the barbecue.

She whirled and stalked into the store, tearing off her apron.

"Lizzie!" Hank hurried after her, his voice sharp with concern. "Are you all right? Where are you going?"

"I'm going to find George Bates," she managed around a lump of dread and panic. *Please let this be a misunderstanding. Or a dream. Or a lie.*

C. J. wouldn't do this. He wouldn't.

*   *   *

But he *had* done it. Or so George and Henry had told her.

An hour later, Lizzie sat in a rented buggy at the entrance to the Circle D, her face buried in her hands. She felt limp and wrung dry, drained of emotion. She wished she could feel numb, but she felt every breath as a stab in her lungs, every whisper of the breeze as a slap against raw flesh.

Still, she resisted believing it, even as George and Henry's words echoed through her mind.

Neither man knew why C. J. had made the offers, but George had admitted that C. J. had paid him by letting him use Goliath as a stud.

C. J. had paid Henry twenty dollars to take her to dinner. Bribery. Plain and simple.

C. J. had said he loved her. Why had he done it? Why? It made no sense. Could George and Henry both be lying?

Pain and betrayal and a desperate desire to hear C. J. deny it all slashed through her. He'd said he loved her. She closed her eyes, her stomach clenching in agony. Reason battled with apprehension.

She wanted to believe in him, in the words he'd uttered only hours ago. If he didn't truly care for her, why had he come straight to her when he returned? How could he so tenderly coax her to trust him with the most intimate and vulnerable part of herself?

She trembled with rage and reaction, trying to keep her worst thoughts at bay. Though George and Henry's words were damning, Lizzie wanted to talk to C. J. She wanted to hear it straight from his mouth.

She wanted him to deny it.

He was going to ask her to marry him.

Late afternoon sunshine slanted into the barn, gilding the drab wood to a warm sheen, turning the red earth floor to copper.

Any reservations C. J. had about letting the ranch go had

disappeared when he'd looked into Lizzie's midnight blue eyes. And even Grandma had understood how much he loved her. Minerva had accepted his decision, and C. J. hoped the rest of the family would as well.

After he unsaddled Goliath and rubbed him down, he joined Lee in the barn, where his brother was checking the shoes on the horses.

Now stripped to the waist, C. J. stood with his back to the door. Dirt and pieces of hay streaked his chest. Sweat slicked his back and slipped into the hollow of his spine beneath the waistband of his denims.

He tapped on Aristotle's left rear leg and lifted the hoof for inspection. His movements were instinctive and sure, but his mind wandered to Lizzie.

His skin still tingled from the feel of her. Thoughts of her eager wonder teased him and made his nerves hum with anticipation. The peace and sense of rightness he'd felt with her still persisted. His only regret was that she hadn't been able to relax about the scar. But she would; he was sure of it.

She returned his feelings. The surprise of it lingered. Why had it taken them so long to see the truth of their feelings?

"How long are you gonna look at that shoe?" Lee spoke from a few feet away.

C. J. started and released the stallion's leg. "I've got something on my mind."

"Like what?" Lee knelt next to a roan mare.

C. J. grinned. "Marriage."

"Marr—" Lee broke off and his eyebrow crooked upward. "To who?" he snorted.

C. J. rested one arm against the stallion's rump. "Lizzie."

His eyes somber, Lee's body uncoiled like a rope stiff from disuse. "Just so you can claim the prize?"

"No." C. J.'s jaw clenched at Lee's assumption. "Because I love her."

For a long moment, Lee stared, then his eyes narrowed.

"And it doesn't hurt that you'll get whatever Grandma decides to give you."

"I forfeited," C. J. ground out. He wanted Lee to know exactly what Lizzie meant to him, and he also wanted to wipe that smug "big-brother" look from Lee's face. "The ranch."

"The . . . what?" Lee's mouth dropped. "The ranch was your prize? How do you know that?"

"I overheard Grandma at Wiley Vernon's office."

"And you forfeited?"

"You don't mind about the ranch going to me?"

"I wouldn't have, no." Lee looked pleased, albeit dazed. "No one's ever forfeited before."

"I know." Satisfaction surged through him. "I told Grandma how I felt about Lizzie." For an instant, he remembered the softness in Lizzie's eyes when he'd admitted his feelings. "I explained that she means more to me than having the ranch."

"I can understand that," Lee said quietly, his face softening. C. J. knew Lee was thinking of his wife, Meredith. Admiration gleamed in Lee's eyes as he glanced at C. J. "Well, I'll be damned." He picked up the mare's hoof again and leaned over it, but stared out at the prairie beyond. "Do you think Lizzie will say yes?"

"I hope so."

"Well, here's your chance to ask." Lee straightened and dropped Athena's hoof. "Isn't that her?"

Releasing Aristotle's leg, C. J. turned toward the barn door. A small buggy raced toward the barn, and C. J. could see the driver was Lizzie.

His heart swelled. She hadn't been able to wait until tonight to see him. He grinned, feeling the same impatience.

Taking a bandanna from his back pocket, he wiped at the sweat on his face and chest and walked out to meet her. She pulled the buggy to a halt in front of the barn, scattering rocks and debris and stirring up a cloud of dust.

"Hi, honey." C. J.'s voice was soft, for her ears only, as he lifted his arms to help her down.

She didn't answer, just dropped the reins against the horse's back and levered herself out of the buggy, ignoring his outstretched hands. "I need to talk to you."

Fear and panic edged her voice and he frowned. "What is it? Has something happened?"

Hurt flashed through her eyes, then they went cold. She stared at him as if he were a stranger. "I . . ." She took a deep breath, as though forcing out the words. "I heard something in town."

"Something—like what?" Her skin was pale and waxy, her eyes dark with apprehension. Concern charged through him. "You're starting to worry me."

"Hi, Lizzie." Lee walked up and leaned against the barn door.

Her gaze flickered to him. "Hello, Lee."

"Lizzie?" Alarm started a slow waltz across C. J.'s nerves.

Her gaze, tortured and pleading, met his. "Jed Bostick told me you offered him money to sit with me at the picnic."

His panic was complete. "Lizzie—"

"Tell me he's lying out of spite because of what you did to him."

He couldn't lie to her, not after he'd bared his heart to her earlier. He would explain. She would understand about Grandma.

"It's true!" she cried out. She glanced away for a second, and C. J. saw her chin quiver. Then she angled her chin at him. "Why?"

"It's not what you think. It doesn't have anything to do with the way I feel about you." C. J. struggled to find the right words, feeling as though he moved in a slippery darkness.

"You're not denying it." Her voice was harsh with anger. "Why? Why did you do it?"

His hands shook. His whole future with Lizzie wobbled in

front of him. Taking a deep breath, he forced a measure of calm into his voice. "There's a tradition in our family." He explained how each child was assigned a task on their twentieth birthday.

"And I was your task?" Her stomach lurched. "Tell me why. Was it to humiliate me? To get a gentleman caller for 'poor Lizzie'? What was it?" she yelled. "Tell me."

"Lizzie—" C. J. broke off, alarm pumping through him. A fine sweat broke out on his brow and his throat worked as he considered the best way to tell her.

Dread flitted through her eyes, a desperate need to know the truth. "Tell me what it was," she whispered.

He licked his lips, his gaze bleak with agony. "It was to find you a husband," he said hoarsely.

For an instant, she stared at him. Her face turned as pale as chalk and pain slashed at her features. Denial followed by humiliation passed through her eyes. Then betrayal. "A husband? That's sick!" She paused, her breath labored. "And what about the bribes? Did she tell you to do that, too? What about George and Henry?"

George and Henry. C. J. reeled, realizing with shame and disgust how the entire thing must look to her.

"Deny it." She leaned into his face, her features mottled with rage, her voice coldly calm. "Deny that you offered George the use of your stallion if he would ask me to the dance. Deny that you paid Henry Taylor to take me to supper." Her voice faded to an agonized whisper. "Deny it."

C. J.'s heart thudded painfully. Betrayal clouded Lizzie's eyes. He reached out to her, but she stepped away.

A knife twisted in his heart. He was vaguely aware that Lee had slipped back inside the barn to give them some privacy. "Lizzie, all that happened before I realized how I felt about you."

"Tell me why, C. J." Her voice quivered and tears of anger flashed in her eyes. Her lips tightened mutinously and her face was chalky except for two bright circles of color high in her cheeks. "I want to hear how you could do that to me. *To me.* I thought we . . ." She gasped for breath, holding her side as though in pain. "I thought you . . ."

The words trailed into excruciating silence. Dread sliced through him and he rushed to explain about the task. "It's an oddity that's been a family tradition for years."

"Why me? You didn't have to do it."

"No, I didn't. I wanted to."

Disbelief and agony creased her features.

"It's not what you think." He flinched at the hurt on her face. "It was Grandma's way of getting me to acknowledge responsibility for your scar."

"I knew it." White lines of fury bracketed her mouth. Her eyes stood out like obsidian in her pale face. "I guess you told me that much of the truth."

"What I feel for you is *not* responsibility. Well, it is, but in a different way now." He reached for her, but she backed away. "I told you in the beginning it was related to the scar, but not now."

"And you expect me to believe you?"

His heart split with pain. "I was supposed to find you a husband and I tried. But I fell in love with you myself."

"You fell in love with me?" She drew herself up, gathering into herself, withdrawing her spirit. "And your reward for this . . . this generous act?"

The bitter pain in her voice slashed at him. For the first time, he cursed his knowledge of the prize. He didn't want to tell her. He knew how it would sound. "I didn't know at first—"

"Tell me." The words hung in the air, rife with the same condemnation as if he'd agreed to take thirty pieces of silver. "Tell me what you get in return for finding me a husband."

He swallowed. He would've felt less evil taking the thirty pieces of silver. At least he had forfeited the task. She would understand that. She would believe him. "I was supposed to get the ranch," he said quietly. "But now—"

"I see." She stilled, light disappearing from her face like the sun behind a cloud. A bitter laugh erupted from her. "I should've guessed."

"No, Lizzie, you don't understand."

"You told me how much the ranch meant to you." Her voice quivered. "That you would do anything to get it."

"No, that's not the way it is," he yelled, trying to control the panic that gnawed at him. "I mean, what you said was true. I did those things, but it was all before I realized I loved you."

"You bartered me away like some prize watermelon! The whole idea makes me sick. You make me sick!" She spun and headed for the buggy.

C. J. lunged in front of her. "Please, Lizzie, listen to me. I love you. I do. If it hadn't been for Grandma, I might never have realized it."

"Love?" Misery creased her features, and C. J. thought she looked ill. "This is not what I consider love, C. J. With all your experience, though, perhaps it is to you." Her eyes glistened with tears as she turned to get into the buggy. "I call it manipulation, cruel manipulation."

She braced herself as though preparing for a blow. Her eyes were empty, masked against further pain. "There's no one to marry me. What a shame you'll get nothing."

"That's right." He latched onto her words and moved in front of her, desperate to make her understand. "I gave up the ranch. When I left you this afternoon I went to Grandma and I forfeited."

She hesitated only a heartbeat, doubt passing through her eyes, then she climbed into the buggy.

"Lizzie, no!" He grasped her elbow, but she pulled away. His gut clenched and his heartbeat ricocheted painfully against his ribs. "We can work this out. You can talk to my grandmother. You've got to believe me."

"I think I did that once too often." She climbed into the buggy, her hands shaking and anger flushing her face.

Sheer panic gripped him. "No! Don't go. Don't leave this way." He touched her shoulder.

She jerked under his hand and pulled away. "Don't touch me. Ever again. I can't believe I ever let you." Her voice broke and a tear slid down her cheek. "That I practically begged you to."

"Don't do this, Lizzie." His throat ached with a hot rawness. "I know you're hurt. I know it was wrong, but you've got to believe me. I forfeited the task because I wanted you. I still do. I gave up the ranch."

"Well, you won't have me. Nor will any of your paid gentleman friends." A bitter smile edged her lips and tears glistened in her eyes. "I imagine this is what a whore feels like, except she at least has some say in who will pay."

"I never looked at it that way," he said savagely. Frustration and anger ripped through him and he gripped the side of the buggy. "Stay and hear me out. Believe me. Believe in us."

"I stopped believing about an hour ago." She stared straight ahead, her fist blanched white around the brake.

"Talk to my grandmother. She'll tell you."

"Why would I listen to her?" she cried. "This whole mess was her idea!"

"She was only thinking of you."

"No!" Her head swerved toward him, and her gaze blazed with fire and tears. "I think she considered only you."

"You're angry and I understand that, but how can you turn your back on me, on what we have?" He flushed, enraged himself, but more afraid he would lose her forever. "It was wrong, but you've got to trust me. The task brought us together. Can't you focus on that and forgive the way it happened?"

"No, I can't." Her voice trembled for the first time with something other than anger. When she looked at him, he saw the deep pain and betrayal she felt. "Your manipulation might have been for different reasons, but it was no different than Jude's."

"No, Lizzie." His throat clenched. "I would never treat you that way."

"At least he never hid his actions. He made threats, but you went behind my back, sneaking around, making plans. We were supposed to mean more than that to each other. I thought we were at least friends."

"We were. We still are, and I love you. Don't leave. Don't walk away from me."

"I can't stay."

His chest ached with the terror that she would never come back. "Are we through, then?"

"I don't know." She lifted her head, tears streaming down her face. "I don't know if we ever really began."

"We did, Lizzie. You know we did."

He held her gaze, willing her to believe, to see into the deepest part of his heart and know he spoke the truth. He saw hesitation and uncertainty in her eyes, along with the flare of agony.

She snapped the reins against the horse's rump, and the buggy lurched into motion.

C. J. stared after her, feeling naked and alone, his insides crumbling to ashes.

Fifteen

DESPERATE FEAR CHARGED THROUGH HIM. C. J. STOOD FOR LONG moments, pain slicing through him like the cool blade of a straightedge. She was leaving. *Leaving him.*

His stunned mind could barely register the fact. Then he pivoted and rushed into the barn, straight for Goliath.

"Hey, man, I'm sorry," Lee said heavily. He stood in the corner behind the door, his face carved in sober shadows. "I'm really sorry."

"I'm going after her. I can talk to her. She'll understand." C. J. grabbed the bridle and bit from the wall and hurriedly fit the stallion.

Lee moved out of the shadows, concern furrowing his brow. "I hope you're right. She looked pretty upset."

"She'll listen to me. I know she will." But he didn't know. Not anymore. In one fluid motion, he grabbed the reins and leaped onto Goliath's back. One swift kick sent the stallion bolting through the door.

"Good luck," Lee called after him.

C. J. hunkered down over Goliath's neck and gave the stallion free rein. He had to reach her. He had to make her understand.

Goliath's hooves thundered over the ground, gouging

dirt, spraying pebbles and twigs in their wake. C. J.'s heart pounded in the same rhythm. Faster, harder, more desperate. He had to reach her.

His chest burned as though it had been ripped open. Desperation lashed at him. He blanked his mind, simply watching as the brown earth and green grass skimmed by under Goliath's hooves. A tree. The creek. His heart kicked doubletime in his chest. She had to listen, believe him.

He reached town and shot across the back field, straight for her house. Goliath slowed as they neared, seeming to instinctively know their destination. Or perhaps C. J. had reined in the horse. He couldn't be sure.

All he knew was that his heart was being pulled out, one agonizing inch at a time.

He dismounted in front of the tiny house and hesitated. The buggy sat quietly, veiled with a thin film of dirt. Lizzie hadn't even returned the rig to the livery, another sign of her distress—if he needed one. The horse, a sorrel mare, eyed him as he approached. Sweat gleamed on her coat. Urgency razored through him, driven by the fear that Lizzie might not listen.

Pushing aside his doubts, he strode to the front door and pounded. "Lizzie, let me in. We need to talk."

No response.

He pounded again, the door rattling under the force of his blows. "Lizzie, answer me! Come to the door. Please!"

Again there was no response, and he pushed the door open, stepping inside. Empty. Without a hint of noise or evidence that she'd even been here. Suddenly C. J. knew where she was.

He spun and sprinted outside, around the back of the house to the shed. A few feet from the small building, he skidded to a halt, his breath catching in his chest.

The door to the shed stood ajar, and though he couldn't hear her, he knew she was there. He walked up and peered inside, squinting against the sudden dimness.

"Lizzie?"

The sound of his voice triggered a flutter of wings and a movement to his left. Domino growled.

"Go away." The words were harsh, thick and rusty. She was crying.

He turned his head, barely making out her silhouette in the dark light. She was holding the injured cat. "We need to talk."

"I've said everything I needed to."

"I know you're hurt. And I don't blame you. But can't we talk about it?"

"There's nothing to talk about. I found out, and now you're free of your obligation." She moved further away, into the corner between the dog and the raccoon.

"I don't care about the task or the prize," he said hoarsely, his breastbone aching. "I care about you." He stooped inside, hunching his shoulders to fit in the small space. The dog bared his teeth and moved between C. J. and Lizzie. "Can't we focus on the fact that we're together and not how it happened? That all that matters is that I love you?"

'Stop . . . saying . . . that," she gritted out, her voice shaky.

"It wasn't about hurting you. It was about making me take responsibility for something that happened a long time ago."

"I told you this scar wasn't your fault," she screamed.

"That's not what I meant." He could see her eyes now. They were wild and frightened. He thrust his hands into his pockets so he wouldn't reach for her. "Grandma thought we would've patched things up by now and we hadn't. She thought it was my responsibility to do something about it."

"It doesn't change the way I feel."

"I was hoping it would." He sighed, unsure how to continue. "I was hoping that you could forgive me and maybe in ten years we'd laugh about this."

Rage mottled her features and her eyes gleamed with a fierce light. "I feel used, betrayed."

"That was never my intention."

"You *bribed* those men. Do you know how that makes me feel?"

"I'm trying, honey. I am." He eased another step closer to her, encouraged that she was at least talking to him. The dog growled, but didn't move. "It wasn't about hurting you. It was about me. I'm ashamed to admit it, but I was trying to find the easiest way to do what Grandma wanted. It was wrong. I know that. I knew it then and tried to back off."

He paused, searching her features for any sign that she might believe him. He could read nothing on her face. "I could see you were friendly with Tom, and I thought things might work out between the two of you."

"Then why didn't you just leave me alone?" she asked brokenly, her voice tired and uneven.

C. J.'s heart burned at the hurt he'd caused. "Because I love you. I couldn't stay away."

Her eyes welled with pain. Even if she forgave him, C. J. didn't know if he could forgive himself for causing her so much pain. "I forfeited the task because you mean more to me than the ranch. You've got to believe that."

She stood stiff and unyielding, her body poised in a protective stance, ready to flee if necessary. The realization tore at C. J.

"I remember when you said you would do anything to get the ranch." Her gaze held his, empty and dull. "I believed you."

"You know how much the ranch means to me. You've got to know that I'm giving it up for something even more important. I did that for you. For us." A new shaft of pain arrowed through him and C. J. closed his eyes against it. "Because of our feelings for each other."

"I don't know what I feel anymore." Her face was pale in

the shadows, eyes gleaming as brilliant points of pain. "And I don't know what you feel, if I ever did."

Anger surged through him and his voice rasped out like flint on stone. "I won't beg you to believe me, Lizzie. We've got to start trusting each other."

"How can you talk to me about trust?" she flared. "Why didn't you tell me when you realized your feelings had changed? When you saw that mine had? I don't see how I can believe any of it."

"When I realized I loved you, I'd already decided to forfeit." He shook his head, frustration clawing through him. "The ranch didn't matter anymore. All I had to do was talk to Grandma."

"You should've talked to *me.*"

"I'm sorry, Lizzie." His voice broke. "I truly am."

"Did you ever consider telling me?"

"Yes, early on." Regret thumped at him. "When I saw how George had hurt you."

"That was nothing compared to this. When I think about those men you bribed—" She broke off, wrapping her arms protectively around her middle.

C. J.'s temper flared. "Forget all that! What about this?" He reached for her, intending to haul her to him, but she flinched. Domino's growl deepened and he poised to lunge.

His heart cracked open and slowly he dropped his arms, wanting to take back the action. "I won't hurt you," he said quietly.

"You already have."

Her words echoed those in his own mind and he looked down, battered by the bleak realization that he had failed.

"I can't forget about George and Henry and Jed," she whispered. "You lied to me. How do I know you're not lying now?"

The words ripped into him and he rubbed his chest, stunned at the pain he felt clear to his soul.

She wiped at her cheeks and drew herself up. "I think you should leave."

He stood unmoving for a moment, a muscle flexing in his jaw. Silence drummed around them, thick as summer rain. How could she turn her back on him? How could she doubt what they felt for each other? Why couldn't she believe that he'd given up the ranch and would do it again? Anger and frustration funneled through him. "You're all too willing to believe the worst. I won't let you. Yes, be angry. Yes, you have a right to hurt, but I'm hurting, too. I won't let you push me away."

"I want you to go." Her eyes flashed with pain and anger. She walked to the door, clearly dismissing him.

"Don't do this, Lizzie. I'll give you time, as much as you want, but don't shut me out."

"Go." She gripped the door frame, her knuckles blanched white, her head bowed.

"I've told you how I feel, Lizzie. The rest is up to you. Don't let me walk out that door."

"I think it's best if you don't come back," she whispered, her voice catching.

C. J. stared for another long second, wishing he could make her understand, wishing he could break through the wall of hurt. Wishing he'd never agreed to perform this stupid task.

He swallowed around a lump of hurt and regret and bitterness. And walked out of the shed.

Agony ripped through her, mingled with confusion. She stood in the door of the shed and caught a shuddering breath. Her gaze centered on C. J.'s retreating figure. He'd admitted everything. How could he have done those things? How?

Oh, she knew his reasons. They tumbled through her mind, opening new wounds, numbing the old. Her breath lodged in her chest. What a fool she'd been!

"Lizzie?" Tom's voice penetrated her dark thoughts. "Are you okay?"

She scraped the tears from her cheeks and turned. Tom stood at the edge of the house and watched the retreating figures of C. J. and his horse. His concerned gaze moved to her. "What's going on?"

Tears burned her eyes again, but she squeezed them back. The words came out hollow and raw. "You wouldn't believe me if I told you."

"Hey," Tom said softly, squeezing her shoulder. "I'm here if you need a friend."

"I do." She bit her lip to stop her chin from quivering. "Thanks."

"Love's hell, huh?" Tom smiled and pushed his plate away. Over coffee and pie, Lizzie had told him everything including the humiliation of learning about the bribes.

"You weren't part of that plan, were you?"

"No," Tom assured her.

She shrugged. "I had to ask."

"I'm really sorry, Lizzie. What are you going to do?" He tapped a finger on the table.

She sipped at her coffee and wished the ache in her soul would go away. "What would you do?"

"I don't know." He hesitated, studying her carefully. "Do you believe what he told you about the task and his grand-mother?"

"It's too absurd not to believe."

"I'll second that." His smile was grim. "I've never met anybody like the people in that family."

Lizzie raised an eyebrow, but said nothing, praying for blessed numbness to settle over her.

Tom wrapped long fingers around his coffee cup. "Do you believe he loves you?"

"I'm not sure." If he really loved her, wouldn't he see her differently than other people? It wasn't the scar. She didn't hink that had bothered him. But what about the way he viewed her as a whole person? Would a man who saw her as capable and normal resort to bribing other men to call for her?

Admittedly, she hadn't had any friends before Jude had died, and perhaps that was the reason C. J. had offered those men money and favors. But she had put forth the effort and had friends now. She had a place in Paradise Plains. And people knew that she wanted a different life than the one she'd had with Jude.

C. J. had been her friend. She wanted to dismiss him, forget the memories they had made, and go about her life as if he'd never been a part of it. But he'd changed her, made her believe she *was* different, that she could be a part of the social world and have a better life.

She brushed the thoughts away, unwilling to dismiss the hurt she'd suffered. Even though her friendship with C. J. had helped her, it couldn't dim the echoes of the past.

Voices rushed through her mind, clashing, jumbling, confusing.

You're scarred, Lizzie. No man will ever take you to wife.

Your face ain't so pretty under here, is it?

I want to love all of you. Would you deny me any part of yourself?

She raised her gaze to Tom, confused and feeling more like the girl Jude had caught at Peabody's than the one who had thought to escape him. "What should I do?"

"I can't tell you that, Lizzie, but I will say this." He waited until she nodded for him to continue. "C. J. came after you. If he really only cared about the ranch, he didn't have to come."

She had thought the same thing, but hearing it aloud unsettled her. And sharpened her confusion.

C. J. reined Goliath to a halt inside the barn and slid to the ground. During his ride from town, the sense of loss had broadsided him. The future was bleak and empty. All because of that damn task.

Now he took refuge in anger. He was angry at himself and at Grandma—and even at Lizzie for not believing him.

Lee was still in the barn, pitching hay into one of the end stalls. He leaned the pitchfork against the wall and walked over to C. J. "How'd it go?"

"She wouldn't listen." Rage pumped through him, fired by indignation and pride. "By Thor, I did everything I could think of. Begged, pleaded, threatened. She knows where to find me."

Lee stood to one side as C. J. paced in front of him. "Pride won't get you anywhere."

"Brother, right now it's all I've got." He reached to pull the bridle over Goliath's head.

"I know a way to get her back."

C. J.'s head swerved toward his brother. *How?* Oh, he was tempted to ask. But pride warred with the urge. If he and Lizzie were ever to have a future, they needed basic trust. She needed to come to him on the strength or weakness of what he'd told her. Of what they felt for each other. He hadn't thought their feelings would be tested so early or so easily, but they had been.

The next move was hers. He was willing to meet her halfway, but she had to want it, too. He shook his head. "Thanks, Lee. But I think it should be her call."

"It's easy," he wheedled. "And relatively painless."

C. J. hesitated. The easy way had backfired on him before. Not again. "Thanks, but I don't know what could change her mind. If she doesn't believe me—"

"Have Grandma deed the ranch over to someone else."

"What?" C. J. froze, rocked by his brother's suggestion.

Lee grinned and leaned back against the stall gate. "If you have proof that you've given up all claim to the ranch, she'll have to believe you."

"How could you ever think you were dumb?" C. J. asked

admiringly. He considered Lee's brilliant idea, but the thought of having to prove his claim chafed. "I think she should believe that I forfeited because I said so. What do we have if she doesn't?"

"Well, it looks like I'm the only one believin' you." Lee eyed him speculatively. "Come on, what do you think?"

C. J. was tempted. A simple piece of paper might settle everything, but his pride bristled at the idea. He'd meant what he said to Lee. What did he and Lizzie have if there was no trust?

He shook his head slowly. "Thanks, Lee, but I don't see how it could make any difference. It's just putting in writing what I've already told her. She didn't believe that I forfeited. Why would she believe a piece of paper?"

Lee shrugged. "All right. I tried. I hope you change your mind."

He'd said he loved her and she had believed that. Before she'd learned about the task.

He'd said he forfeited. She wanted to believe him, but that could be another lie so she would marry him and he would still receive the ranch.

She couldn't believe he would tell such a lie, but she was hurt and confused.

One minute fury burned through her. The next, doubts hammered at her. What if C. J. really did love her? What if he had forfeited? That still didn't give him the right to interfere in her life or to manipulate her.

But her feelings for him hadn't been manipulated. She had fallen in love with him.

The pain of betrayal lay heavily inside her, lingering like a racking case of pneumonia, settling as a permanent ache in her heart.

Part of her wanted to go to him, but a stronger part, the wounded part, wanted to hide away, protect herself, try to forget him.

She kept seeing his eyes, tender with love as he told her he loved her, dark with pain when she'd confronted him about the task and the bribes. She wanted to remember only that, but other memories slipped in.

Like how often he'd been supportive of her. Even if it had been for the purpose of checking on her marriage prospects, she hadn't imagined his concern or the anger he'd felt at George for leaving her at the dance and Henry for talking about Daisy all night. Or had he been upset at them only because they kept him from achieving his goal?

She'd told C. J. not to come back. And she'd meant it. But as the days passed, she wavered.

She couldn't believe she had been so wrong about her feelings for him. Or his for her. Even though she had not surrendered the most protected piece of herself, she still felt ripped open and humiliated. Her pride stung and she wanted to cling to the belief that he had used her, that he had bribed men to call for her so he could marry her off and win that stupid ranch. His voice played in her memory and she again heard the steely determination when he told her he would have the ranch, that it was his life.

But she also remembered the way his eyes shone at her with wonder and a new heat, the charmingly uncertain way he'd told her things were changing between them, the frantic way he'd come after her. As if he really cared.

For two days, she waged a battle between old insecurities and the life she wanted to have. Because she was hurt and betrayed, her old insecurities had come crashing back. Jude was right. No man would ever want her for herself.

She didn't want to believe it, but the pain had worn her resistance thin. Still, a faint voice in her head urged her to forgive, to reconsider. To trust.

And though she wouldn't admit it even to herself, she wished C. J. would come into the store once more.

She tried to shove the thought away, but a growing part of her wanted to be persuaded, swept up in his charm and that weak-kneed response he always invoked. Forgiveness came hard, but Lizzie had to fight the urge to see C. J., at least one last time.

At the end of the week, she sat in the back room of the store and tallied the figures from yesterday's sales for the fourth time.

Hank and Maybelle had been concerned and angry over Jed's accusations, and Lizzie hadn't been able to reassure them. She had explained that she wasn't seeing C. J. anymore, but didn't go into details.

Hank and Maybelle had exchanged sad, disappointed looks, but didn't pry. Instead they had silently supported her, and she knew she could count them as true friends.

Lizzie's concentration was ruined, the numbers in her head interspersed with memories of C. J., his lips on hers, the achingly sweet way he'd kissed her scar. Humiliation stung as she relived the depth of her surrender to him.

She redoubled her efforts to concentrate on the numbers in front of her.

"Hello, Lizzie."

Minerva Daltry. Lizzie straightened and froze. Her heart kicked into a rapid staccatto as she turned.

The older woman stood in the curtained doorway of the storeroom, studying Lizzie with sharp gray eyes. There was a wariness there, as though she knew she might not be welcome, but also a grim determination.

Lizzie frowned and slowly rose from her chair. Her curiosity was stemmed by a sudden worry. Had something happened to C. J.? She wanted to ask if he was all right, but bit back the words. If something had happened, she would've heard.

Minerva stepped toward the desk. "May I come in? I'd like a word."

Her imperious attitude annoyed Lizzie. She said softly, "I'm rather busy right now."

"This won't take long," Minerva said briskly. "It's about C. J. and this mess."

"I really don't care to discuss it."

"Please, honey, give me a chance to make things right." The older woman's voice was gruff, but Lizzie heard the plea under the words.

She eyed Minerva with a wary readiness.

The older woman's gaze flickered away for an instant. "First off, I'd like to apologize. I'm sorry for hurting you and for involving C. J."

Lizzie agreed, so she remained silent.

"He seems to be in the same doldrums you are."

"I'm fine," Lizzie informed her stiffly. She wanted to rage at the woman for her meddling, but anger battled with an inborn respect for her elders.

Minerva walked to the desk, running a paper-thin hand over the dark wood. "I'm here to plead his case. He's too proud to do it." She sighed. "And, by rights, it is my mess."

"C. J. and I have spoken." Lizzie's heart ached. She wanted to know what he was doing, *how* he was doing. Had she done the right thing or not? "It's a mutual agreement."

"Mutually miserable, I'd say. This is my fault, girl. You shouldn't hold him responsible."

"He played a part, too." Lizzie held her gaze.

Minerva conceded the point with a tilt of her head. "The way he handled the men was wrong."

The hurt welled to the surface. "I don't understand how you could've done something like that."

"He asked the same thing," the other woman muttered. She lifted her head, her gray eyes steely. "I was trying to remedy a bad situation and teach my grandson something in the process. I felt he hadn't taken responsibility for what had happened to you, that your life had been altered because of what he did or didn't do."

"It has now." Lizzie stroked the wood of the desk behind

her, searching for balance or reassurance. Just hearing C. J.'s name elicited a grinding pain.

The older woman winced. "Touché."

"I don't want to be rude, Mrs. Daltry, but I have work to do." If she heard C. J.'s name once more, she would fold.

Minerva leveled a hard gaze at her. "Don't turn your back on him just because of an old lady's eccentricities. I admit my way might not have been the way to go about things, but something wonderful came of it. C. J. loves you. He wants to build a life with you."

If C. J.'s grandmother believed there might still be a future for them, could it be possible? But he wasn't here and Minerva was. "That's between us."

"Well, he won't come. Damn stubborn male pride," Minerva burst out. Then more quietly, "Give the boy another chance. This is my fault, not his."

"He didn't have to bribe those men."

"No. No, he didn't. He also didn't have to fall in love with you. By doing so, he lost his right to the prize, the ranch."

Lizzie had no rejoinder for that. If Minerva were to be trusted, then C. J. really had forfeited.

"We both know his reputation with women. I warned him strongly about toying with you."

"He should've listened."

"Don't you see, my dear? He's not toying. He could've left you alone, let you become involved with some other man, and he would've had the ranch. But that's not what happened."

Lizzie wanted to send the woman away, but she also knew that her pride was the only thing hurting, the one thing that kept her from believing that C. J. really loved her.

Minerva stepped closer. "He tried at least twice to get out of it because he didn't want to see you hurt. I didn't make it easy on him. Besides which, no one in our family has ever forfeited."

Hope welled up inside her, but Lizzie couldn't trust

blindly again. "Why are you telling me this? It doesn't really matter, does it?"

"I'm telling you because he loves you and I think you should talk to him at least one more time."

"Did he send you?" She held her breath, wishing, hoping.

Minerva's gaze flickered away for an instant. "I'm supposed to tell you that he'll be at Tom English's ranch tomorrow. Will you see him?"

Lizzie glanced down, not wanting Minerva to see how much she needed to look into C. J.'s eyes and determine if there was love there, or if she had killed it. Her knowledge about the task and the bribes still stung, but pride was only a cold satisfaction.

She was hurt. No matter how much she wanted him, she didn't know if she could sustain another wound like this one. She knew the next move was hers. He had said so. If she did nothing, she wouldn't see him again.

She wanted to see him again, wanted to see if there was a future there. He *had* come after her. Didn't that mean he loved her? Wasn't love about forgiveness?

She had told him not to come back.

She could take a chance and go to him, find out if he still wanted her. Or she could be stubborn and pigheaded. And alone. She hesitated, unable to say the words.

Minerva Daltry turned to go. "I hope you don't regret this, Lizzie."

She stepped away from the desk. "I'll go."

C. J.'s grandmother smiled. "Tomorrow morning. You won't be sorry."

The days had slipped by in an endless toil of heat and sweat and pain.

C. J. worked in the far pasture, branding cattle, staying up until all hours playing cards with the ranch hands. His eyes were gritty; his muscles and nerves strung taut. And a relentless, nagging ache burned across his belly.

He'd felt it constantly in his soul since the day of his confrontation with Lizzie. The pain gnawed at him, destroying his sleeping and waking moments. He couldn't escape it through work or sweat or liquor. Only Lizzie could ease it.

He hoped she would change her mind and come to him, but she didn't. He didn't see a hint of her shadow, didn't smell one vague whiff of rose water. His pride died, leaving a sharp numbness that penetrated his soul. He couldn't give up on her. Not yet.

Digging his heels into Goliath's sides, he sent the stallion racing through the pasture, dodging an oak stump, leaping a gully, and racing toward the house. And Grandma.

He wanted Lizzie. And if he had to deed the ranch to Lee or Atlas or even Goliath, he was going to do it.

Minerva was in the dining room with his parents. All three sat at the table. Odie was drawing plans for a new chair while Jane and Grandma shelled peas into a chipped ceramic bowl.

"Grandma?" He halted in the doorway, gripping the door frame with both hands. "Can I talk to you?"

She glanced at him, a smile hovering on her lips. "Come sit down."

He walked into the room, but didn't sit. Impatience surged through him. "I want you to deed over the ranch to Lee."

His mother looked up from her peas. His father's head snapped up and he ceased his mumbling.

Minerva frowned. "Lee doesn't want the ranch."

"All right. Atlas then. Or Pa. I don't care. Just somebody."

"Why do you care—oh. This is about Lizzie." She dropped a handful of peas into the bowl and looked up.

C. J. palmed his hat from his head and wiped at the sweat on his forehead. "It's the only way I can think of to prove I was telling the truth. *We* all know I forfeited, but how is she supposed to know? This will prove I love her for herself, that I'm willing to give up all claim to the ranch."

"Are you sure of your feelings?" Jane asked quietly, her eyes trained on him. "This is a big decision."

"Yes, Ma, I know, but I want Lizzie."

"You're not talking about giving up the ranch entirely? Or leaving?" Odie shook his head as though dazed and set down his pencil and compass. "Lee might need you to run the place."

"Lizzie and I will get our own place, just like Lee and Meredith." C. J. turned his attention to his father. "We can start our own ranch and do it together."

"Can you be sure of her, son? Does she want the same thing?" Jane asked quietly.

C. J. knew his mother was concerned that Lizzie might hurt him, but he knew better. "I don't know if she'll have me, but she's not like Diana. She would never commit unless she truly meant it."

"Don't be hasty, son." Odie pushed away from the table. "The ranch has been in this family for a long time. Lee might someday want you to have it, and you can't forget how you love this land. Just like a part of yourself."

"I know, but I can start over with her. I can do anything with her. She's strong and brave and she loves me, even if she is being stubborn about it right now. We love each other. Please say you'll do it, Grandma."

Odie exchanged a proud glance with Jane, who smiled softly at their son.

Minerva sat quietly, her face unreadable.

"Grandma?" C. J. gripped the chair back. "I know I have no right to ask for anything since I forfeited, but—"

"I'll deed it to Lee. I just hope it isn't too late."

"It won't be." He reached down and hugged Minerva tightly. "Thank you, Grandma. You won't be sorry."

"I hope this works."

"So do I. When can you do it?"

"You want me to do it now?"

"Yes. I want to show it to her. She can't dispute it if it's in my hands."

Jane frowned. "Don't you think Lizzie should believe in you as much as you seem to believe in her?"

"Yes. And I think she does. But I also think she needs a little convincing. If you're willing, so am I."

The sound of a horse approaching drew C. J.'s attention and he strode to the window behind his father.

Odie mumbled, "It's Tom English. Wonder what he wants?"

"Why don't you see him, C. J.?" Minerva suggested. "I'll check on the deed. It's in my room." She rose and patted his arm, then walked to the stairs. "I hope this works."

"So do I." C. J. reached the front door just as Tom knocked. "Hello, what brings you by?"

"Hey, Daltry." The other man peered inside the house and C. J. stepped out onto the porch. "I've got a new mare that needs breaking and I was wondering if you could give me a hand."

"I'd be glad to, but I've got some business to take care of right now."

A smile lurked in Tom's eyes, and C. J. wondered about it. "You're grinnin' awful big. She must be a beauty."

"What? Oh, yeah." Tom settled his hat lower on his head, and a latent tension crept through his body. "What do you say about tomorrow morning?"

"Sure. That's fine."

"Great. See you then." Tom's secretive grin resembled the one Grandma had worn on her way upstairs.

Who could figure? C. J. shook his head and went back inside.

Minerva stood at the bottom of the stairs with Jane and Odie. All wore troubled expressions.

He said in alarm, "What is it?"

Grandma frowned. "I can't find the deed."

"What!" C. J.'s hopes burst. "Where could it be?"

"I don't know." She turned and walked back upstairs. "I'll keep looking."

"Thank you." He exhaled and shared a long look with his parents. Dread filled the room. If Grandma couldn't find the deed, he could forget about Lizzie.

Sixteen

C. J. tossed all night. What if Grandma couldn't find the deed? He needed something, some tangible proof that Lizzie could see and believe. Restless and irritated, he rose at dawn, dressed, and knocked on Grandma's bedroom door.

She hadn't found it, but promised to look again.

"What am I going to do?" Frustration and desperation battered at him.

Grandma smiled sleepily. "Go on to Tom's. I'll bring it over myself when I find it."

"All right." C. J. thrust a hand through his hair, trying to tamp down his impatience. "Thanks, Grandma."

"You're welcome, boy." She tugged off her nightcap and swung her legs over the edge of the bed.

C. J. walked down to eat breakfast with the ranch hands. He was halfway to the bunkhouse when he realized he hadn't told anyone he was going to Tom's. Now, how had she known that?

Lizzie reined the buggy to a halt, letting the cool newness of morning wash over her. In only an hour, thick, muggy air would settle over the land like a hot, damp blanket.

She chewed at her lip and eyed Tom's house, nestled between a stand of pines at the bottom of the hill. His house was a single-story sprawling frame, modest compared to the Daltry ranch, but impressive all the same. Behind the house sat the barn and corral.

The sound of men's voices drifted across the plain, and her heartbeat quickened. Was C. J. down there? She urged the buggy to the edge of the rise, able to make out two men. One stood on the fence, hollering and waving his hat. The other rode a bucking horse inside the pen. Lizzie could see the wheat-gold gleam of his hair and knew it was C. J.

Indecision sawed at her. What would she say? Would he listen? She'd said hurtful things, but the humiliation of what he'd done still stung. She closed her eyes and imagined more of the hollowness she'd experienced in the last week. Even if C. J. rebuffed her, she had to try.

She couldn't survive with that emptiness the rest of her life. She'd learned other things about herself. That if she wanted happiness, it was up to her to reach for it. She wanted that with C. J. She had to at least try.

Things couldn't stay this way between them. She had existed in a torturous limbo and she needed to look into his eyes, see if his love had died or if he had ever really loved her at all.

She drove the buggy down the hill and reined up between the house and the corral. Tom saw her and waved, stepping down from his perch on the fence. C. J. sat atop the bucking horse, his attention fully centered on the writhing animal as he grappled to keep his seat. Dirt sprayed beneath powerful hooves. Saddle leather creaked and the horse huffed loudly.

The scents of sweat and dirt and horseflesh tinged the air. She pulled the brake and climbed down from the buggy before Tom could assist her.

"Hi, Lizzie." He trotted up, out of breath and wearing a triumphant smile. "What brings you out?" He wiped his hands on his denims and took her elbow to walk her to the corral fence.

"I need to talk to C. J."

He inclined his head toward the pen. "You came to the right place, as you can see."

She halted at the fence, her gaze locked on C. J. Man and animal moved in a rugged ballet, the horse's angry movements taking on a certain grace. Sinew stressed in magnificent relief and muscles corded on C. J.'s arms and thighs. Long, ropy muscles flexed in the horse's flanks as man and beast battled for dominion.

She stood mesmerized by the raw power in the primal contest. Gradually the horse slowed, worn down by C. J.'s firm hand and patience.

She became aware of Tom's gaze on her and glanced at him. He grinned, a knowing gleam in his eye that made her wonder what he was up to.

C. J. dismounted and wiped his arm and sleeve across his face. Sweat dampened his shirt, making it cling to his shoulders. He turned toward the gate where she stood and froze.

Her gaze met his and her mouth went dry. Pain flitted through his eyes, then disappeared.

He walked toward the fence. "Lizzie?"

She waited for him, her heart strumming a ragged beat.

He climbed over the fence and plucked his hat from the post, plopping it on his head. He moved to stand in front of her, his shadow a long wedge in the sunlight. Uncertainty clouded his blue eyes. "Did you come to see Tom?"

"No." She frowned and doubt crept in. He hadn't known she was coming? "I knew you'd be here."

"You did?" With his bandanna, he wiped at the sweat on his face. Pleasure heated his gaze.

She pursed her lips, uncertain now about coming. "Your grandmother told me."

C. J.'s mouth dropped open. *"Grandma* told you I'd be here?"

"Yes." She shifted from one foot to the other, suddenly

wondering at the conversation she'd had with Minerva. "She said you wanted to see me, but were too proud."

"Why, that old sneak!" He chuckled, then tipped his head back and laughed, full and deep and rich.

Lizzie frowned. "What's funny? Should I leave?"

"No." Tom and C. J. answered at the same time.

Lizzie and C. J. turned surprised gazes on Tom.

Tom grinned and moved a step away. "Y'all excuse me for a minute, won't you?"

Lizzie watched Tom walk away, suddenly feeling exposed and self-conscious and as if she'd walked into a trap. She slid a glance at C. J. and found him watching her warily.

Taut silence edged around them, striking memories and doubts in Lizzie's heart. She searched his eyes for tenderness, a hint of the love he'd professed, and found instead a latent hunger and his features drawn into a tight, unapproachable mask.

They stood in the yard, surrounded by rolling green hills and immense blue sky. C. J.'s voice rumbled out. "It looks like Grandma and Tom set this up. Tom asked me last night if I'd help with the mare, but I didn't tell Grandma. Yet she knew I'd be here."

"Why do you think they did it?"

He leveled his gaze on her, steely and piercing. "You tell me."

She swallowed. He sounded nervous and uncertain, just as she felt. The realization spurred her on. She met his gaze, her throat tight. "I want to apologize."

Relief and tenderness flashed through his eyes. "Me, too," he breathed.

Hope surged in her breast. "I said things I didn't mean. My pride was hurt. I was hurt."

"I never, ever meant to hurt you, Lizzie. It's been killing me."

"I'm trying to look beyond that. I want—" She paused, searching for strength and the right words. "I believe you."

"About forfeiting the ranch?"

"Yes."

Relief etched his features. He took her hands, his gaze fervent and heated. "I love you, Lizzie."

"I love you, too." Her hands tightened on his. "Does this mean you'd like to start over?"

"Yes. And I'd like to start here." He leaned down for a kiss and she met him. Warmth and exhilaration and joy welled inside her.

His kiss was tender yet possessive, stirring a fullness in her soul she had never experienced. The ground vibrated beneath their feet and Lizzie became aware of the thunder of horse's hooves. C. J. pulled away, brushing her cheek with his knuckle before he looked up. "It's Grandma."

Lizzie turned, surprised to see Minerva riding up on a dapple-gray mare. She glanced at C. J., who pulled her close to him. "I want you to be sure of me, to never doubt me again."

"I am sure," she told him, still swamped by feelings of love and relief.

"I have something for you, something to show you so that you can always be sure."

"I don't need anything but you." Lizzie put her arm through his and squeezed. "You were right. It doesn't matter how, only that we found each other."

Minerva reined up and C. J. moved to help her dismount. "Did you find it?" Lizzie heard him say.

Minerva glanced at Lizzie and grinned. "Doesn't look like you need it." Her eyes twinkled as she held out a piece of paper to C. J.

Tom walked around the barn. "Hey, Missus Daltry!"

"Tom, how are you today?" Minerva's voice brimmed with satisfaction, and C. J. grinned as Tom walked over to join them.

"Looks like it worked," Tom said to Minerva in a low voice.

She laughed and tapped her cane on the ground. "It was a good plan, even if I do say so myself."

"Remind me to never trust the two of you," C. J. teased.

Lizzie smiled. "But we thank you anyway."

He smiled and walked back to her, pushing the paper into her hands. "Read this and know that I love you, that I want only you and there's nothing else tied into that."

She unfolded the paper in her hands. It was several seconds before she realized she was looking at the claim to the ranch. Deeded over to Hercules Daltry.

"C. J.?" She lifted her gaze to his, disbelief and alarm shooting through her. "What have you done?"

"Grandma deeded the land over to Lee. So you'll not have cause to doubt me."

"But you can't do this." Lizzie choked back a rush of panic and tears. "No. Please don't do this because of me."

"I'm doing it for us."

"No, C. J. You've worked too hard. I never wanted to take anything away from you. I only wanted to be sure you loved me for myself."

"You're taking nothing away. We can start over, you and I. We can buy another ranch or whatever we want, but whatever we do, we'll do it together."

"No, no." Lizzie swiped at a tear slipping down her cheek. "I never wanted this. I can't let you do this. I don't want to be the cause of your losing the ranch."

"You're not," he said firmly, gripping her shoulders. "I want to start over with you, for the two of us to build something together."

"C. J., this isn't right. I can't let you do this."

"It's already done, honey." He gathered her to him and hugged her tight. "I'd rather have you than the ranch any day."

"But—"

"Hush." He planted a soft kiss on her lips. "If you feel that bad about it, why don't you try to make it up to me?"

"How?" she asked earnestly, feeling the heat stir through her body. "Anything. Tell me."

"Marry me."

Her heart skipped a beat and something stirred low in her belly. "Oh."

"Is that a yes?"

"C. J., are you sure?" Excitement swirled through her, though dimmed by the fact that he'd given up his legacy for her.

He wrapped his arms around her and lifted her in his arms. "I've never been more sure. Now, tell me, yes or no?"

"Yes. Definitely yes."

He kissed her, hard and unrelentingly and triumphantly. When he raised his head, his eyes glinting like flames, she caressed his cheek. "I never thought I would find someone like you, someone who makes me whole and better. And has given me a place to belong. I want to make you happy. Like you've made me."

He glanced over her shoulder at his grandmother, then whispered in Lizzie's ear, "Let's go to the barn and you can make me as happy as you want."

She laughed softly and looped her arms around his neck.

C. J. wanted to be married on Independence Day, vowing to replace all her bad memories with happy ones. For the next month, Lizzie was swept up in preparations for the wedding.

Lizzie's new family joined in the festivities, making everything easy and joyful for her. The only thing to mar her happiness was the bleak realization that C. J. had given up his life's desire for her. It made her feel ashamed and selfish. She had tried to talk to him about it again, but to no avail.

He'd insisted that he was eager to find a new place, just the two of them, and start over. Still, Lizzie had fretted until the day before the wedding, when a solution had presented itself.

The Fourth of July was a sweltering summer day. By late afternoon, the ceremony had been performed, toasts made, and the cake eaten. The guests had left, and now the new husband and wife sat at the Daltry dining table with the rest of C. J.'s family. The bride and groom had been honored with a dinner specially prepared by Persy.

Lizzie sat between C. J. and Atlas, giddy with anticipation about the night to come. After dinner with the family, she and C. J. were going into town to spend the night at her house. Finally they would become husband and wife in the physical sense, although she already felt a part of him.

Persy and her husband, Jake, sat across the table. They had arrived from a stay in Boston just in time for the wedding. Lee, Meredith, and Jimmy sat next to them. Jane and Odie took one end of the table with Venus while Minerva sat in her usual place at the opposite end with Allie.

Conversation around the table was loud and boisterous and Lizzie reveled in it. Her mealtimes had been quiet, lonely affairs.

The talk tonight was divided between memories of the wedding earlier and the decision to hire a cook so that Persy could travel with Jake without worrying about her family getting proper meals.

Minerva tapped her fork against a fine crystal goblet and silence descended. She rose, looking regal and proud as she gazed at C. J. and Lizzie. "Lizzie, my girl, after seeing how happy you are with C. J., I've decided I'm not nearly as sorry for that task as I should be."

Lizzie smiled. C. J. reached under the table for her hand and squeezed it.

Minerva nodded at Odie, who disappeared into the kitchen. Then she continued. "I'd like to present you both with a wedding gift. I hope you'll enjoy it together and know each time you see it that you were destined for each other."

Lizzie exchanged a questioning glance with C. J. before her attention was snagged by Odie backing into the dining room.

"Pa?" C. J. craned to see around his father.

Odie turned, his features creased in a proud smile. He tugged a large sheet-covered oval in front of him, then pulled off the sheet to reveal an exquisite pecan wood mirror.

A collective gasp rose from the room. Lizzie sat stunned. The polished glass winked, shooting shards of light around the room. Delicate detailed fleur-de-lis and birds were carved into the dark frame.

"You made that, didn't you, Pa?" C. J.'s voice thickened with emotion.

Odie grinned. "Sure did, son. With your ma's help on the flowers."

C. J. squeezed Lizzie's hand, searching her eyes.

She read his worry clearly. He alone knew of her aversion to mirrors. He was afraid that she wouldn't like the gift, that she wouldn't be able to accept it.

She realized with surprise that her reflection no longer represented the bad memories of her life. C. J.'s love had torn down the last of those barriers. This gift symbolized the beginning of their new life together.

All eyes were riveted on Lizzie and C. J., concerned, waiting, anxious.

She smiled, tears burning her eyes. "It's the most beautiful thing I've ever seen. Thank you so much."

Atlas and Allie clapped and the room erupted in sound.

C. J. leaned over to whisper, "You don't have to do this for me."

"I'm not." She smiled into his eyes.

He rubbed his thumb over her wrist and stroked the sensitive skin there. She smiled, anticipating the night to come, but excitement of a different sort tickled her nerves.

She sought Lee's gaze over the table and he grinned at their shared secret. Lizzie could hardly wait to give C. J. his wedding gift.

Amid a cacophony of good wishes and teasing and rice, C. J. and Lizzie took their leave. After wrapping his family's wedding gift carefully and placing it in Lee's old room for safekeeping, C. J. climbed into the buggy beside Lizzie.

"C. J., Lizzie, congratulations." Lee moved to the buggy and shook his brother's hand. He lowered his voice. "I don't want to ruin your night, but I thought you should know that the ranch has been sold."

Lizzie felt C. J. stiffen. "What?" He leaped down from the buggy, his features sharp with disbelief. "What are you talking about? How could you sell it?"

Minerva walked up with Jane and Odie. C. J. rounded on his grandmother. "Grandma, I can't believe you'd let Lee do this. Why?"

C. J.'s features were hard with anger and confusion; Lizzie was ready to tell the truth, but Lee spoke up. "I wouldn't have told you tonight, except it happened pretty fast and I didn't want you to find out from somebody else."

C. J. shoved a hand through his hair. "This makes no sense." He frowned at Jane. "Ma?"

"I'm sorry, son."

C. J. looked at his father, who shook his head and looked away.

"No!" He pivoted and strode back to the buggy, muttering to Lizzie. "They've lost their minds, every last one of them."

Lee clapped him on the shoulder, pursing his lips as though to keep from laughing. "Sorry, brother, but Grandma liked the bidder. It was just too good to pass up."

"She's selling because she liked the bidder?" C. J.'s jaw dropped. "I can't believe you're all serious about this."

A chuckle escaped Odie and Minerva. C. J. spun. "What?"

Lizzie bit her lip, wanting to step in, but she had promised to let Lee handle it.

Lee laughed. "Don't you want to know who it is, C. J.?"

"What the hell difference does it make?"

Lee folded his arms across his chest. "It might make a difference."

C. J. frowned at his brother, but Lee was staring at Lizzie. She waited as C. J.'s gaze followed Lee's.

She smiled, giddy with the secret.

He shook his head. "I don't understand."

"This should help." She opened her reticule and pulled out the piece of paper. Excitement jangled her nerves.

"What's that? The marriage certificate?"

"No. But almost as good." She pressed the paper into his hand.

He glanced at Lee, then Minerva, while unfolding the paper. The family moved forward as a unit and closed in like a band of soldiers. C. J. lifted the paper to read it in the flow of moonlight. For a long minute, absolute quiet surrounded them. Lizzie's heart ticked off the seconds.

Then his gaze lifted to meet hers and she read wonder and denial and disbelief. *"You* bought the ranch."

"We bought it."

He glanced down, then up again, his fingers tightening on the deed. "My name is on here."

Chuckles erupted from Minerva, Lee, and Odie.

"I expect to take full advantage of your expertise." Joy sprang through her, and her throat tightened at the disbelief in his eyes.

"Lizzie, I can't let you do this. You used your money, didn't you? The money you were saving to buy part of the store?"

"Yes, I did."

He shook his head, refolding the paper and shoving it back at her. "I can't."

"You can," she said gently, pushing the paper back at him. "It's our future, don't you understand?"

He climbed into the buggy, his eyes fervent. "You saved that money for the store. I don't want to take that away from you. It was your dream."

"I was holding that money for a future, for a chance at a different life." She cradled his face in her hands, urging him to believe her. "I'll have that with you. We can have it together."

"But, Lizzie—"

"You wouldn't let me talk you out of giving it up," she reminded, stroking his cheek.

"That was different," he said, his jaw locking and determination tightening his lips.

"What's mine is yours," she whispered, planting a kiss on his lips. "My heart, my body, my soul. Why wouldn't I give you my money as well?"

"Not like this."

"You gave up your home for me. Now I'm sharing my future with you. Please understand and accept the gift."

His gaze held hers, uncertain, speculative. He glanced down at the paper in his hand, and a slow smile curved his lips. "You are something else, Elizabeth Colepepper."

"Elizabeth Daltry," she whispered against his lips, melting into his kiss.

"Here, here!" Lee shouted, punching a fist into the air.

Meredith, Jane, Persy, Venus, and Minerva laughed.

"Yea!" Atlas and Allie and Jimmy chorused in unison.

C. J. ended the kiss and leveled a mock glare on his family. "Y'all are crazy and rotten—" He smiled. "And I love you."

Jane and Minerva leaned in to kiss him on the cheek and pat Lizzie's hand.

C. J. picked up the reins. "Excuse us, but I've got something to show my wife."

With a wicked glint in his eye, Lee slapped the horse on the rump and the buggy jerked to a start. Lizzie grabbed the sides of the cab for balance and waved at everyone who had gathered in a tight knot behind them.

C. J. pressed a kiss on her forehead. "I still can't believe you bought the ranch for me."

She smiled, holding close the joy she'd experienced at seeing his reaction when he'd learned of her gift.

C. J. had carried her across the threshold and now they stood inside the bedroom of her tiny house. Dusky light washed through the window and danced with the lamplight, a palette of fading gold and smoky shadows.

His hands closed lightly around her waist. "I love you, Mrs. Daltry."

"I love you, Mr. Daltry." She smiled, unable to believe they finally belonged to each other. In a short time, they would truly be one flesh.

He tugged her closer and dropped a kiss on her nose. A muscle flexed in his jaw and Lizzie saw his throat work.

"C. J.?"

He gazed down at her, love and gratitude and yearning gleaming in his eyes. "You gave me the ranch and yourself, Lizzie. Both my heart's desires." He took her hand and pressed it to his heart, his gaze turning hot with promise. "I love you, honey."

He leaned down to place a tender kiss on her lips, seeking, testing. She gave herself up to the sensations unfurling low in her belly.

He was going slow. For her, she knew. She could feel the leashed power in his arms, the rigid restraint in his tender kiss, and love ached in her chest. He kissed her, long and lingeringly, drawing out flashes of desperate desire. She wanted him. Oh, how she wanted him.

Her stomach jumped and her skin heated, even while brief thoughts flitted through her mind. Hope that he wouldn't be disappointed. That she would always be all he ever wanted. That her legs wouldn't give out.

Sensation rippled through her belly and centered between her legs to thrum with the pulse of her heart. C. J. shrugged out of his shirt, his coat already on the floor. His hands worked at her bodice, peeling away the white satin dress as easily as he'd peeled the layers of hurt from her past.

At last, she knew a sense of complete belonging, a settling of her heart, and tears pricked her eyes.

"I want to know all of you, Lizzie," he murmured against her temple. "And I want you to know all of me."

"I want that, too." A flush heated her skin, but she wouldn't turn away from him in shyness. She wanted to know every part of him. And wanted him to know every part of her.

His hands skimmed over her, leaving her dress and new flimsy chemise in a puddle on the floor. His boots thudded against the floor as he shucked them off. His kisses grew more fevered, tangling her thoughts, cinching an invisible wire of passion deep inside her.

Hard, hot hands splayed over the flare of her hips and down to the curve of her bottom. Her skin felt like satin next to the smooth leather of his, and his arousal throbbed against her abdomen. Excitement and uncertainty blurred with each other. "Shouldn't we . . . douse the light?"

"No." His lips whispered over her skin, down the slender column of her neck. "Don't hide from me, sweetheart. Not anymore."

She didn't want to hide; she wanted to surrender everything. If she could. She swallowed hard and nodded.

One calloused palm cupped her breast and he gently thumbed her nipple to an aching peak. A sharp sensation throbbed low in her belly.

C. J.'s breath rasped out. "Lizzie," he groaned. "You are so perfect."

Lizzie felt as though she were spinning, whisked blindly into the vortex of a storm. She was aware of the moist heat of his lips on her neck, the demanding hands at her breasts. Swept into a rush of heat and power, she dragged her hands over his warm satin skin, reached greedily for his mouth. He was hers. She was his.

His hands slipped under her hair, splaying warm and firm against her scalp. His lips left hers to trail delicate kisses along her right jaw.

He nipped at her earlobe and a shiver rippled down her spine. She gasped.

"You like that?" he whispered, his breath caressing her ear and sparking more heat between her legs.

"Yes." She tilted her head to give him better access and clutched at his shoulders, impatient to enjoy but also to explore him, test her tongue in his ear.

He kissed his way down her jaw, brushing a light kiss across her lips. Then on her cheek, her brow, her eyes. His hand stroked her neck, inciting a wicked dragon of heat to spiral through her.

Long fingers tangled in her hair. "I love your hair, Lizzie."

"You *do?*" She stilled, trying to catch every beat of the sensual pulse in her blood.

"I love everything about you." His breath misted over her, bathing her with gentle heat. He backed her toward the bed, and his lips moved across her cheek. Up her temple. Down toward her left jaw. And the scar.

She stiffened. She couldn't help it. She wanted to surrender completely, show C. J. that she trusted him absolutely, but she couldn't relax, couldn't give over that last secret part of herself.

He stopped, his heartbeat thundering against hers, his

voice rough with passion. "Please, Lizzie. I will deny you nothing of me." His gaze, deep and fervent, held hers.

She couldn't look away. Her body ached, clamoring for him to return and resume his tender onslaught, but still her mind struggled against it. It seemed the ultimate surrender, the boldest intimacy. Yet she longed to belong to him in every way.

She needed him in a way she had never needed anyone. Instinctively she knew he could complete her, because he knew the essence of her, had seen shadows of her that no one else had ever suspected.

There was none of the past between them, no resentment, no responsibility, no guilt. Only need and an unfurling wonder. Her throat drew tight with the need for him. It echoed through her body in a relentless throb of her senses.

She knew she would be safe with C. J., and suddenly, amazingly, her fear melted away. She nodded and closed her eyes, praying he wouldn't find the scar horrible. She wouldn't be able to bear that.

Love glowed in his eyes. His breath fluttered against her cheek, and her heart clenched. One long finger tipped her chin, angling her head for his touch. He kissed her gently, claiming her mouth first. For the briefest instant, her heart stopped.

Then a sense of freedom washed through her. She was uninhibited, focusing all her energy on the man in front of her, the godlike beauty of his face, his generous nature, the gentle stroke of his hand.

Then she felt—*oh*.

His lips moved slowly, carefully along the scar. Heat and silk. Butterfly caresses that branded her, yet soothed and healed at the same time.

Tears burned her throat and she opened her eyes, searching his for revulsion or hesitation. She saw only desire, impatience, a struggle for control.

His gaze burned into hers. "I love every part of you, Lizzie. Maybe this part more than any other."

Her heart shattered. She looped her arms around his neck, searching blindly for his lips. A quiver started in her belly and splintered outward.

His hands moved over her carefully, inciting a flicker in her blood, a restlessness that caused her to arch against him. His muscles corded as he struggled to control his pace.

They fell onto the mattress together. His weight settled on top of her and a new impatience exploded at the satiny friction of bare skin on bare skin.

She closed her eyes in wonder at the way her smooth body felt next to his hair-roughened one. The feel of him against her stoked a languorous fire deep inside, and she arched against him, seeking union, led by an instinct she didn't fully understand.

And then he was there, between her legs. He braced himself above her. "I'll go slow, Lizzie, but it will be uncomfortable at first."

"I love you." Her gaze locked on his and her breath knotted painfully in her chest. "I want to belong to you."

He kissed her, long and slow, cupping her hips in his big palms. Inch by slow, full inch he filled her. Her body stretched to accomodate him, feeling slight discomfort, then a stab of heat. "Oh," she gasped, throwing her head back.

"Are you all right?" He paused, concern drawing his features even more taut.

She pressed him to her. "I'm fine." She could barely speak. Emotions tangled in her throat, love and possession and wonder. Her eyes locked with his. For the first time, she felt total trust and total belonging.

He began to move and tears blurred her vision. They were joined. Forever. She found his rhythm and moved with him, faster and harder toward a completion she had never experienced. Giving up herself, her fears, her past, in a motion of total surrender, they climaxed together.

Afterward, C. J. shoved the quilt down to the foot of the bed and they lay naked on top of a sheet. Darkness had fallen and now faint tracings of moonlight laced the window, overwhelmed by the stronger light of the lamp. Lizzie felt drowsy and deliriously happy.

C. J. hugged her to him and smiled against her hair. His hands stroked over her hip and she felt wrapped in a cocoon of contentment and warmth.

Suddenly a loud screeching noise split the air, followed by a series of pops.

Lizzie jerked upright, her gaze darting around the room. "What was that?"

C. J. grinned and threw the quilt over her. He scooped her up in his arms and carried her to the window in the front room.

"C. J.!" She grabbed at the quilt to keep it from falling. "What are you doing?"

"Look."

She followed his gaze out the window.

Suddenly a brilliant burst of light showered through the slate-colored night, followed by more crackling explosions.

"Oh, my." She squirmed in his arms, angling for a better look. A gold light streaked across the sky, then burst into a myriad of blue and purple showers. "Fireworks!"

"Yep. For our wedding."

She grinned up at him. "It *is* the Fourth of July. Don't you think they're part of the town celebration?"

"Tonight they're for us," he said firmly. "I worked it out with Hank."

"Oh, C. J." She looped her arms around his neck and kissed him.

'Mmmm." One hand slid over her back and down to the flare of her hips, pushing the quilt out of the way. A sliver of heat sparked in her legs and arms. "We'll have them every year as our personal celebration. It'll be a nice way of reminding ourselves how lucky we are. What do you think?"

She tightened her arms around him and planted another kiss on his lips. "I think I love you, C. J. Daltry."

"I love *you*, Liz." He rested his forehead against hers. "Don't ever doubt it."

"I won't." Their lips met in a bond of joy and promise and the tentative touch of the future.

When they finally surfaced for air, C. J. chuckled.

"What is it?"

"Despite all the maneuvering and mistakes, I ended up with a double prize."

She smiled up at the golden shower of sparks raining down from the sky. "Then I'd say you are truly blessed."

"Absolutely, Mrs. Daltry. Absolutely." He pressed a soft kiss to her lips. "Let's go back to bed. Fireworks aren't the only thing I want to show you."

Recipes from the heartland of America

THE HOMESPUN ❧ COOKBOOK ❧
Tamara Dubin Brown

**Arranged by courses, this collection of
wholesome family recipes includes tasty
appetizers, sauces, and relishes, hearty main
courses, and scrumptious desserts—all created
from the popular *Homespun* series.**

Features delicious easy-to-prepare dishes, such as:

Orange Nut Bread

2 cups flour	1/3 cup orange marmalade
4 teaspoons baking powder	grated rind of 1 small orange
3/4 teaspoon salt	1 egg
4 tablespoons sugar	1 cup milk
1 cup chopped nuts	2 tablespoons melted butter

Sift dry ingredients. Add chopped nuts, marmalade, and grated
rind. Beat egg into milk and stir thoroughly into flour mixture.
Add melted butter. Pour into well-buttered and floured bread pan.
Let stand 20 minutes, then bake 1 hour at 350 degrees. Do not
cut until cold. Make thin sandwiches with butter and cream cheese
for afternoon tea.

A Berkley paperback coming February 1996